The Seventh Day
of Christmas

The Seventh Day of Christmas

A Story of the End Times

Stephen Hicks

iUniverse, Inc.
New York   Bloomington

The Seventh Day of Christmas
A Story of the End Times

iUniverse books may be ordered through booksellers or by contacting:

iUniverse
1663 Liberty Drive
Bloomington, IN 47403
www.iuniverse.com
1-800-Authors (1-800-288-4677)

ISBN: 978-1-4502-5676-6 (sc)
ISBN: 978-1-4502-5677-3 (ebk)

Printed in the United States of America

iUniverse rev. date: 10/15/2010

Special thanks to:
God
Marina, my wife
Pastor R.
Kevin

And my proofreading team:
Jane, my mother
Megan
Jill
Teddy
Sarah
Vivian
Kiara
Acacia

Chapter I

The family huddled together in the attic, cold and afraid. Angelica, the mother, had her arms draped around her two children, and gripped them close to her when she heard noise from downstairs. Someone was in the house.

The silence was so deafening that the only thing she could hear more clearly than the footsteps, those ominous footsteps, was the pounding of her own heart. She didn't think she had been born simply to die in her own attic, hunted like an animal and executed like a criminal. She found herself praying that her kids would keep quiet now. They were good kids. They knew better than to draw attention to themselves. But even still, kids were kids. God, she pleaded, keep them quiet.

Like a flash, she realized that she should be praying about everything. The silence of the kids was just a bonus. There was nothing in the world too big or small to bring before God in prayer.

Her mind raced. 'Let it be Josh!' she cried silently. 'Let it be my husband, rather than someone who followed him home. Let him be alive. Let him be returning to us.'

The footsteps were getting louder now. This mysterious person, this possible harbinger of death, was climbing the stairs. The access to the attic was secluded; the only way in or out was through a narrow hole in the ceiling in the closet of a secondary bedroom. Someone could only find it if he knew where it was. Yet the footsteps drew closer still.

'It must be Josh,' she reasoned. 'The steps are too deliberate. Unless it's Josh's killer, coming to finish the job.' Another family of terrorists wiped out. The planet would be four people closer to the artificial salvation prescribed by the government. The world had many names for this government, which had risen to supreme power over all the nations on earth, claiming both political and ecclesiastical authority and prescribing torture and death to those who dissented. Angelica and her family, however, used only one name to refer to all the facets of this international beast, whether religious, military, economic or otherwise. They used the name that had been written in the Bible, warning against this power for millennia: Babylon.

She heard this unknown person walk into the bedroom, and toward the closet. The only thing separating her family from possible death was a quarter-inch piece of wood with stucco on one side. Her heart seemed to slow. Each second stretched into a year. Time seemed to freeze. She realized she wasn't breathing.

Then, like a light, the sweet relief of life in the face of death, came the knock.

Knock, then the agreed-upon pause, then *knock knock knock*, then another pause, and a final *knock*. 'Praise God,' she thought. 'It's Josh.'

She released her children, and heard them gasp for air. They hadn't been breathing either. She pulled the wood off from over the covering of the attic entrance.

"Is everyone OK?" asked Josh. "I came back as soon as I could."

"Everyone's fine," answered his wife. She lowered down the shaky rope ladder they had fashioned out of bed sheets. The family used this to ascend and descend their attic fortress, as there were no stairs to help them. They feared that a stool in the closet would give away their hiding place if ever their home were invaded by the soldiers again, and so they opted for the rope instead, though it was not convenient. Angelica found herself scared for the safety of her children whenever they had to use it. She realized that before the world changed, before Babylon took over, she would have scolded her kids for using such a dangerous device. And yet this was their present reality.

Josh was wearing a backpack that once belonged to his son. What had, in the past, carried around the tools to his son's education now transported supplies, mostly food, from wherever they could be gotten to his family's new home in their own attic. A small hole had worn in the bottom corner, and Josh was constantly fearful that something would fall out without his even knowing. Yet he could not purchase a new one. The world didn't work that way anymore.

As Josh climbed through the attic portal, the contents of the bag clinked together. Seth, their twelve-year-old son, heard the clink and seemed immediately interested. Josh always brought home berries or, at best, bags of snacks like potato chips. A clink was unusual, and even Angelica was curious about it. When Josh carefully set the bag down and set himself to replacing the cover to the attic entrance, Seth seemed hardly able to contain himself.

Josh unzipped the bag. He had brought home an unusually large number of things today. First he pulled out the standard assortment of berries: raspberries, blackberries, and blueberries. The family owned a sandwich sized plastic bag that Josh used to carry berries home each day. He used to put the berries directly in the backpack, but this proved troublesome. Often the berries would squish during transport, which not only meant less food for the family, but also caused the bottom of the backpack to become quite sticky. Josh had since washed the bag as best he could, but water was scarce, and closely watched by the military. He didn't dare go to any public sources of water like the town pool. The creek nearby was heavily patrolled. There was a river that was usually safe to use, but it was nearly five miles away, and the family no longer owned a car. Traveling that far on foot was quite dangerous under the best of conditions. He would surely encounter the military, or law enforcement of some kind, if he went out during the day. And so the only time to go was under cover of darkness, but even still the patrols kept coming. When he went to the river, there was no guarantee of coming back. There was never a guarantee of coming back from anywhere these days.

So in order to wash the bag the family had used some of the water that remained in the toilets in the home. Within 24 hours of the family being declared part of the terrorist group, the water had been shut off by the town, and the enforcement wing of the new Babylonian authorities had thoroughly ransacked the entire home. By God's merciful grace they had left the building standing, which all by itself was unusual. These monsters tended to burn their victims and their possessions. So the water remaining in the toilets and the water heater was the only resource that remained in close, safe proximity to the home, but it was dwindling. The decision to wash the bag with it was not a light one. But the bag served a larger purpose, and so the family agreed to this course of action.

Even the decision to wash the bag had been made in faith. Why waste the water, they reasoned, when it would get sticky again as more berries would be needed? As a family they raised their eyes to the sky in acknowledgement that they simply could not provide for themselves on their own. Then one evening, on his way out to gather food, Josh found a solution right there on the front doorstep: a sandwich bag. It was a single bag, perfect and unused, like a gift just for them. When Josh found it, he dropped to his knees and gave thanks. And so the use of the water to wash the backpack, though impractical and coming with the threat of future thirst, was justified in faith. God provided the bag. God wanted a clean bag for them. God would continue to provide water as needed.

So today, Josh pulled the bag filled with berries from the backpack. He passed it to Angelica, and she passed it on to the children before taking any for herself. Angelica's nature was very self-sacrificing and noble toward her family. She would sometimes show her fear in her eyes or on her face, but never in her actions.

He also pulled out a sealed bottle of water! What a treat! Josh's daughter Phoebe squealed in delight. Phoebe understood well the horrible circumstances that had befallen the whole world over the past year, and showed remarkable maturity for her seven years, but her weakness was thirst. She was always thirsty. She complained every day that she wanted more water than she was given.

After this Josh removed a large package of dried apple chips from the backpack. Angelica's eyes shone with wonder. "Where did you get all this?" she asked.

Josh turned to her. "It was all right there under the berry bush. Just waiting for me." The plentiful berry bush was, all by itself, a miracle, since it was winter, and not the season for any of this fruit. He handed the dried apples to Seth. "Be careful with that," he said to Seth. "It will taste good but it will make you thirsty if you eat too much too fast."

"I will, Dad," replied his son. "Thanks."

Next out of the bag was a two-pound package of spaghetti. There were no amazed stares or squeals of delight at this gift. Spaghetti was a mixed blessing at best. When they had last had spaghetti, water was just as scarce as it was now, and so they kept reusing the water from batch to batch, which caused the cooked pasta to be extra sticky over time, and lose much of its flavor. The water eventually turned into a soup, and smelled, and would no longer boil, and had to be discarded. But the water problem was not even the biggest one – since that time they had lost a mechanism to heat the water, and thus had no way to boil the pasta for cooking. Dried pasta hardly seemed like food to the family, especially the kids. To everyone except Josh, the pasta seemed as edible as a rock.

But then Josh removed a small bottle of propane gas from the backpack. Among the items they had moved to the attic before the home was ransacked was a small propane torch. They had used this to cook with until the gas ran out, and now it was lying useless in the corner. But the introduction of gas meant they could cook again, and it had been so long since the family had eaten warm food that even the difficulty of the reused water no longer seemed like an obstacle. Suddenly the bag of pasta seemed much more promising than it had a moment ago.

"All this was just under the bush?" asked Angelica in disbelief. How could they be so blessed?

"Technically some of it was under each bush. But yes. And," he turned to his kids, "I have one more thing for each of you."

He reached into the bag one more time and withdrew two glass bottles of soda. The silence that came from his children was not born of disappointment, but rather of awe. Sugar in a bottle was a weakness for children of all ages.

"Merry Christmas, kids," he said to them, delivering their presents. "From me, and from God. I hope you thank Him before you drink these."

Angelica saw a flaw in the situation, however. Glass bottles didn't often come with twist off caps. And her heart told her that was true of these bottles. "I don't suppose God provided a way to open these goodies, did He?" she asked. Her choice of words implied a skepticism that she immediately realized and repented. But the question stood.

Into the bag Josh's hand went a final time, and withdrew a small bottle opener. It had a beer logo on it. He smiled. God had a sense of humor. "Of course He did," he answered his wife, handing the opener to his kids. "Ye of little faith."

"What's a Heiner-kin?" asked Phoebe, reading the logo on the opener.

"Something that would have gotten you in some trouble in another ten years or so," answered her dad. "And something that won't exist for too much longer." Seeing the lack of understanding in his daughter's face, he summarized simply, "Ask God when you see Him. He'll tell you all about it."

Chapter II

The attic was never meant to be inhabited. For about a year after buying the house the young family didn't even know it was there. They went about their business: raising kids; earning money; paying bills; slowly but ever surely running out of space in the house for their growing amount of goods and necessities. The house seemed smaller to them now than when they bought it eight years ago; three bedrooms for the two of them and their young son had seemed enormous. Yet even then it had felt like only just enough space for the things they'd accumulated.

As Seth grew and Phoebe was born, the home grew smaller, and smaller still. As he grew, Seth lived in the smaller, second bedroom. Phoebe was given what had once been the study and guest room. What had seemed very large to them at first was now too small for them to even have company over. They had to buy a pull-out couch.

It wasn't until Seth was five, which was seven years ago, that Josh noticed how the ceiling panels in Seth's closet didn't fit together quite right. It was only as he dug in frustration through his son's pile of toys and other childhood debris one day, as one toy after another emerged from the diminishing pile that refused to produce the thing Josh was actually looking for, that he looked upward at the ceiling and noticed it. A panel, he guessed about two feet by eighteen inches, was sitting in an equally sized hole in the ceiling. Something was up there.

Over the years, as Josh reflected on this discovery, he felt embarrassed that it had taken him so long to figure it out. The master bedroom ceiling was much higher than the ceiling in either of the smaller bedrooms. The ceiling outside was pitched frame construction, not flat like the bedrooms. What had he ever thought was up there?

Shortly after he realized it was there, Josh set himself to exploring it. He made Seth clean his closet (the first time any such thing had ever happened, beginning a trend Josh quite enjoyed, but Seth did not), armed himself with a flashlight, a face mask for breathing, and a small can of bug spray, and hauled the ladder upstairs from the garage. He used the top of the ladder to nudge the panel out of the way, set it against the side of the resulting opening, and ascended into the darkness.

When he poked his head into the attic, his first inhale left him breathless. The air was so stale, so very musty, that he felt as if trapped in a coffin, breathing in his own grave. He pulled the mask over his face in a hurry, then shone the flashlight around.

The floors were bare, and had uncovered pink insulation resting between exposed floorboards. The pitched ceiling rose to a point, and then disappeared behind a wall that he recognized as the other side of his master bedroom wall. The ceiling itself had no insulation. 'No wonder it's always so cold in the house,' he thought. There was no opening anywhere except where he was standing. No sunroof. No window. No place for light or air to enter, or leave.

At first he was surprised how few bugs there were. It had taken a great deal of faith and courage for him to attempt this in the first place. He was not a friend of bugs, especially spiders. But, though there were the telltale remains of spider webs in the corners, by and large this attic space was clean of life, insect or otherwise. He guessed that made sense. Even bugs need to breathe.

The space was surprisingly large. From the shared wall with the master bedroom to the exterior of the home was approximately nineteen feet, though the roof met the attic floor at an angle so the last two feet were difficult to use due to height restrictions. The opposite length, representing the combined width of the two children's bedrooms, was about twenty-five feet. The only entrance to the attic was in Seth's room, though the strange space did extend over Phoebe's room as well. At its greatest height, the attic roof stood about six feet above the floor.

Josh climbed all the way into the attic and began to explore in depth. He stepped only on the rafters, being careful not to step on the uncovered insulation. A heating duct rose from the floor almost exactly in the center of the room, which he realized was right above the furnace, and stretched across the space before disappearing into the master bedroom. This was how his bedroom was heated.

It was while he was considering this that Josh had, what he referred to in later retellings of the story, a Holy Spirit Moment. With no forewarning, suddenly his mind envisioned floorboards lain across the rafters, covering the insulation and providing stable floor space. He saw a hinged window cut into the roof and opening into the attic space, installed at the very top of the ceiling as far away from the sight of someone on the ground outside as possible. He saw modest furnishings of chairs, rugs and sleeping bags, with candles for light and small toys for the children's entertainment.

Josh felt a tingling in his chest, like a release of adrenaline hitting his heart. His mind was crystal clear suddenly, and though he had never studied electrical work or plumbing, he was nonetheless quite excited to begin his project of thoroughly converting this attic space into another living space. It wouldn't be comfortable, and would certainly not compare to the rest of the house, but he got the distinct impression that wasn't the function of this room.

The renovations took more than three years. Josh went to the lumber store without studying the dimensions of the wood he would need or how much of it to get, and instead bought what he thought looked good in a quantity that seemed sufficient and was, more importantly, within budget. He became an overnight expert in insulation and window installation. Just about everything he did seemed to work on the first try. He felt invincible as he transformed his grave-like attic into his family's fancy secret.

But it was slow work. Josh worked full time at the bank. Though he had no particular fondness for money or business transactions, and even had a belief that a day would come when the banking institutions of the world would fail beyond recovery, he pursued this career because it allowed him not to work from sundown Friday to sundown Saturday. By the time his bank began offering Saturday hours, he was already senior enough to claim privilege against working this shift. He was prepared to invoke religious preference in order not to work during that time, but he never had to.

So, whereas the career was a great means to be able to remember the Sabbath, it still kept him away from his pet project for most of the week. Though some nights could be devoted to his construction, most were occupied by the simple tasks of preparing dinner, and raising two kids. So this left him the weekend to work, but out of sheer principle he refused to labor in his own attic during the holy period of rest, so he was limited, most weeks, to working in the attic from sundown Saturday through the end of Sunday. One day of work per week, no matter how diligent, was a slow way to reach the goal.

In addition, the construction was at times fraught with trouble and inconvenience for poor Seth, who hardly understood what was happening. When Josh cut the hole in the roof to install the new opening skylight, he had not purchased the right material to seal the window in the opening. So he was forced to cover the hole with plastic sheeting until he could correct this problem, but the following day was Monday, and with Mondays came work. He bought the material Monday night, but could not find the time again to finish the installation until Thursday. This caused Seth's room to be cold and noisy for the intermediate days as the wind blew the sheeting around in the attic above his bed.

But largely the construction was a success, and just after Seth's ninth birthday Josh held the grand opening of the space for his family. Though he had never forbidden them from entering the attic, they had each chosen not to. They had never offered a reason as to why, and Josh had never asked.

Josh had thought that the kids would enjoy it quite a bit, and at first they seemed to. Seth told stories of creating a secret club headquarters in the space and spying on the rest of the family. Phoebe, though only four at the time, agreed with everything her older brother said and declared boldly that she would spend even more time in the attic than Seth. In reality, however, neither of the children spent much time there. Seth complained only a week later that it felt lonely to him, and when he stopped climbing up there Phoebe did too. The attic went largely unused until the day when the family moved there permanently.

Chapter III

Angelica at once began to prepare the pasta. Josh had descended back into the home and gone out to the water heater, which was non-functional, but that still had a few dozen gallons of water in it. He had managed to draw from it a pot's worth of water, and brought it back up to his family. He had then fit the new gas tank into the propane torch while his wife portioned the spaghetti and broke it into smaller lengths to boil.

Angelica kind of got lost when she prepared food. She did not particularly enjoy the task, and in fact felt that even the joy of watching her family eat the meals she provided was not enough to overcome the amount of time she had to give to prepare the food in the first place. But as the years went by she came to accept her role as the primary provider of prepared food, and she was able to disengage her mind from the routines of food preparation. Her hands cooked the meal, but her mind wandered elsewhere.

The pot with the uncooked pasta rested on an oven burner above some flat rocks that had been gathered from outside. The torch's nozzle could be tucked in the space under the burner, between the pot and the rock, and the flame could easily heat the underside of the pot this way. They were careful to open the window in the attic, so as to not be poisoned by the gas exhaust, but neither parent was particularly concerned about this. Since

God had provided the gas in the first place, He would not let them asphyxiate as a result. Angelica was able to rest the torch in such a way under the burner as to free up her hands while the water boiled. Then she stirred as needed, and drifted away in her mind.

She had never imagined this scenario for herself before she met Josh. She had been raised in a Christian family, but her church had more questions about the end of time than answers. The story they had taught her about the Messiah's return was quite different from, she later learned, how the Scriptures described it. Since she and her church learned their end-time theology primarily from novels and movies on the subject, she had never seriously thought at all about the world coming to a close. Any idea of a 'time of trouble' would happen to someone else, or at worst she would be whisked away to heaven before that happened. She grew into adulthood with no clear ideas about, or fear of, these end-time events; but, if she were being honest, she had no clear idea of the nature of God or of what her relationship was to Him either.

She and Josh had met in college. They were both reasonably attractive young people, she with black hair just past her shoulders and he with a conservative cut to his dirty blond hair, parted on one side and trimmed short around the edges. Angelica studied literature, and Josh studied business. Neither of them had any particular aspirations for themselves in the course of their various studies, and both credited their college education to something their parents had ascribed to them and expected of them, rather than something they had actively wanted to pursue themselves. Since Josh found himself working in the banking business to earn money during school, he saw himself simply continuing there after graduation since it gave him weekends off, and he already knew that observing the Lord's holy time was more important than following any specific career path. Angelica, similarly, always enjoyed reading so she chose a literary major. But she never fooled herself into thinking she would be a great writer, or a great professor, or even an awesome high school teacher. She intended to pay her bills working somewhere, anywhere really, until she could start a family.

Having similar professional goals gave the two of them a common interest, and they found immediately that they enjoyed each other's company. They met in a film appreciation class, and learned about melodramas of the 1950s together, all while joking between themselves about how useless all of the things they were learning would be in the rest of their lives.

Through all the months that the young couple dated, no differences in their respective theologies were ever discussed or even mentioned until the day she met Josh's family during a weekend visit to their home. The visit went very well. The family seemed quite impressed with her. Then, one morning, without any prior discussion, as if it were completely normal and naturally expected of everyone, the family got up and went to church. This would not have been a problem for Angelica, except that this was happening on a different day than she was expecting. When she was able to get her boyfriend to herself, to discreetly ask what was going on, Josh had looked at her confusedly, as if the question was silly in nature, and said, "Church."

"But church isn't until tomorrow," she said.

Understanding shone across his face, and he stated simply, "Church is today. Get ready quick. You might learn something today."

And so she did. Over the next two years she learned things she hadn't even known there were to learn. Her very idea of the faith she claimed to follow was turned inside-out, upside-down, and on its head as she came to understand the pagan history of many of the things she had been taught in contrast to the plain truths of Scripture. Her view of the world became radically changed as she began to see things through God's perspective. She saw current events in a totally different light as even otherwise mundane things became evidence of things described in God's Word. Her vocabulary changed to incorporate the concepts and ideas she was learning. And, she came to realize, the only thing that had caused this to happen was that she came into real knowledge of the Bible, a book that she had always had on her bookshelf for her whole life, but had never actually read. It was the book her family and church claimed was so dear to them. It was the book they all said they believed literally, and verbatim. Yet she came to understand that she hadn't known it at all. Not until she knew Josh.

But with this new knowledge came visions of the future through the prophecies contained in the Bible, and this future didn't seem so very far off. She always liked to keep it at a distance, maybe placing it far enough in the future to be beyond her lifetime, but she was aware that it was coming, and believed it. From time to time, however, this knowledge frightened her: 'And there shall be a time of trouble, such as never was since there was a nation even to that same time.' She would hear the words of her Savior, the perfect teacher, echoing the same sentiment several hundred years later: "'For then shall be great tribulation, such as was not since the beginning of the world to this time, no, nor ever shall be.'" When her children were born, she was tempted to throw these prophetic words even farther into the future than she had previously, because she disliked thinking that her children would live to see such a day. But the events of the world consistently proved to her that a simple wishing of the delay of these events would not cause it to be true.

And so, when her husband undertook the remodeling of the strange attic space, she accepted it. She had no confusion as to why he was doing this. Even their children knew, vaguely. This is why none of them had even gone into the attic during the construction. Without even being conscious of it, each one of them saw the day when that dark space would be their home.

Angelica was vaguely aware that the water was boiling now. She struggled to bring her thoughts back to the present day, with its dangers and discomforts. Her appearance hadn't changed much over the years. She was a little heavier now after bearing two children, and her hair was a little shorter, but as a whole she retained the look of vibrant youth she had back in college. Her eyes were hazel, and had a haunting appearance against her black hair, as if she could see right into a person's heart. These days she wore her hair in a ponytail most of the time for convenience. Josh commented frequently that this hairstyle reminded him of the young girl he fell in love with so many years ago.

Angelica decided she had cooked the spaghetti well enough, and it was time to serve it. She closed the valve of the propane torch, and grabbed the pot's top for draining.

"Get the basin for your mother," said Josh to his son. Seth got up and went to the corner, where the bucket they had used to store the water between batches of pasta had been stored since the last time it was used, when they ran out of propane.

"I can't see," said the boy. Josh shone a flashlight into the corner, illuminating the area in a way the outside light could not, shining as it was through the small roof window, the only source of light they had most of the time. The flashlight revealed the bucket, and Seth picked it up. He commented as he brought it to Angelica, "It smells funny, like old food."

"Ewww," said Phoebe, scrunching her face in disgust as she imagined what old food must smell like in a bucket.

"Don't think about it too much," advised Josh, "unless you want to go hungry."

Angelica deftly drained the pot by placing its lid only slightly askew over the pot's opening. She somehow, in that magic way that only mothers know how to do, kept each and every tiny strand of spaghetti locked in the pot, while the water drained into the bucket to be reused next time spaghetti was on the menu.

The family feasted on sticky, plain pasta, yet the food felt so good to them that it tasted like gourmet. Tonight was Friday, and they had entered into the Lord's holy period of rest. Christmas was just around the corner, next Tuesday. Resting with a belly full of hot food, Angelica felt at peace.

Chapter IV

The family went to bed early these days, as their only source of natural light was the small skylight at the topmost corner of the roof. When the sun went down, there was not a whole lot left to do. Flashlight usage came at a premium, since their supply of batteries was limited. They had a reasonable stash of candles, but even they were used sparingly. Generally, once the sun set the kids turned in for the night, and the adults soon followed.

That night, no one in the family remembered their dreams. It was such a rare delight these days to sleep uninterrupted by hunger, or thirst, or explosions, or cries, or strange visions that lingered on in consciousness even after sleep departed. Each one of them felt secure as they fell asleep. This was the one night in seven when they didn't worry. They chose to do nothing active. They chose to put their trust in the One who had created the holy time in the first place.

As they slept, the world kept spinning.

But the world didn't resemble what it had only a short time ago. Each member of the family remembered fondly what their lives had been like even one year prior. There had been life, and joy, and promise. The economy kept getting worse and worse but ultimately they managed to get by just fine. The world seemed to be spinning out of control, with wars and rumors of wars, but their little lives were stable.

During that time, however, the world as a whole experienced daily life much differently. When the banks began to fail, the global markets kept getting worse and worse. Governments from around the world kept pouring money and resources of all kinds into the various failing institutions, but nothing seemed to work. Every minor improvement in economic conditions was followed by a larger worsening. Each time there seemed to be stabilization, the very earth itself would shake, and there was just never enough money to clean up the devastation. Long dormant volcanoes erupted around the globe, weather patterns grew more and more severe, and catastrophes of all kinds, both natural and manmade, fell like plagues on even the most wealthy and powerful nations. There were elections, and re-elections. Little wars broke out all over the world, primarily among the poorer nations, and the constant threat of larger wars hung over the more advanced nations as well.

Then everything went mad all at once. The world's largest terrorist attack ever seen was launched and successfully executed.

Beginning in the late twentieth century, the United States of America had formed an alliance, secret at first but unashamedly exposed as time went on, with the world's only government that also claimed the identity of a church. Together, this alliance had effectively put an end to the Soviet bloc of communism. The powers continued to work closely together as presidents came and went, and their influence spread over Europe, Asia, and even the Middle East a little bit at a time. In the beginning of the twenty-first century, when the domestic attacks by Al-Qaeda against the United States launched "terrorism" into everyone's everyday vocabulary, this same alliance continued to work to meet the new threat.

But eventually the terror attacks were launched against the church government itself, and the man at the head of this religious power was killed. This assassination was only part of the attack, however, and in very short succession large explosions were carried out around the world against buildings, airliners, and other places where massive casualties were recorded. Some of these explosions were nuclear. Even the wealthy nations like the United States were targeted. Overnight, the rulebook governing life on earth changed.

After the attacks, as the minutes turned into hours, and the hours into days, no person or group stepped forward to take responsibility for this carnage. Even the most hated terrorist groups of the world seemed to take offense at these explosions, as if even they could not fathom doing such a thing. A strange sort of peace settled over the world, as everyone temporarily forgot their enemies and remembered that they were all human.

Temporarily.

Unfortunately, this peace did not last. Someone finally took responsibility for the carnage. It was a previously unknown alliance of high ranking government officials in the Middle East region whose stated goal was to bring about global chaos in order to fulfill a prophecy of their religion. They claimed that their Savior, who was not Jesus Christ but who would come with Christ at his side nonetheless, required a globe in chaos in order to appear. Therefore the attacks, as horrific as they were, supposedly had the good of humanity as their driving motive. This group had its goal met. The world erupted into a global-scale conflict the likes of which had never been seen. East fought against West in a repetition of the ages-old warfare between ideologies, theologies, and cultures that had plagued Europe and the Middle East for centuries, but this time with modern warfare techniques and technology. The United States immediately came out strongly in favor of its church/state ally, and pledged its military strength on its behalf. This unholy alliance pledged not to rest until the threat of Jihadist terrorism was wiped out for good, and proceeded to blanket that corner of the globe with bombs of all types. The idea of protecting against innocent civilian casualties was lost.

The nation of spiritual Babylon, foretold in the Scriptures for millennia, was finally born.

Josh's heart ached as he watched this unfold across the world. The violence and revenge was being wrought in the name of his Savior, yet he knew the Scriptures well enough to know such a thing would never be ordained by God. He felt personally violated every time the war was described as a Christian war. But no matter how he hated this turn of events, he knew it was foretold long ago, and in fact that this was just the beginning of the end.[1]

As the conflict grew, no nation was spared involvement. This came to be known as the greatest war of all time, completely eclipsing the horror of both of the conflicts previously known as the World Wars. All nations of the world began to conscript their people into their militias. Overnight, there was no such thing as freedom in many parts of the world, even where freedoms used to abound. Nations were constantly invading and being invaded. In some parts of the world, blood ran like floodwater in the streets. Largely, burial became a thing of the past. Now the dead were just litter.

All throughout this time, large and powerful earthquakes shook each corner of the globe. They began at infrequent intervals near the beginning of the new century but increased in frequency and severity as time drew on. These quakes at first roused a sense of urgency among those who feared God but as time continued even they seemed to fall asleep at the Lord's warnings, choosing instead to believe that they were part of a natural cycle of the earth or any one of a number of excuses posed by scientists and geologists as to why nothing was out of the ordinary. The quakes grew in power along with the storms, fires, floods, and other "natural" chaos around the globe, but aside from an increased frenzy to curb greenhouse gas emissions from vocal politicians (a cause so passionately trumpeted that it continued on even amid the global religious war) there was little response to the

---

1   A prophetic view of these end-time events can be found starting in Daniel 11:36

devastation. Only a very small group remembered the promise from God written long before, that the earth shall reel to and fro like a drunkard, and shall totter like a hut; its transgression shall be heavy upon it, and it will fall, and not rise again. Despite their warnings to the world regarding this promise, they were marginalized, ridiculed, and ultimately ignored in their urgency, as most of the world continued their frenzy to commit genocide to everyone who seemed even remotely related to terrorism.

As time wore on, it seemed clear to most that victory in this global conflict would eventually fall to Babylon and its allies, which had come to claim all the violence and genocide in the name of Christ, and openly called the war a crusade. As such, a nervous sense of surface happiness settled over entire societies in the "Christian" areas of the world, despite this chaos. Each morning, the anchors on the morning news would smile into the camera as they reported massive slayings, senseless violence, astounding war tolls, and human hunger and suffering on a global scale. The stories seemed so increasingly bizarre and senseless, yet all the reporters pretended to remain calm, as if the world at large needed them to appear in control of themselves, in order for the remains of the nations' social networks to remain intact. The weather reports also were increasingly alarming, as though each day the earth itself were rejecting its inhabitants in another part of the world. Record-breaking storms of all sorts became commonplace. The large-scale earthquakes stopped being the exception and, with increasing frequency, became the norm. Days without weather-related havoc somewhere on the globe were rare.

Similarly, economic news settled into a format of its own over time. Most days brought with them some horror of massive layoffs, or crumbling businesses, or even entire governments collapsing. Entire supply chains were disrupted because of various military conflicts relating to the great war. Everywhere, governments flooded markets with currency in the desperate hope that something somewhere would stabilize. Yet when these things were reported to an anxious audience, no bad news was ever stated without framing it in such a way as to offer a comparative "big picture" perspective in which the immediate calamity was not really so bad, and would eventually pass, and in fact was necessary to usher in the new age of economic prosperity that, it was always reported, would definitely come. After all, every former economic crisis had eventually passed.

However, six months into the great war, the entire economy across the whole globe failed. Like everything else, it happened swiftly, and without the understanding of the people who were supposed to control such things. Suddenly, with no warning at all except the daily slayings of hundreds of thousands of people worldwide, everyone stopped buying everything. Money from all nations became worthless. Weapons manufacturers could not sell their arms. Clothing manufacturers could not move their garments. Farmers could not unload their crops. Cash from every nation could be found in significant quantities, totally ignored and discarded by an entire world finally recognizing that money had no intrinsic value and could not fix what was broken. Whatever was left in anyone's investment accounts was suddenly gone. Businesses boarded up. Emergency crews stopped responding.

And violence was everywhere.

In the streets, right in the open, were beatings on every corner. Though some areas of the world suffered worse than others, not even the United States was immune from the destitution. Begging, which had become common as things began to fall apart so dramatically, became the only commerce anyone could engage in. Although no one ever gave anything, the begging continued. And each small area of open space in which to beg became prime real estate. Men were beaten to death over a begging corner, and their corpses were left there while the murderers begged for food in the presence of their victims.

Yet no food ever came. The food producers had quickly begun hoarding their crops, therefore it was not long until the commercial farms began to burn. Entire towns would form huge posses and descend on a local field, ravishing it like locusts and completely destroying any building, equipment, or person who was still there once the food was gone. All the while, almost no one thought to plant more food, or to care for crops that were growing but not yet mature. So within one season, the world had consumed and destroyed nearly its entire food chain. And no more food was coming.

People became desperate. They killed and ate anything that moved. Species of wildlife, already in sharp decline due to the changing climate, were decimated to extinction within months. The world ceased to have frogs. The world ceased to have deer. Household pets became family meals. And eventually, families even turned on themselves, using the weak to feed the strong.

As everything went so massively to pieces, however, Babylon remained solid. Babylon had the world's largest supply of gold. People across the globe stopped putting their faith in colorful pieces of paper with deceased politicians on them, but no one ever stopped being interested in gold. It was shiny, and useful. It could be made into things. It could be worn. It was a testament to the true nature of mankind that nearly a million people met their deaths each day due to starvation or murder, yet the elite still adorned themselves in the same shiny trinkets and baubles that had always dazzled the minds of humanity.

Babylon, even before its military alliance with the United States, was a church, and a government, all at once. It was the only entity in the world that lay claim to both titles; it claimed to simultaneously offer men their earthly salvation through wealth, and their eternal salvation through God. As nations failed, this power grew. As governments failed, this power grew. Everyone in the world blamed everyone else for the global misfortunes. But no one blamed this power. No one dared. And sure enough, as time wore on, Babylon brought about the end to the global conflict, and claimed victory. Islamic fundamentalist terrorism, they claimed, had become a thing of the past. Large areas of the Middle East lay completely desolate, and entire nations were destroyed. The vast oil fields in those regions had been breached during the fighting, and massive oil spills unlike any the world had ever seen were witnessed. Other wells had been set aflame, and the air in those countries seemed permanently polluted beyond healthful living. Moderate Islamic countries, which had at first seemed supportive of their ethnic brethren, quickly changed their position when Babylon showed its amazing military might through its alliance with the United States. In order to save their own people from extinction, they bowed down in subjection before Babylon, and paid lip service to its supposedly Christian ideals.

Babylon never faltered. It claimed, as it had for centuries, that it was ordained and ultimately governed by God, and would exist as such until the very end of time. Its loyal followers were cared for. Food was provided by this power. It introduced a new global currency, one backed by its immense gold reserves, and each loyal nation eagerly accepted it as their sole means of doing business. Therefore, economic infrastructure was restored everywhere in the world that pledged loyalty. Earth began to resemble a long-forgotten ideal of normalcy, with one major difference: a global presence by the new religious government of the world.

Within the organization, a hierarchy quickly formed. The existing pecking order of clergy remained as it always had, though these men were now expected to assume the role of spies. Nothing ever said to these people was confidential. Confession at church became the quickest way to end up in a dungeon, or worse. At the very head of the hierarchy sat the most visible leader of this church and state union power, newly elected after his predecessor's assassination. He was the most powerful man in the world.

Under the clergy was a small but growing group that had come to be known commonly as the Loyalists. In exchange for various favors, all of which were at the expense of common people, these Loyalists were given as much luxury as the world still had to afford. Most commonly these people were military enforcers. Many others served as money changers. The Loyalists came to profit from everything.

The bottom of the hierarchy consisted of the common people. This was the largest group, and it was heavily persecuted by the church government. As the church's territory expanded ever farther, the militaries of any cooperating nation became subject to use by the church itself. As such, the enemies of the church became the enemies of the state, no matter where the offender lived. To avoid this, each person was allowed to pledge their individual loyalty to the religious power. Once loyalty was assured, they would be spared the wrathful arm of the military. But they received no preferential treatment. They were mostly poor. Many starved, or killed each other over meager portions of food and alcohol.

The church government began to actively shape global politics. As the months passed after the great war, in an effort to restore order to their own chaotic nations, the powerful governments of the world, including the United States, began cooperating with Babylon and utilizing its currency. The theocracy thus established dominance around the globe. As its power and influence grew, it trumpeted a single position over and over, which was a position it had been heralding for hundreds of years: all the world's problems would be solved by shutting everything down for twenty-four hours each week. This would force everyone to distance themselves from their work, and to reconnect with their families. It would force even the most menial of workers to participate in much needed rest.

In addition to all the political and economic grandstanding that Babylon paraded across the world, there also began to be strange phenomena for which Babylon took complete credit. Charismatic men and women offered inexplicable healing, and claimed to be Christ incarnate. In some parts of the world, these miracle workers would utter pre-determined prayers and cause rain to fall; in others, those same prayers would make the torrential rains cease. These solutions were never permanent, and the populace that received these strange blessings always went back to the same misery as before once the miracle workers moved on. However, because the man at the visible head of Babylon endorsed these phenomena as given by God, each corner of the earth that received one of these fleeting miracles always threw its support to Babylon afterward.

During all this, the misbehaving climate continued to wreak total havoc and devastation around the world, and even still no one could figure out anything to do about it except to keep blaming greenhouse gasses. The United States of America quickly accepted Babylon's plan and legislated that all commerce within the US borders would, indeed, cease on the prescribed day. This was supposed to fix the destructive weather, since automatically it would reduce carbon dioxide emissions by over 14% when all machinery would cease every seven days. There was a small transition period when this forced rest was suggested but not mandated. Until this point, each nation had retained a certain degree of autonomy, despite its dealings with the church government. But the USA did something different. By accepting this demand, the President claimed the church's laws as his country's own. The United States of America became not just a party to Babylon's power, but a part of Babylon itself.

Amazingly, very shortly after the United States took this position of loyalty to the global religious government, a strange storm descended on the nation's capital, with unnatural dark clouds but no rain. This caught everyone's attention immediately, including the government of Babylon. Video of the phenomena was everywhere on earth instantly. Babylon immediately issued a statement saying that this storm was a sign of approval from God regarding the choice that the United States had made in pledging loyalty. When the President reiterated his loyalty, suddenly this storm unleashed a small but intense stream of fire that was awesome to behold but fell harmlessly to the earth. Shortly after, the fire ceased and the clouds departed. Since no one could explain how this had occurred, nearly all the other governments of the world very quickly followed suit in pledging their uncontested loyalty, and Babylon was made ruler over all the earth.

When Josh saw that his beloved United States had taken the final step of loyalty to what he knew from the Scriptures to be an evil world power whose authority came not from God but rather from the enemy, he read the thirteenth chapter of the Revelation of Jesus Christ. He noted that the entire world was foretold by God to follow this beastly power. He knew it would not be long before he and his family would have to move into the attic for good.

Although nothing actually changed, the world seemed to need to believe that this loyalty and forced day of rest was the answer. No one else had any answers! So, despite how the terrible storms kept coming, how the flooding continued, how the pollution remained, how the poverty and random violence did not decrease even a little bit except for those with the strongest ties to the religious government, still the world decided and stood firm in the conviction that obedience to this theocracy would ultimately fix everything.

When most of the world pledged allegiance to Babylon, this terrible power decided to take matters into its own hands and force the rest to get in line. In an amazing act of self-righteous violence, this power mobilized its own long dormant military, and invaded what remained of Israel, which had been an ally of the religious government during the great war. The United States, now in full alliance with Babylon, followed suit with an invasion of its own.

When Josh heard about these invasions, he gathered his family to read the eleventh chapter of Daniel. In it, he read how this religious government of great wealth would enter also into the glorious land of Israel. He explained the context of this prophecy to his family and they all saw how it fit perfectly the current events of their day.

Josh taught his family how, despite the craziness around the world, this too was not the end of the destruction. Babylon would still set out in a great rage to destroy and annihilate many.

Phoebe had started to cry, and Josh knew enough to pray for her understanding. Like so many others throughout time, Josh thought, she would be comforted about this topic by simply hearing how the story ended. Though this terrible power, this beast as described in Scripture, would reign with mighty violence and carnage for a short time, ultimately he shall come to his end, and none shall help him, because Jesus Christ would return to rescue His people at that time. Josh endeavored to show his children that these things must take place. The Great Controversy between good and evil must come to a close. It was their great privilege, not damnation, to be alive to see it.

Babylon invaded Israel as a scapegoat of sorts. Though it had prescribed to the world a particular day of rest, there were those who refused to play along. Israel, like Babylon's bizarre twin, also believed, as a nation, that the answer to the world's problems could be found in a day of rest. Unlike the great persecuting power, however, they stood fast in their convictions that the proper period of time was from sundown to sundown, not midnight to midnight, and it fell at the end of the week, not the beginning. Much to Babylon's dismay, Israel even seemed to prosper in this belief. Therefore, unable to change the practice of the Jews by economic or political means, they simply chose to invade, and did so under the pretense of wiping out those who were preventing the world from returning to normal.

And so today, huddled in his sleeping bag and drifting off to a peaceful sleep, Josh was still keenly aware that the weekend had come, and two days of special danger lay ahead. If he were to be witnessed observing the "Sabbath of the Jews," (or, as in some of the more colorful circles, "Jew Day,") as the world had come to call it, he would be imprisoned as a traitor. Worse still, if he were to be witnessed NOT observing the "salvation day" (another clever nickname, courtesy of the world), he would be executed as a terrorist.

It was with these thoughts that his eyes closed, and he drifted into unconsciousness, where for at least a few hours, nothing could scare him. The last thought he remembered before his brain disengaged was the hope that today was the last day, that he would awake to the glorious trumpet of God and be delivered home. But, he knew, there was more prophecy to fulfill. The end wasn't yet.

Chapter V

At this time of year, when the daylight reached the peak of its brevity and began adding minutes rather than subtracting, the sun rose each morning at the time that Josh used to know as 7:00AM. Josh could sense somehow that sunrise was about an hour away, but he had been awake for a couple hours already. Angelica and Phoebe were awake, too. Only the boy remained unconscious. Seth had always been a gifted sleeper.

It was natural for them to be up before the sun, as their days tended to end at or around dusk, shortly before what the world still called 5:00PM, which left the family in the dark for about fourteen hours each day. Seth was the only one with the ability to sleep that long for several consecutive nights. Finding ways to keep themselves occupied in the early morning hours before the sun rose had been a bit of a challenge in the early days of living in the attic.

But Phoebe had taught her parents a valuable lesson without even trying. One morning, about two weeks after they moved in, Angelica awoke to find her daughter praying. But Phoebe wasn't on her knees. She did not have her hands neatly pressed together as in a yoga pose. She wasn't reciting carefully memorized verses. Phoebe lay huddled face down on her sleeping bag, her knees tucked in to her chest, her dirty blond hair like her father's resting on the floor around her head with her hands folded over her head like a covering. Her eyes were closed, and her lips were moving, though no sound was coming out.

The image frightened Angelica, though it wasn't the first time she had seen this kind of thing. In fact, she sometimes prayed this way. Sometimes she didn't know what else to do before the Lord except to come as low to the ground as possible. Sometimes she had no strength to do anything else.

Angelica was frightened because she had never seen her daughter pray this way. In her home, the way things used to be, Angelica always saw prayer as a very private matter. The parents had always encouraged their children to get to know their Creator, but the specifics of how exactly to do that they generally left up to the kids. The adults themselves had different methods of worship, which were unique from each other's and always changing.

So no one had ever taught Phoebe to pray this way. This seemed like a very fragile moment to Angelica. There was a spirit of intimacy in the air, like the very heart of the universe was reaching into their attic, and into her daughter's mind.

There had been a full moon that night, and Angelica watched in amazement as her daughter communed with the invisible in the soft moonlight glow. This continued for some time. Angelica was not sure exactly how much time had passed, but eventually Phoebe stirred, exhaled loudly, and got up.

The little girl had not heard her mother wake up, and was surprised to see that someone was watching her. "Hi Mommy," she said. "Having trouble sleeping?"

As all four of them now lived in such close quarters, and without walls, privacy had become largely a thing of the past. The parents had fallen into the habit of discussing private things after the family had all gone to bed, when the children were sleeping. The adults would whisper to one another about their impressions from the day that had just passed, or their expectations for the day to come. That night, Angelica explained about Phoebe's prayer time to her husband.

Not much time passed before the entire family fell into the habit of using the time between when their bodies arose naturally and when the sun shed its light on the world to pray. It seemed like the perfect way to begin each day. And everyone in the family felt a greater strength after this began; even Seth, who was awake before sunrise the least frequently out of them all.

Therefore that morning, the morning after Josh's big find under the berry bushes, Josh spent the couple hours after he awoke praying to the Lord. He offered thanks for the food and water provided the day before. He gave praise for another day being able to breathe. He poured out his gratitude that his family was safe, and had not been torn apart or destroyed like so many others. Josh never found himself at a loss for what to say, because each time the words failed to come, he simply listened. The only thing better than talking to God, he found, was hearing God talk back. He could spend hours at a time in this type of dialogue. Each day when the sunrise broke the inky blackness of night, he felt a little disappointed that he had to stop to turn his attention to the immediate needs of his family. He longed for the day when the dialogue would never end.

But today he quit earlier than usual. He knew he had to leave the house today, and he wanted to do that before the sun came up. Each time he entered or left his home, he ran the risk of someone seeing him, and being led to their hiding place. Travel was best under cover of darkness. This was not always possible, but was always striven for.

He had chosen to go to church that day. At one time in his life, this would have been done without question, as he felt strong in his conviction to remember the Sabbath, and chose to do this in the most visible way possible, by corporate worship. But terrible times had come over the world since then, and now it was no longer safe to worship in public during the "Sabbath of the Jews." The soldiers had a cell or a bullet for those whom Babylon felt were disloyal to its cause, regardless of ethnicity, gender, or position in society. After the invasion of Israel, this became anyone in any country who worshipped on the seventh day and not the first.

Because of this inherent danger, the issue of attending corporate worship became a struggle for Josh and his family. Each of them felt as strongly about the issue of Sabbath observance as he did himself, and each of them desired to continue their attendance at church even when it was no longer safe. At first, they did this. But it didn't last long. Each week fewer people would show up at the church, and often those who kept coming had news, sometimes even eyewitness accounts, of the fatal misfortunes of those who went missing. One Sabbath, the group arrived at the church and found all the doors and windows broken, and the inside thoroughly torn up and vandalized. That was the last time anyone showed up for awhile.

Benny Ramirez was the pastor of Josh's church when Babylon came to power, as he had been for a half decade before that. Benny was a man of great faith, and had never known a life outside of service to the Lord. He took his role as pastor very seriously, and viewed each day as a divine mission to spread the good news of the kingdom however he could. When he discovered that the church had been vandalized, he was devastated. When his members had dispersed, he begged for his life to be taken from him, for he had never felt so alone, or so defeated.

But God, as He sometimes does, refused to grant this prayer. Benny had work left to do. And after a Saturday night and Sunday in mourning, Benny regrouped, and set to work rebuilding the church.

He knew that the property would be patrolled from time to time, so he was cautious about when he would go there. At first he went only under the cover of darkness, and he spent many nights in a row picking up and stacking the chairs, organizing the Bibles and other books that had been destroyed, and putting the interior space back together as best as he could. But he did not rebuild in such a way as to allow for large public worship; he knew those days were gone. He organized the main sanctuary, but did not rededicate it for use. Rather, he created a small area for worship down the hall from the sanctuary, in a room with no windows, where small groups could come together without fear of being seen from outside. He left the sanctuary organized but vacant, as a testimony to the adaptive and overcoming power of the people of the Lord God. This way, Babylon would know it had failed to eradicate these people, even as it remained unable to catch them.

Benny, of course, did not live at the church, and had to travel to and from it at his own peril, as did everyone else. The work of cleaning it up was slow. Benny worked a little at a time for seven weeks. There were nights when he would travel all the way to the church from his home, a distance of about four miles on foot, only to see from afar that there were soldiers at the building. Facing certain capture and near certain death if he confronted them, he instead chose to walk all the way back to his home. Yet another night would go by with no place for his flock to call home.

But after seven weeks everything was ready again. Benny recognized that, in the old world, some form of advertising would be needed in order to announce the grand re-opening of his church. But in this world, no such thing could ever happen again. So, like everything else in this process, he left the details of bringing people back to church up to God.

The very next Sabbath, people showed up.

They did not all come at once. Benny spent the entire Sabbath, from sunset Friday until after sunset the following day, fellowshipping with his brethren, worshipping their Creator, sharing joys and trials they had faced, and encouraging each other for the times yet to come. He would speak with them as they arrived, alone or in small groups, and speak with them until they left, and there was a near constant trickling of believers for the entire day, even during the late night hours.

So it was each week from then on. Not everyone came every week. Some stopped coming entirely as time went on, and Benny feared the worst each time. Often his fears were founded, as his members had met with misfortune. But he knew their deathly sleep would be short, and soon enough they would breathe the pure air of heaven, when this world was finally passed away.

It was Phoebe who decided on behalf of the family that they should return to the church, seven weeks after it had been ransacked. No one else in her family thought it was a good idea, especially not her father. But she had been adamant. She insisted they would make it there safely, and return without harm. She would not take 'no' for an answer, and it wasn't until she moved to leave the attic by herself and attend the church even without her family with her that they relented. Josh noted her stern expression with determination like fire in her eyes that he could not ignore, no matter how much he wanted to.

After that time, the family's attendance, like everyone else's, was inconsistent. Increasingly, Josh or Angelica would go alone, while the other watched the kids at home, as they both felt that the risk was simply too high to bring Seth and Phoebe outside. Sometimes no one went at all.

But that morning, Josh knew he was going. The previous week, he and Pastor Benny had made an agreement, and he was going there today to make good on that agreement. He and the pastor would worship together in praise of the success of their plan.

Josh lifted open the covering of the attic entrance as he was ready to leave. Not even Seth could sleep through the noise of the bubble of the attic being broken. Each time that hole was open, danger was present.

"Daddy, come home soon," said Phoebe. She was sitting up with her sleeping bag wrapped around her to protect her from the chilly winter air.

"Be careful Dad," advised his son, still lying down half asleep.

"I love you, Josh," said Angelica, refusing to consider that this would be the last time she saw him. "Please come back."

"I love you too, Angel," he said. "Pray."

When he climbed down the rope ladder, he didn't fear for his return. He looked around, and remembered so many warm memories that had occurred right here in his son's room. These memories stood in sharp contrast to the barren, vandalized reality in front of him. 'I will not miss how empty this room feels,' he thought to himself.

He moved immediately, without waiting for Angelica to reseal the attic entrance. He moved into the hallway and down the stairs, and through the kitchen to the back door. The door had been forced open, and the handle and lock were now separated from the rest of the door, which now swung loosely on its hinges, and was never fully closed. Josh exited through this door. He felt as if the chances of being seen were the slimmest here.

The church was a little over a mile from his home, and took only about five minutes to drive to, which had been very convenient before the world fell apart. These days he had to walk there, and never by the open road, so he had to take a slightly roundabout route by following a small creek bed, which had long since dried after the rain stopped coming a couple years back, along much of the distance. Even still the journey was dangerous; he made each step deliberate so as to cause the least amount of noise possible, and took ample time to listen for any signs of humanity nearby. He made it to the church in about forty-five minutes. The sky was still quite dark, but had the slightest hint of the coming daylight, like subdued electricity in the air. Josh had hoped to be on his way back home before first light. He was running behind.

He waited for nearly five minutes just behind the tree line that ran the perimeter of the parking lot of his church. He had been asked to do this by the pastor any time he came, to watch for spies or soldiers. Being caught would not only endanger himself, but also the pastor and anyone else inside. So Josh watched as the sky threatened to get brighter by the second, waiting the agonizing few minutes as he looked for signs of movement. Finally, eventually, the time passed, and he emerged into the open.

Once exposed, there was nowhere to hide before reaching the building, so if Josh had been wrong about the safety of his approach, it was too late to do anything about it. Josh advanced into the clearing with boldness, figuring the goal was to get to the church as soon as possible, whether he was a target or not.

He reached the front door, which had once been a glass door with a metal frame but had long ago become a simple metal aperture, as the glass had been destroyed during the raid. He paused long enough only to look inside to scan for anyone who didn't belong there, and to take a good listen for any signs of life. As satisfied as he could be, he entered.

As he had in Seth's room, he suddenly had memories of joyful times spent in this church sanctuary, times of worship and fellowship. He had seen the baptisms of many people he knew now to be dead. He had seen the baptism of his wife.

But he did not hesitate. He went to the back of the room and down the hall, into a room marked 'library.' There was total darkness, and he turned on his flashlight for the first time. The room was crowded with boxes and debris. Josh carefully stepped over the boxes and made his way toward the back of the room, where a black curtain hung in front of the back wall, and stacks of paper and plastic boxes, as well as loose articles of all sorts, were stacked up in front of the curtain. Josh went to the right side of the room, knelt down on the ground, and crawled through the small opening at the bottom of the stack of boxes. This revealed that the curtain did not cover the room's rear wall but rather concealed the secret room that Pastor Benny had created for those who still chose to come for worship. The room was not large, but could comfortably fit a handful of people.

As Josh moved to part the curtain, he called out, "Pastor, it's Josh Ragizzo. Are you here?"

"I'm here, Josh. Come on in."

Behind the curtain, the pastor was sitting in a chair with his Bible open, and the room was illuminated by a dozen lit candles. Benny was an older man, clean shaven with a head full of gray hair attesting to his life experience. He stood about five-foot-eight at full height, and due to his short stature his head always seemed slightly too large for his body. He was almost always smiling and had more energy than Josh expected a man of his age to have.

"Good morning, brother. Happy Sabbath. How's your family?"

"Fine, pastor, thanks. How are you?"

"I am blessed and highly favored, my brother. I've lived to see this day and I have hope to live to see the next. We must be so close now. It can't go on like this too much longer."

"Amen," answered Josh. "Each day I hope it's the last one."

"Let me show you something," said Benny, and he grabbed a newspaper that was under his chair. "Take a look at the front page."

Ever since moving into the attic, Josh's family had only gotten their current events from the church. They were completely cut off from the outside world. No newspapers came to their home, and even if they did it would be too dangerous to actually collect the newspaper, as this would be evidence that the house was not vacant. The TV stopped working when the power was cut. And Josh, in an oversight that caused him many nights of sharp regret and self-reproach, had never thought to put a radio in the attic. He had no idea what was going on in the world. He knew Babylon must fall, that he would not be delivered home to heaven until this happened, but had no way to know if this was happening or not.

Josh took the paper in his hands, and read the headline. **REPORTER ARRESTED AFTER CRITICAL INQUIRY**. The article told the story of a high profile newspaper reporter who had been arrested by the authorities. The reporter had recently published a controversial report that was critical of many of the policies that were being enforced by Babylon, most notably their persecution of anyone at all who dared to challenge the government's claim that it was equal to God Himself. This was dangerous to do. All persons who openly criticized the authorities went mysteriously missing. But this reporter had become a hot news topic because of his article, and there had been other news organizations present with him when the police came to arrest him. Babylon's officials were not able to make this man disappear quietly into the night. There were simply too many cameras that caught them in the act.

So he had been arrested. Josh knew what this meant. The end result would be the same as always. The man would meet certain death, and likely only after much pain. But the very fact that the controlling powers had been irrefutably caught imprisoning a man who had drawn negative attention to them was different from any other past incident. Though everyone knew who was responsible for the people who went missing, no evidence would ever be tied to their involvement in these people's disappearance. Now evidence existed.

Josh recognized that a significant event had taken place, but he didn't necessarily see the point. "Is this good news?" he asked.

"It's the beginning, Josh," answered Benny. "The sixth plague that will fall upon the earth is the drying up of the Euphrates. Remember what water stands for in prophecy?"

"Peoples. Nations of different tongues."[2]

"That's right," said the pastor. "And the Euphrates runs right through Babylon. So when the symbolic river dries up, the people who support this terrible power will withdraw their support. They will understand that the emperor has no clothes."

"And you think this reporter is the start of that?" asked Josh.

"Only God knows for sure. But I know that the more attention can be drawn to the darker side of the devil, the better. So I praise God for this," said Benny, pointing to the paper, "and I pray that He have mercy on this poor soul, the reporter, and that this man may receive a just reward for the sacrifice he's made."

"Amen," Josh agreed. There was silence for a moment. "Benny, did you bring what we talked about last time?"

---

2 Revelation 17:15

"I did." Benny motioned to the unconcealed area outside the curtain. "Follow me."

The men crawled through the small opening on their knees. Benny was not a young man, and Josh could see the discomfort in his face. Though he looked to be only fifty-five, Josh knew the man was over seventy. On the other side, the darkness was complete, so the men navigated their way by the light of the pastor's lone flashlight. For a moment, Josh had turned his on as well, but Benny had waved it away. Any light at all was a danger.

The pastor lifted a large plastic container off the top of a stack of boxes piled against the wall, and laid it on the ground, then did the same for the container underneath. The third container from the top was larger than the others, and Benny opened it. Inside were several, Josh guessed a half dozen, collapsed sacks with straps to carry them. Benny lifted one out and gave it to Josh. As Josh examined it, the pastor resealed the large box, and lifted the two other boxes back on top.

"It's amazing," said Josh. The sack was made of a brown waterproof vinyl, and the two straps attached to it allowed the wearer to carry the entire thing on his back. Inside the vinyl outer sack was an inner container of sorts, made of a black material that felt like rubber. This was a water pack. About five gallons of water could be poured into the rubber container, and could be easily transported like a backpack. "Brother Benny, this is great. And the timing is perfect."

"Nothing like the end of the world for a refreshing drink of water," joked the pastor.

"All this water will make a perfect Christmas gift for Phoebe," said Josh, already picturing his daughter's face, alight with awe at fresh water that didn't smell like cooked pasta or porcelain.

"Don't be stupid with this," cautioned the pastor. "Josh, I'm serious. I could only get so many of these, and not enough for everyone who still comes here. I had to prioritize based on family size and need. Don't be careless. Don't get yourself killed."

"I'll certainly try, by God's grace," said Josh. "I would hate to have made it this far and not be part of that group, of those who are alive and remain when Jesus comes, as Paul said."

"True," said Benny, "but let's never forget the justness of the Lord. He promises us that the dead in Christ shall rise first. First, Josh. You'll get to see it even if you have to sleep through death beforehand."

The men looked at each other in silence. The moment was heavy, and solemn. All moments were that way these days. Finally, Benny said simply, "Come, let's pray."

The men went back into the small worship room, again descending to their hands and knees to crawl through the tiny opening. When they sat, the pastor picked up a Bible from the floor and handed it to Josh. He then opened his own and turned toward the back of the book. "Turn with me to Matthew's gospel, chapter 26."

As Josh flipped through his book, he stated as a simple fact, "The last supper."

"That's right. Did you find it? Please read verse 29."

"'I tell you, I will never again drink of this fruit of the vine until that day when I drink it new with you in my Father's kingdom.'" Josh didn't see the point. "Is that the right verse?" he asked.

"Indeed," answered the pastor. "Brother, when was the last time you had anything to drink besides water?"

"It was …" he began, then realized he didn't remember exactly. He was about to say it was before moving into the attic, but that wasn't true. He had brought some potable supplies with him. Even still, he had no memory of consuming those things. He simply could not remember the last time he had eaten or drank like a normal person. "Pastor, I don't remember."

"Would you like to have some grape juice now?"

Josh's eyes lit up. "You have juice?"

"No, Josh, no, I wish. I am the same as you. It's been so long since I've tasted anything joyful that I've forgotten what juice tastes like. I was merely asking if you desired some juice now, if it were available."

Josh thought for a moment, and realized that his whole insides felt like a desert, and a thirst that seemed unquenchable was suddenly upon him. "I do. I would have it now. I would never stop drinking it."

"Did you always feel that way?" asked Benny. "About grape juice, I mean. Did it always have this strength over you?"

"No," answered Josh honestly. "I never really cared for it. It was never my top choice of drink."

"And yet at the thought of it being here now, I saw your eyes jump nearly out of your head. Why?"

Benny did this type of thing often. His method of teaching was to bring his audience all the way to the conclusion through questions, but not offer the answer himself. Josh knew this, and had himself come to teach in largely the same way. He knew he was being presented with a riddle, and that there was a specific answer that the pastor was hoping for.

But this was easy, as far as Benny's riddles went. "Because it's been so long since I've had it," said Josh. "Since I've had anything sweet, for that matter."

"And yet Christ has not had this drink since the supper, so many hundreds of years ago. How do you think He feels?"

Josh saw the point, and yet argued. "Christ is God. It cannot be the same for Him. He is in heaven. He can't want for anything."

"Be careful, Joshua. While it is true that Jesus has access to the tree of life, that His life is not in danger, and that your situation and His are very, very different, you must remember His humanity. He, like you, has tastes. He is fully human. And He wants, more than anything else, for you to be there with Him. He misses your company in heaven much more than you miss grape juice."

And Josh, as he always was when his understanding was broadened by the Scriptures, felt humbled.

"But imagine," continued the pastor, "how joyful it will be for you to have your first meal in paradise. Turn to Revelation 19."

As he had with Matthew's gospel, Josh said without even thinking, "The wedding supper of the Lamb."

"Amen, brother," said Benny. "Verses four through six. 'And the four and twenty elders and the four beasts fell down and worshipped God that sat on the throne, saying Amen; Alleluia. And a voice came out of the throne, saying Praise our God, all ye His servants, and ye that fear Him, both small and great. And I heard as it were the voice of a great multitude, and as the voice of many waters, and as the voice of mighty thunderings, saying, Alleluia: for the Lord God omnipotent reigneth.'"

"This is right before we all become eternally wed to Christ," said Josh.

"Yes, that's true, but I want you to notice something in verse five. Who is it who sits on the throne?"

"God," answered Josh.

"Yes, but which person of God? The Father, the Son, or the Ghost?"

"God the Father is on the throne," said Josh. "Christ is at the right hand."

"So who is it that the elders and the beasts are worshipping in verse four, when they worshipped God that sat on the throne?"

Josh paused. He hadn't considered this before. "I suppose it would be the Father."

"And yet," continued Benny, his eyes wide with a certain gleam that always appeared when he got excited about the Scriptures, "a voice then comes out of the throne. Who is the voice of God?" Josh was silent. "Okay, then, who is the Word of God?"

Josh knew that answer. "Christ is. John 1, 'In the beginning was the Word, and the Word was with God, and the Word was God. The same was in the beginning with God.'"

Benny continued, "Therefore, who is it speaking from the throne in verse 5, commanding everyone to worship?"

"It would be Christ."

"Exactly! And what does He say? 'Praise our God!' He says 'our' God! Christ is part of both groups here! He is, all at once, part of God in His throne, yet He is also part of the wedding ceremony, part of us, one of the servants of God. And so, I can't prove it from the Scriptures, but I've always seen Christ being part of that great multitude in verse six, which cries Alleluia: for the Lord God omnipotent reigneth."

"That's really interesting, pastor."

"And," Benny continued, on a roll, "that means that Christ is in full celebration mode, just as we will be. He is as excited about His marriage to us as we are about our marriage to Him. And what will we do to celebrate this great marriage?"

Again Josh paused. He felt like his answer was too simple. Yet it was all he could think of, so he said simply, "Eat?"

"Eat!" cried Benny loudly, for a moment seeming to forget that danger lurked all around, and could in fact be listening at the door. "It is the marriage *supper* of the Lamb! After all this time with meager food and plain drink, will it not be as marvelous a supper as you've ever had?"

"Amen," agreed Josh, with his eyes closed. He could just taste the divine food of God now. For a moment he forgot that he was not there already.

"And yet for Christ, it will be the first time He has had this drink in millennia. The juice will be sweeter still on the lips of our Savior than it will on your own. Consider that."

Josh considered. He felt such a grand awe that the author, creator, savior and redeemer of the entire universe could enjoy such a simple task as the drinking of juice. He felt completely humbled that He who knew no beginning and no end would desire the company of lonely, broken humans, and would desire to partake with them in such a mundane activity as a meal. Yet this would be the grandest meal any man or woman had ever seen, and it would be the inaugural celebration of paradise. Welcome to the old heaven, he could just hear God whisper to him now. Yet this is not yet the end. A new heaven awaits you still.

"You should probably go," said the pastor, "though I enjoy your company."

Josh woke from his thoughts. He realized he had stayed at the church longer than he had anticipated. The sun had surely risen by now. Getting home would be a danger, and his family would be worrying. "You're right, pastor, I should."

"Would you like to have prayer before you go?"

"Of course," said Josh. He leaned forward and clasped Benny's hands.

"Heavenly Father," began the pastor, "Lord, thank you for your many blessings. You have shown us such great mercy by preserving our lives until today, and providing us with what we need to endure this terrible time. Lord, I ask a special blessing today for your son Josh and his family, so he can make it back home to them safely and continue to provide for them until you come to take us home. And we ask you specially, God, not to tarry a moment longer than you must, for we all long to come home with you, to taste the special supper you have prepared just for us, and to walk in the light of paradise with you forever. Please preserve us now, Lord, as we await that great day, when we hear the great trump of God and see you face-to-face. In Christ's name I pray, Amen."

"Amen," agreed Josh. He opened his eyes and looked at Benny, and waited just a moment before saying, "Thank you, Benny. I hope we meet again."

"We will definitely meet again, brother. Don't forget about next week!" said Benny. "Personally, I hope we next meet up there, and not again down here. I want to go home. But if not, then I hope to see you here again next Sabbath, with your family." Since Christmas was only a few days away, the remnant of this congregation had planned to meet at the church on the Sabbath after Christmas Day to celebrate the birth of their Lord.

The men got up and exited the small worship room. They hugged a final time and then Josh left the church with his new bag strapped to his back and began his journey home. The way home was quiet, and uneventful, and he took the journey without worry, for he felt elevated, and close to the Lord. He felt confident that his steps would not fall into snares, and that his way would be sure. His thoughts, all the way home, were on the coming of the trumpet call of God.

Chapter VI

The Ragizzo family lived in the small refurbished attic space of a two-story townhouse in a medium-sized complex with other homes of similar construction. Their home was sandwiched between two others so he had to walk the perimeter around one or the other to reach his back door. His home was also at the far end of the complex, so he had to pass one row of homes and cross an open area in the middle of several others all facing toward it before reaching his own. Josh stood behind the tree line on the far side of the street from the entrance to his housing complex, hesitating before entering into the open to cross the street, resting in the last safe place before he reached his destination. Like at the church, if anyone was watching, there was nothing he could do about it once he left the trees.

He prayed. 'Lord, keep me safe as I make this final journey back to my family.' Then, taking a step of faith, he entered into the open, and ran toward his home.

The journey was only a few hundred feet, but Josh felt like he was traveling for miles. Each step seemed to take a lifetime. Even when he finally saw his home across the once-well-maintained common area of his complex, the steps he took seemed to shorten the distance only minutely, as if in a dream, and he felt sure that a sniper's rifle was trained on his head, or his back. Maybe he would get to his door only to be intercepted by military. Maybe he would be tackled to the ground and shot before ever reaching the door. His forehead began to sweat, but Josh doubted it was from the exertion.

He finally reached his neighbor's home that he had to walk around to reach his own. The front window of his neighbors to the east, the Cain family, revealed clearly the contents inside, since no one had drawn the curtains the night before. Inside the home, he was able to see a dining room table and two couches pointed to a flat screen TV. Everything looked in place, though he saw no signs of life. The Cain home had not been ransacked like his own, and he felt envy about this. A flash of hatred ran through him, and he hoped the Cains would have the same sort of tragedy befall them as had happened to his own family. If they were still alive and living in this kind of luxury, he reasoned, then they had aligned themselves with Babylon, and would surely report him to the authorities if they saw him. He wanted to burn the home down, especially if they were still inside.

Yet he did not. He knew that the earth was reserved for fire, being kept until the day of judgment and destruction of the godless, and that God would be much more just with His divine destruction than Josh ever could be on his own. He managed to swallow his rage and continue home. He did not know if his neighbors even still lived there, and he recognized that he was judging them unfoundedly.

Seeing the flat screen TV called to Josh's mind the strange days before Babylon's meteoric rise to power, when the world was at war and everything seemed hopeless. The United States had not been spared the desperate famine of food, but the severity of it was not like in other countries. Josh's family, in preparation for such a thing, had stored non-perishable food in significant quantities and they lived primarily on this during that time. The grocery stores nearly all closed their doors since the food stopped coming, and even right here in Josh's quiet town there had been reports of brutal, fatal beatings over tiny morsels of bread. Though this chaos had not lasted very long, and though the United States was among the first to adopt Babylon's currency and thus return to a sense of normalcy, still it seemed strange to Josh to see his neighbor's home so neatly arranged and implying such luxury. Comfort of that scale didn't seem right to him, in a town where lives had been lost over scraps of bread.

At one time, Josh's family had been friendly with the Cains, though they had never been terribly close. A few times they had joined company to have dinner, or play board games. Their kids had played together at the park once or twice. Josh wondered if the family were followers of God, and would be present with him in heaven for a divine reunion, or if in fact they had received the mark of the beast and been deceived into damnation through false worship like most of the world. Josh remembered a time when many people were sitting happily on the fence of indecision, not ready to take a stand for or against God. But the world didn't allow for middle ground anymore.

Inside the Cain home, Josh noted, was no Christmas tree. This surprised him, because he knew Babylon gave away trees for free to its followers. Did that mean that the Cains were not Loyalists? Yet their home remained untouched. Further, their status as Loyalists was the only good explanation Josh could think of as to why his own home hadn't been burned when Babylon's military invaded it.

He realized he was dawdling, and this was dangerous. He resigned himself to not fully knowing the fate of the Cain family until he could read their record in the books of heaven. He felt pity for them though the appearance of their home indicated nothing about which to feel pity. He silently prayed to God as he walked around their home to get to his own, 'Lord please bless this home and the people inside it. Shine your light of truth upon them and help them to know you.'

Josh reached his back door, broken and hanging loosely on its hinges, glanced around quickly and didn't see anyone watching, and entered into his home. He had made it, to be united with his family again.

Josh did not see that a person sat hidden in the bushes nearby, watching. He could not have seen, even if he were looking directly at the bush. Unbeknownst to Josh, this person had been watching Josh enter into and leave his home for many days.

Chapter VII

While Josh had been away, the family had an adventure of their own.

One modification that was conspicuously absent from the attic refuge was a system of septic plumbing. Angelica found it very strange that her husband had thought about many small details of the attic's layout including painting the walls blue, yet had somehow forgotten to provide a way to relieve themselves comfortably. The family as a whole found themselves needing a restroom less often as a result of the dramatic decrease in food intake, but even still the natural urge did come upon them from time to time, and since there were four of them the need came just about daily to at least one member of the family. That day, it had been Seth's turn.

When the family had first moved into the attic, these needs were both more frequent and more embarrassing. Josh had brought a small curtain from the wreckage of the home and hung it in the farthest corner of the attic, allowing for a small amount of privacy. Certainly, there was no mechanism to disperse the odor that ensued. Over time, the sheer immodesty of the situation forced their self-consciousness to fade.

When Josh was present, he would descend from the attic and stand guard downstairs near the back door. The front door was intact and locked, so any attempted entry from that point would cause a ruckus and take some time, but the back door was broken and could be used easily and noiselessly. Josh would take his watch at the foot of the stairs, with a sheltered view of the back door. Angelica would come down from the attic and use a bucket to relieve herself in the bathroom. (Water was too precious a commodity to actually use the toilet.) If a child had to go, he or she would use the bucket in the bathroom while Angelica took her post at the top of the stairs, waiting for any alarm from Josh. When Josh had to go, he and his wife would change posts.

But they agreed that this arrangement would only work when both parents were home, and while the sun was out. Otherwise the danger was simply too high. So at night, or while Josh was out (Angelica never left the house, except to occasionally go to church), the bucket would be used in the small curtained off area of the attic, and emptied whenever the opportunity next arose.

Seth felt the call of nature while his father was at church that day. Per the family agreement, he used the corner of the attic. Normally, Angelica would wait until Josh's return to descend from the attic to empty the bucket, but that day the smell was rather strong, and the idea of waiting to be rid of it was especially revolting. Angelica had removed the covering to the attic entrance, and climbed down the rope ladder into the home. Seth had reached through the opening and delivered the bucket to his mother to be emptied. Angelica then took the bucket and intended to bring it downstairs to be placed by the back door, so Josh could bury the waste in the back yard under cover of darkness that night.

But when she reached the top of the stairs, she heard a commotion below. She froze, and listened intently. It was footsteps, definitely footsteps, that she heard, and she was rather certain there was more than one set. People had invaded the home.

This surprised Angelica, since the sun had not yet risen, and Josh had been gone only a short time. She worried that these people had seen Josh, or worse. Terrible imaginings raced through her mind, of her husband dead, of the impending death of her children, and herself.

She didn't dare move. If they heard her moving, her cover would be blown. But then again, if they came upstairs she would be given away regardless. Her heart pounded in her chest. Her face grew hot and flushed. She felt as if she couldn't catch her breath.

Without thinking, she moved back into Seth's bedroom and addressed her kids. "Seth!" she called in as loud a whisper as she dared. "Close the attic! Someone is here!"

"Come up first!" he whispered back.

"No, there's no time!" She did not want the intruders to find her climbing up the ladder, and proceed to eliminate her kids. She would rather die alone than subject them to the torment of the followers of Babylon.

"Don't leave us here alone!" called Seth, desperate. With his dark shaggy hair showing signs of recent rising from bed, Angelica perceived her son to look five years younger than he actually was. She fondly remembered caring for him as a younger boy, when he seemed so helpless every day.

Phoebe appeared. "Mom, I'm scared!" she whispered.

"Just do it!" ordered their mother. Sensing that they would not give up unless forced to, she disappeared from their sight and went back to the top of the stairs. Shortly, she heard the soft *thud* of the cover being slid back into place, sealing off the attic.

The footsteps drew closer. She heard voices.

"There's nothing here," said a female voice.

"Gotta be something," replied a male voice. "There's always something."

"There's nothing!" cried the woman. "Look at this place! Someone's been through here before."

"Shut up," demanded the man. "There has to be something. If we don't find something to sell, we won't eat today. You want to eat, don't you?" There was no answer. "Of course you want to eat. You always want to eat. I wish you weren't so fat! How many times did I tell you, 'lose some weight?' Now we're scavengers."

Interlaced with this conversation was colorful language from both parties. Angelica hoped her children couldn't hear.

"Why do you have to be so mean?" asked the woman, sounding hurt, even to the terrified Angelica. "God, I just hate you sometimes."

"*You* hate *me?*" cried the man, incredulous. "You sleep with everything that moves, and *you* hate *me?* I can't even look at you most of the time!"

The woman lost it, and began yelling. "What do you want me to do? Those men were going to kill us! Would you rather be dead? I'm soooo sorry that I thought you'd prefer to be alive!"

"Why? So we could starve to death instead?" demanded the man. "I wish you'd just die. I'd never go hungry again with all your fat to eat."

Angelica flinched at this. As scared as she was, she could just feel the fear inside both of these people's hearts. No one deserved to go hungry. And no one deserved to be treated this way. 'God,' she prayed, 'forgive them these sins. They know not what they do.'

Sounds of a struggle drifted up the stairs. Angelica imagined the woman attacking her abuser. She heard the man declare, "Get off of me!"

"I hate you!" cried the woman. "I wish *you* would die! I could finally get some peace then! And I'd find some man, a good man, to take care of me while you rot away in hell forever!"

Angelica felt a new pity for these people. Hell was a particularly dreadful thought. No wonder people turn away from God when they perceive Him to be so petty and vengeful as to condemn His enemies to an eternity of torment. If only they would read God's Word, she thought, they might turn from their ways and repent. They would have the terrible burden of the pagan "hell" lifted from their shoulders. They would see God as their savior, not condemner. How, after all, could any "hell" be worse than this world?

The woman continued to yell. "I never should have married you! My mom told me not to, she said you were no good, and she was right! You're the worst thing that ever happened to me! I wish you were never born! I wish we never met! I hate you! I hate everything about you! I hate..."

"Shut up!" shouted the man, though the cry did not sound like a reproach to Angelica. It sounded like he was changing the subject. "Just shut up! I found something!"

From the top of the stairs, Angelica heard footsteps come closer. She withdrew a few feet backward, as quietly as she could. She heard the telltale creak of someone standing on the bottom step. "Look, a remote," said the man.

A brief pause followed, then the woman said, "You think there is a machine still here?"

"What am I, a psychic?" asked the man, dripping with sarcasm. "Look around. This looks like a DVD remote. If we can get a DVD player, we'll be set for a few days."

There was quiet, and Angelica heard the intruders searching through the wreckage of her home for their bounty. 'Please let them find it,' she prayed to the Lord. 'Let them take it and leave us alone.'

"Here it is!" shouted the woman. There was a joy in her voice that seemed unnatural to Angelica, as she and her husband had been ready to tear out each others' throats just a minute before. "I found it! Saul, I found it!"

The intruders conferred for another moment, then left the home. From the backyard there was a crashing noise, but they did not return, and the danger seemed to have passed. Angelica offered a prayer of thanks to her God, both for the safety of herself and her children, but also that these poor people would eat for another few days. She knew from the updates she had received through Benny and other members over the past few weeks and months that Babylon had begun a campaign of media dissemination designed to promote loyalty to itself and condemn those who kept the "Sabbath of the Jews" as enemies of the New World Order.

As such, media playing devices fetched a premium. The various branches of the Babylon government were the only places anyone could engage in commerce these days. All buying and selling was done through this government entity. Angelica knew that these people would have to go to a government office in order to sell this DVD player. They would receive a price higher than the Ragizzo family had paid for it, and it would in turn be sold to a Loyalist for a price higher still. By being the only stable government entity in a world where literally everything else was falling apart so dramatically, and by invoking the name of the Most High God, Babylon had convinced nearly everyone in the world to profess loyalty to it. As such, when Babylon instructed that the world would reach the promised salvation only by following its own precepts, which it disseminated to the people through DVDs, television, and radio broadcasts, the people were generally in a hurry to possess the means of hearing the messages given by their ruler. Watching a DVD produced by Babylon was supposed to cure the world, and secure the viewer a place in heaven; therefore any price paid for a DVD player was worth it. And, as was always the case, Babylon profited from every sale of everything.

Angelica was thankful that Josh had foreseen this. The DVD player had been carefully placed in a visible area after the home was ransacked, and the remote was purposefully left on the stairs as a clue. Josh had hoped that by offering free loot to invaders, they would be distracted enough to leave his family alone. It seemed to Angelica in that moment that her husband was a very wise man.

She stood there at the top of the stairs for several minutes, waiting for any sign of the intruders' return. When she was satisfied that they had gone, she went downstairs and placed the bucket under the kitchen sink. After the excitement of that morning, she no longer felt comfortable leaving the bucket simply by the back door, visible to anyone who entered. Then she went back upstairs, to rejoin her children, and reassure them that everything was alright.

She, like her husband upon his return from the church, did not notice the spying eyes hidden in the bushes nearby, that had seen the entrance and exit of the hungry intruders, and that saw Angelica move in her destroyed kitchen through the unveiled window that looked out into the world. She retreated to her attic still unaware that this hidden person had been watching them all for several days.

Chapter VIII

From the bedroom below, Josh tapped the familiar code. *Knock*, pause, *knock knock knock*, pause, *knock*. Angelica grabbed the attic covering and pulled it away, allowing him entrance to their living space. She tossed down the rope ladder and he climbed it quickly, eager to share his good news with his family.

Once Josh saw them in the attic, however, he knew something was wrong. His wife was wearing a look of concern that he recognized, as if she were giving her full attention to a single issue that must be dealt with immediately. That expression usually preceded bad news. Seth's eyes were wide open; his body twitched with nervous energy he did not know how to expend. Phoebe sat with her arms wrapped around her knees, huddling to herself and clearly afraid. There was unmistakable anxiety in their voices when they greeted him.

"There was somebody here, Daddy," said Phoebe, not looking at Josh as she spoke to him.

Angelica tried her best to keep calm as she told the story of the home invasion, but she was not entirely successful. Josh felt his heartbeat quicken as he heard about the intruders on the stairs, then arguing among themselves, and finally being distracted by the carefully placed bounty. Angelica and the kids were all so excited by these events that they didn't even notice that Josh had come home with a bag he did not have when he left.

Josh examined his role in how the intruder incident played out. When the idea had come to him to leave the DVD player as bait, he had second-guessed himself and wondered if it would actually work. He realized that he was betting his family's safety on the greed of humanity, and there was something about that entire mentality that felt wrong to him. Yet he could not shake the idea, and so had executed it. Now this morning, while he was at church having worship with his friend the pastor, the day had come when this idea had paid off.

Josh was proud of himself. He had protected his family, even in his absence. Seeing proof that planning ahead could, indeed, stave off disaster, he felt a renewed urge to think ahead and do similar things. God would honor his actions! This seemed very plain to him now.

He was so lost in his own mind that it was his son who finally noticed that he had brought something home. Seth asked him about the bag.

At the question, Josh's mind reset to the present. "This," he began, sliding the straps off his arms and handing the bag to Seth, "is why I couldn't miss church today. Pastor Benny told me a few weeks ago that he would probably be able to get his hands on a few of these, and today he came through."

"But what is it, Daddy?" asked Phoebe. In a flash, Josh remembered a time when Phoebe wasn't so matter-of-fact all the time. But since moving to the attic, she seemed to have grown much older than her age. She had, in very real ways, become the spiritual leader of the family, and she often had advice and instructions for her family that seemed to materialize out of nowhere. She also was never wrong. 'Your sons and your daughters will prophesy,' promised the Lord to His servant Joel so many hundreds of years ago and recorded in the Bible. God kept this promise through Phoebe often, right in their midst.

"It's a bag for carrying water," answered Josh. "I will be able to bring home much more water than before by using this. We might not have to use the same water over and over for cooking."

The kids seemed to like this idea, but Angelica still wore the familiar concerned look. Josh knew he had troubled her somehow and regretted it.

As the Sabbath wore on, Angelica's features relaxed and the family grew more at ease. They eventually put away the bag, had some food, and studied the Scriptures as their worship. On that day, they turned to the book of Ruth and studied how God uses mundane events like death and passion to promote His plan of salvation. The lineage of King David, the ancestor of Jesus Christ, could be traced back to a romantic encounter in a field between a poor woman and a rich landowner. What an amazing God, who is so interested in the everyday workings of humanity that He would be willing to hinge the fate of all humanity on such a chance encounter. The lesson, the family learned that day, was that there was no such thing as chance. Even the deaths of Ruth's husband and brother-in-law had been used by God in order that Ruth should one day meet her second husband Boaz, and become part of the holy lineage of Jesus. The entire book, Josh taught them that day, was written as a beautiful chiasm,[3] which emphasized the plan for Ruth and Boaz to marry. The chiastic literary structure of the book of Ruth was designed to shine a spotlight on this union of marriage as a solution to everyone's problems. As Boaz redeemed Ruth's family, so too would Christ redeem the entire

---

3   A chiasm is a literary structure which begins with a theme, progresses to a central theme, and ends with a theme related to the first. The opening and closing themes counterpoint one another, but the central theme has no counterpoint. Larger chiasms will have additional sets of related themes progressing throughout the story. The theme without a counterpoint, in the center of the chiasm, contains the purpose or climax of the literature, in much the same way that Western literature focuses its climax at the end. Much ancient literature was written in this way, and the Bible has many examples of this structure, including the entire book of Revelation.

human family. As Boaz married his bride Ruth, so too would Christ marry His bride, the church.

Eventually, the sun set, and another Sabbath day was over. These few hours between sundown Saturday and the ensuing midnight held a strange sort of peace. Those loyal to the Word of God no longer participated in their day of worship, and those who chose to worship the prophetic beast Babylon had not yet entered theirs. It was the only period in the whole weekend when neither the God of the universe nor the entity that claimed to be His representative received worship from their respective followers. If there was a Sabbath keeper who had managed not to find himself on a terrorist watch list, this was the time when he could enter into the world without fear.

Yet for the Ragizzo family, it was time for bed. They had long been declared as enemies of the state, so there was no time in any day when they could show their faces. As the sun set, so did they. And before too long, the children slumbered.

After the children were asleep, Angelica discussed her fears with Josh. He had forgotten all about the bag as he was immersed in the Scriptures, and the joy of watching his family respond to the Word of the Lord had erased everything else from his mind.

"Where will you get the water to put in that thing?"

Josh considered this for the very first time. He found it strange that he had been planning to get the bag for several weeks and had given no thought at all as to how to fill it once he brought it home. There was a very telling pause between Angelica's question and Josh's answer, but finally he responded with, "The river? I don't know. Where else?"

"I don't want you going to the river," pleaded Angelica. "There must be some other way. The river is too far."

This irritated Josh a little. He had this amazing gift given to him, free of charge, and at the expense of another family who likely needed it just as much, and he was going to leave it empty? "What should I do, then?" he asked. The irritation was evident in his voice. "You want me to leave it here? You want to be thirsty?" he demanded. "You want Phoebe to be thirsty?"

Angelica was visibly hurt by this accusation, despite how both of them knew it was untrue. "No, Josh, I don't want that."

The couple lay there in silence for some time before Josh said to her, "I'm sorry, Angel. I don't know why I said that."

She didn't answer verbally, but instead inched closer to him, and tucked herself in his waiting arms. She nestled her head under his, and the two of them felt, indeed, like one flesh, lying there together.

In that position, the couple fell asleep and slept a pleasant, dreamless sleep until the early hours of the morning, when they awoke at nearly the same time to find their daughter already awake and in prayer, and quickly followed suit.

Chapter IX

A disaster fell upon the family the very next day, when Josh went downstairs and outside to bury the contents of the waste bucket. They had agreed that for the sake of sanitation and comfort, the bucket should be lightly rinsed between uses. Josh dutifully retrieved the bucket from its hiding place (though the odor downstairs had become so obvious that he could have found the bucket even without his wife's instructions), took it outside after being reasonably certain no one was watching, and quickly dug a hole in the earth and poured the bucket's contents in. He buried the waste, and moved to rinse the bucket for reuse.

The family lived in a temperate climate in a central part of California, where snow was a near impossibility but chilly temperatures were still common during certain parts of the year. The construction of the house included a small closet attached to the outside in which was stored the water heater. Angelica often commented that this arrangement seemed strange to her, having grown up in an eastern state with the water heater always inside to avoid freezing.

The idea of a home remodel to move the heater indoors was disagreeable to both parents, however, so each time Josh went to retrieve water, he did so outdoors. This morning with the bucket was no exception.

But Josh uncovered a terrible surprise that morning when he tried to use some of the remaining water inside the heater. The gas had long since been shut off, so all the water was cold, but it was still potable, and useful for cleaning. He had intended to use some today, to wash the bucket, and wasn't even terribly worried about using too much, since he would be heading toward the river at some point in the near future.

He was not expecting, however, to find the heater completely empty. The actions of fetching water from the machine had become so routine to him that he didn't even notice the slowly drying puddle on the ground leading from the base of the heater, representing the remains of their water supply. It was only after discovering that no more water was left inside that he began looking for answers, and found the evidence of something gone terribly wrong.

Even still, he had to prioritize. The bucket had to get cleaned. He went inside and grabbed a cup from the remains of the kitchen. The cup was broken, but could still hold some water in it. He took the cup and bucket to the bathroom, and scooped out two small glasses of water from the tank, which he poured into the bucket. Back outside, he swirled the water around, rinsing the bucket as much as possible, and poured the filthy water onto the ground. The family had their "toilet" back.

But they had no water! How was he supposed to tell this to his family, especially his chronically thirsty daughter? And what had happened? When he inspected the water heater, he found that the pipe leading from the bottom of the tank into the home had been broken, purposefully, and the water had escaped out through the damaged plumbing. Yet it was intact only the day before! No one had …

The realization dawned on him like a revelation. Someone had, indeed, been there. His home had been invaded the day before, while he was out. There was no other way this could have happened, except as a result of these people.

He went inside, but before heading up the stairs he knelt down to confer with God. 'Lord,' he cried out in his mind, 'how could you let this happen? Why would you allow these terrible people to victimize us like this?' He continued in this vein, unloading his frustration on his invisible protector. It was not until he calmed down that he realized he was doing the same thing all people had done since the beginning of time: he was blaming the Creator for sin and its consequences. Never mind that the Creator was coming to put an end to this suffering, or that Josh had witnessed the healing hand of the Almighty God often enough to know that misfortune never came from Him. Right now he lashed out in his frustration, and God, as always, took it.

But that didn't make it right, and Josh knew it, so before he got up to face his family with this news, he offered repentance for his temper and shortsightedness. Feeling right again, he went upstairs.

He climbed the rope back into the attic to rejoin his family, bucket in tow. But his brow was furrowed and his jaw set, betraying that something was wrong. His wife wasted no time determining why.

"The water heater is broken now, and there is no more water for us," he said simply, and paused to let his family absorb this news.

Eventually, Seth asked in disbelief, "No more water?" Phoebe started to cry.

"Well, son, we have the water bottle from Friday, and there is a little bit left in the toilets."

"You're wrong, Dad," said Seth scornfully, as if it were his father's fault that the water supply had dwindled. "The Feeb drank it all."

"Nu-uh!" insisted Phoebe through her tears. "There's some left." She produced the bottle, which had about an eighth of its original contents remaining.

"Phoebe, honey, you were supposed to make that last longer," said her mother gently, but with a hint of irritation in her voice.

"But Daddy said he was gonna get us lots of water with his new bag!" cried the girl, wracked with guilt.

"You're always thinking about yourself!" said Seth with reproach, and punched her in the arm.

"Ow!" she cried, and hit him back square in the chest, causing him to flinch.

"Quiet, you two," demanded their father. "This isn't Phoebe's fault."

Angelica retold the story from the day before, and they tried to figure out when and how this misfortune had transpired. She told the story all the way through.

"Then they left," she finished. "They went out through the back door, just like they came in."

"And you didn't see or hear anything else?" questioned Josh. Pinning down the cause of this mess wouldn't bring back the water, he knew, but he didn't know what else to do besides play detective. He felt completely powerless.

"No," answered Angelica. "I was upstairs. I never even saw them at all, and when they left I stayed upstairs until I was sure they were gone. Especially after ..." Her voice trailed off.

Josh looked her directly in the eye, suddenly interested. An answer? "After what?"

She closed her eyes, as if in defeat. "After I heard a crashing noise from the back. I didn't think about it. I figured they threw something, or I don't know. I didn't think about it much."

And that was that, he reasoned. Vandalism. Or maybe, hopefully, they at least took some to drink. Then it wouldn't be completely wasteful.

So the family set themselves to figuring out what to do next. It was clear, they decided uniformly, that a trip to the river was absolutely necessary, and the sooner the better. But such a trip meant certain capture and death if done during the day, so it would be at least that full day, Sunday, before the trip could occur.

They further decided to wait an additional day until Monday night. Tuesday was Christmas, so they figured there would be a smaller than usual number of people to encounter if Josh went on Christmas Eve. Angelica wisely added that travel would likely be in full swing that night, Sunday night, as people traveled to be with their families for the holiday. So the trip would be Monday night, about 30 hours from that very moment. Josh would then go on his journey to provide water for his family.

They discussed ways to make the water last until that time. For that night, they would forego pasta, and return to their all-too-common diet of berries and whatever else Josh could harvest locally. They would not rinse the bucket after future uses except in emergency situations. They agreed to these and several other restrictions in order to make it through the next day and a half. Phoebe kept quiet though her scowl and crossed arms made it clear she was unhappy.

The time passed in this way. They ate the dwindling provisions they had on hand, as it was completely out of the question to go outside for any reason until the daylight hours of Sunday were over, lest Josh should run into the Babylonian enforcers, who were always out in force to intercept and capture those who refused to conform to the mandatory worship prescribed by the world's government.

Josh had learned, at the beginning of the Sunday prescription, while worship of Babylon was suggested but not yet mandatory, that the government had devised a system of travel passes for families who voluntarily signed up to participate. The only way to enforce such a mandate, the government had realized, was to restrict everyone's passage and activities for the entire day. Once the corporate worship had become mandatory and enforced, no person was allowed out of his or her home except first to travel to and from their designated church, where the pass would then be validated in order to go anywhere else. All vehicles were stopped by the authorities, and inspected. If the vehicle's occupants were without a government issued pass, everyone in the vehicle was detained, and much more often than not never heard from again. From the reports he received from members of his church, he understood that about 65% of the domestic population had voluntarily enlisted their loyalties to Babylon. Another 30% had been forced into it, by coercion or torture or both. The remaining 5% were ultimately declared to be terrorists, and hunted by the authorities. Josh and his family were among that small group.

Even the enforcers of this corporate worship were allowed safe passage only after they each declared their loyalty early in the morning by attending a special worship service only for government personnel. The priests, too, were confined to their churches for the entire day.

So the family waited until Sunday passed. The hours were long, as they always were, but they survived. They played cards, they told stories, and they ate what they had on hand. Eventually the daylight waned, and the sun disappeared behind the mountains. The enforcers dwindled in number after dusk, and the blanket of darkness offered protection. Josh left his home about an hour after sunset, and found an ample supply of berries at his favorite group of bushes, which never seemed to run dry of food no matter how much he took. He also found a box of granola bars and, mercifully, a small bottle of water. He returned to his home as quickly as possible, and shared this bounty with his family, who gave thanks to the One who gave it.

It was Sunday night, the day before Christmas Eve. Josh and Angelica both had a strong suspicion and yearning that this would be the last Christmas that the world ever saw, and gave thanks and praise that this world of death would soon pass away.

Chapter X

Finally, the sun set behind the mountains again, and Christmas
Eve was upon them fully. Across the nation, across the world,
families joined together by their trees to admire their presents and
maybe even open a few. Children shook with excitement, waiting
for Santa Claus to come and reward them for their good behavior.
Fires were lit, carols were sung, and praise was given in the name
of the One whose birth this holiday was supposed to signify.

For one night, the world seemed completely at peace. Nearly
every household in the world was decorated with signs of the
season. Babylon had subsidized a program to provide a Christmas
tree to every household on earth free of charge, and those who
did not participate were heavily investigated and persecuted. The
government had done this in order to take a census of the world,
the population of which had been so radically decimated over the
past few years due to the combination of war, famine, pestilence,
and persecution that had taken place. By forcing everyone to
accept a tree, they could properly categorize everyone who was
left on earth, and focus their energies on the destruction of those
absent from the program. And to those who willingly participated,
the government seemed like the very savior of the earth itself,
providing without charge such a universal symbol of peace and
harmony during a time when very few people had any money at

all. To many, Babylon seemed messianic, and they offered their worship accordingly.

Josh took advantage of this to make his run to the river. He took with him the water bag and the two empty plastic bottles he had found over the last few days.

Before he set out, the family had prayer together to ask for Josh's safe return. Phoebe had begun to cry during this prayer, but kept herself together for the most part. Josh saw the task ahead of him as daunting, and witnessing his family's worry made it worse. It would be a difficult task to travel the several miles to the river and back, but he would also have to move slowly and carefully to avoid attracting attention, and for the latter half of the journey he would be weighed down with several gallons of water.

Yet he knew that he must go, and he placed his trust in his Lord to provide him with the strength and resources he would need to be successful. And so he left.

As he exited through the broken back door, he looked around to see any signs of life, but he didn't look too hard. This was a precaution he took every single day, often several times a day, and like anything in life that is repeated too often it became a routine more than anything else. He glanced around for movement, for anything that seemed out of the ordinary, but he failed to notice the eyes still spying on him from the bushes nearby.

The journey to the river was complicated not because of its distance or geography, but simply because there was not very much cover along the most direct route: a path that had been constructed about fifteen years prior to run through his town and into the adjacent towns on either end. When this project had appeared on the voting ballot, he had voted for it, and was proud of the cooperation between municipalities that was required to bring it to fruition. But now the trail seemed to mock him. Use me, it seemed to cry, I will get you there faster. Just don't expect to get there alive.

The trail was used as a firebreak, though there had never been any fires for which this trail needed to be used. Because of its official designation, it was paved in such a way as to allow large vehicles to travel along it, for the purposes of extinguishing fires. As time passed and the world fell apart more and more dramatically, other vehicles found it to be useful, including those used for patrol by the enforcers. Josh knew he wouldn't make it a quarter mile along that trail before he would encounter someone all-too-eager to take his life.

So instead he had to snake through less obvious routes. When the Sunday laws had been passed but were not yet enforced, he had set out to map his way through the woods and neighborhoods from his home to the river, and had found a route that kept him primarily out of sight of major roads and households. It added nearly a mile to the distance, and he always ran the risk of getting lost in the unmarked woods, but he figured the extra time away from his family was a small price to pay in order to be able to return to them at all.

He had to first dash across the open space in his housing complex, the same way he went to church. He used this route for nearly everything, including gathering food each day. He didn't like it, but he saw no other less dangerous way.

As he ran through this open area, he looked inside the homes that were lit around him. He saw lit Christmas trees in every home, decorated in gold and silver trimming with colored lights and a star or an angel perched at the top. Some trees had the unmistakable mark of Babylon, bearing the distinct colors of purple and scarlet which were the state church's official colors. Josh saw happy families in two homes lounging around their trees, each with smiling children happily playing games while the adults talked amongst themselves. One family even had a fireplace in use, and their short-sleeved clothes against the warm fire stood in sharp contrast to the cold nighttime air through which Josh was about to spend several hours running. He was surrounded by people who believed everything in the world was just fine, and who were willing to overlook the atrocities of their rulers as long as they still got to open presents around a tree. He felt strong envy well up inside him. These people were content, and even more than that they probably honestly believed that Josh and his family were the terrorists whom Babylon claimed them to be. Further, he reasoned, even if they knew what he knew, even if they knew what was coming, they would likely choose to disbelieve or ignore it. After all, who would voluntarily choose to be cold, alone, hungry and hunted when they could be surrounded by loved ones, huddling around a tree they had received for free? He found himself hoping these people never saw the truth, and that they suffered the punishment of Babylon that would inevitably come. It would serve them right. He would look out at them before they were destroyed, through the walls of the holy city that would come down out of heaven from God, and smile at their misfortune as the skies opened up and released the rain of sulfur to devour them. What comfort would their free trees be to them then?

Josh knew these thoughts were wrong. He knew he should pity these people, who had been misled by the ultimate incarnation of evil into thinking they were chosen by God to survive, but he just could not. In that moment, as he was risking his very life to provide his family with as basic a need as water, he could not find pity in his heart for those who pledged allegiance to the enemy.

He reached the edge of the woods and quickly ducked inside the protective boundary of the trees. He was never safe as long as he was outside, but he was safer here than in the open. And his journey began.

It was less than one mile before he stumbled across a body laying there on the ground, unburied. The sight startled Josh. It was dark out, and he could barely see the moonlight through the trees, so he had nearly stumbled over the remains of this poor man. As his mind adjusted to what he was seeing, he had a strong urge simply to flee, to continue his journey since he could be of no assistance to this person now. Yet something stopped him.

The man seemed about six feet tall. His skin was pale, and kind of blue, so Josh was not surprised when he touched the body and found it to be cold. He had been here awhile, but not long enough to smell or decompose. Maybe a day? Josh was not a forensics expert. He lightly patted down the body, hoping to find food or some other useful thing, but found nothing. He did, however, discover that the shirt was sticky, and upon closer investigation found it to be saturated with blood from at least two different gunshot wounds to the chest. What a terrible fate, lamented Josh, to be hunted, then discarded like trash.

He knew this man was no more, that his consciousness had gone to sleep, and that his spirit had returned to the Lord, from which it came. He knew that the ultimate fate of this person would not change no matter what happened now to the vacated body. Yet he could not help but to feel a responsibility to this man, his human brother who had shared the same enemy as he did. He felt that leaving this corpse where it was would be a victory for Babylon.

He decided to bury the man. Josh did not have a shovel. He entertained the idea of fashioning a shovel out of a stone or some other material, but quickly realized this idea would take more time than he had, even if the proper materials were available, which, as far as Josh could tell, they were not. Instead, he followed the example of his Biblical namesake and began to entomb the body in a shroud of rocks. There was no shortage of rocks here.

Josh began with the feet. Despite his knowledge that this man was no longer aware of what was happening to his body, he wanted to save the face for last. He felt a little uncomfortable laying heavy stones on an unprotected face.

As he worked, his mind wandered. Had this man known that the most terrible persecution the world had ever seen was coming upon the earth? Had he taken any precautions? Had he warned his family? Did he have family, and did they miss him? Were they even still alive?

When he reached the man's chest, he realized that he was expecting there to be more blood than there actually was. Drawing on the knowledge he gleaned from television shows on the matter, he deduced that the body had been moved after the execution. That made the whole situation even worse in Josh's mind. This had not been a chance encounter with the enforcers while traveling through the woods. This spot had been chosen as a dumping ground. And that meant that the authorities knew about this place, specifically. Chances are they would return with more corpses at some point. And they would see the grave.

Josh had folded the man's arms over his chest, both to conserve space and to cover the wounds. 'Brother,' Josh said mentally to this body, 'when you awake, these holes will be gone from your body. The perishable will be clothed with the imperishable; the corruptible with incorruption. Your body will be remade in perfection forever. Rest well, brother, for soon you shall hear the trumpet of victory sounding from the very skies.'

After a half hour of labor, there needed to be only one final stone placed to complete the tomb. Josh found a rock to accomplish this task, and rested it as gently as possible over the man's face. Despite the bluish hue, he looked peaceful in his deathly slumber. His suffering had passed. With the placement of the final stone, Josh's work was complete.

He dedicated this spot, asking God to remember to send His angels to retrieve this man when He descends from heaven with a shout to collect His people. Then he set out again through the woods.

Chapter XI

Memories of when he could travel around freely kept coming to him along the way. Each left turn he made when the shorter way was to the right reminded him of how different everything was. Each time he chose to stay under the cover of the trees when he could shave twenty minutes off the journey by cutting through open space was a stabbing reminder of all they had been through. Just shy of the second hour after leaving home, he reached an area with special meaning to him. It was near the first home he and Angelica had purchased after their wedding. It was Seth's first home.

He recognized the area because he and his son had built a fort there when Seth was a little boy. It never did get completed, and the fort was truly nothing more than a pile of rocks in a circular shape. The area was only a couple hundred feet behind their home; father and son had explored into the woods behind their property, since there were no other homes back there. They had discovered this small clearing, and created a scenario where their home required protection from the world. This fort would be that protection. From this fort, they would take on the world.

When Josh came across this little fort, as he knew he would, he had to stop. While it was reassuring to know that he was, indeed, on the right track toward the river, and not wandering further off course by the minute, it was also a bittersweet moment. He remembered how joyful the boy had been stacking rocks one on top of another. Seth had been so young then that Josh was sure he didn't truly realize what was happening. Most of the story of fighting off the world was born in Josh's mind. Yet despite his youth, the boy became visibly excited each time he trekked out to the rock pile. This was perfect father/son time. It was as good as life could possibly be, and it was among the best memories Josh had. He missed those times.

Josh wondered about other fathers. Even those men who were deceived into believing the world's lie, that this terrible government was sent from God to restore order, must realize that the days of fort building with their sons were over. Even if the persecution were to end that very day, the earth could not sustain life the way it used to. *Babylon* kept promising that the world would be healed by obedience to it, yet nothing ever got better. The food kept not growing in most places. The money kept not flowing, except into and through the government. The weather had not relaxed at all. The summers were so brutal now, and each year a new corner of the earth would be destroyed by fire. Several coastal cities had been devastated, even after taking precautions learned from the devastation of New Orleans in the early part of the century. No significant rain had fallen in Josh's town in years, and he knew this was true of many parts of the world as well. It was simply impossible, in Josh's mind, to believe that everything would somehow return to normal. He wondered if there was any father out there who felt differently, and if so, how. Could denial be that strong?

Josh turned right at the fort, toward his former home, even though this was not the way to the river. If what the pastor had said was true, if there was beginning to be public skepticism that the government didn't have all the answers, then maybe the end would come soon. Once the final divine sealing was finished, the earth's probation would close, and the plagues would begin. The series of events that would usher in the end would come quickly, he knew. Maybe this would be his last chance to see his old home. He hoped so.

He crept toward the home, moving slowly so as to not attract attention to himself. He saw the back of the home as he grew closer. He noticed it had been painted. It was a deep purple color now, not the brown it had been when they lived there. This frightened him a bit, since purple was the official color of all of Babylon's propaganda. Josh knew that chances were good that the new occupants were Loyalists. Were they part of the government itself?

Despite himself, he felt an urge that he could not explain, drawing him forward to the home. Long ago he had learned not to fight these urges, that they were the promptings of something bigger than himself. He quickly offered a prayer for protection, and continued forward.

He walked into the back yard, and forward further still toward the home. He saw no lights on inside. As he reached the building, he peeked into one of the windows. It was dark outside, and without lights on it was difficult to see anything in the interior. However, he saw a small glow coming from the living room, which was around a corner from his perspective. He moved to the side of the house for a better look.

From the side, he was able to look through a different window into the living room, where he saw a nightlight plugged into the wall throwing a small illumination onto its surroundings. He saw a piano against the rear wall and a couch sitting opposite the piano. There was a television sitting on a media cabinet next to the piano, with what looked like a DVD player but he couldn't tell for sure. Josh knew that there was a fireplace against the wall through which he was looking, so he moved to change perspectives again to get a better look at this. He turned another corner of the home, and was now at the front. He could be clearly seen from the road, or even from the windows of neighboring homes. He was not sheltered at all.

He looked through one of these windows, and was able to see the fireplace against the side wall. It was just as he remembered it. Hanging from the mantle were four stockings, the same number as there would have been in his own home right now if the world hadn't fallen apart. He felt a twinge of envy at this, that someone else was living in his former home, nourishing his own family and hanging his own stockings from the fireplace that used to bring Josh's family such joy. Josh felt like breaking a window, like invading the home and stealing the stockings. He hated these people, and hadn't even met them.

He figured the home invasion would be easy; the hardest part would be getting through the broken glass of the window without alerting others to his actions or getting injured. But then he would simply go to the fireplace, remove each of the stockings, and …

And he froze. Above the stockings, resting on the mantle and in fact being used as weights holding the stockings in place, were skulls. Josh couldn't see them clearly, as the only light was from the nightlight across the room, but he was nearly certain they were skulls. Human skulls.

He recoiled in horror. What had his old home become? Were these people killers? Had they kept these things, remains of their victims, as souvenirs? Could the people of the world truly have gone so insane that they would not only accept and condone murder on a massive scale, but that they were now keeping trophies? Josh could feel the darkness emanating from his former home like a poison, like tangible sin itself, and he felt sick.

Suddenly, from behind him, someone yelled "Hey!"

Josh turned to look. Across the street and four houses down, a man was standing in his front doorway. He was pointing at Josh, and had clearly shouted to draw attention to Josh's spying. "Hey you! Stop there!"

Josh knew better. He turned back the way he came and fled around the side of the home, into the backyard, and toward the trees. Behind him he heard more yelling, "He went around the house!" Other voices had joined in too. He couldn't make out all the words clearly, but he knew there was a group who was coming to get him, and he very much did not want to stick around long enough to meet them. He dashed toward the trees, but his old backyard suddenly seemed impossibly large, and each step he took seemed to bring him no closer to safety. Then, as if in a movie, he heard the unmistakable *crack* of a gunshot.

Josh swore instinctively, in panic. He did not often swear, but he felt suddenly trapped and endangered. He poured all his energy into making his legs move, one at a time as quickly as possible, and eventually he reached the trees. But it was winter, and the trees were mostly bare, and he knew the cover was spotty at best, so he did not slow down.

He leapt over branches, bushes, anything that was in his way, and again he heard the ominous *crack* of death, though this time it sounded farther behind him. He was just beginning to feel good, like safety was coming, when his foot caught on something, and he plunged face first into the ground. His momentum carried his body forward despite this, and between the initial impact and the ensuing commotion of his body coming to rest in a heap all over the place, he made a tremendous noise.

In addition, as he rose to continue to flee, he felt a pain in his right foot, near his ankle. It wasn't broken, certainly, but he had struck whatever caused his spill quite hard, and had severely bruised himself, if not worse. He resumed his run, more slowly by default, and tried as best he could to swallow that pain. He looked backward to assess the danger. He saw no one, but he did see what caused him to trip: the fort.

He cursed his stupidity but kept running. He could still hear his pursuers, and he was not going to stop until that was no longer true. He ran, limping, until his breath failed and he needed to rest out of sheer necessity.

When he felt his energy giving out, he spotted a small group of bushes nearby, and ran toward them. He fell into them and crawled in desperation out of sight as best as possible. He felt his chest heave over and over again, and seemed unable to catch his breath. His heart was pounding, out of fear and strain, and his mind could not focus on any one thought. His mouth was dry like a desert, and his ankle was pulsing, demanding rest that it had not gotten.

The minutes dragged on like hours, and eventually his breath slowed, as did his heartbeat. His head pounded, and he felt thirsty. But as his body returned to normal, he was able to hear things other than his blood pounding in his ears. He listened, but could hear nothing: no running, no gunshots, no signs of life in pursuit of him. He slowly emerged from the bushes to continue on toward the river.

As he did this, he saw a glimmer in a low hanging tree branch, and upon investigation he discovered three leaves that had fallen in such a way as to hold water. Skeptical, since it had not rained in so very long, he dipped his finger in the puddle, smelled it, and tasted it. He could find no signs that the liquid was anything but water, so greedily he swallowed it down, and the coolness of the liquid felt like the refreshment of life itself against his dry, stressed insides.

When the water was gone, he gave thanks to his Protector, He who provided in all circumstances, and continued on his way.

Chapter XII

Eventually, Josh ran out of woods. Unfortunately for him, he could only stay under this cover for so long, and ultimately there was a little less than half the total distance that he had to cross pretty much out in the open. He knew this, but kept hoping there was some way he would be wrong, that the earth would have opened itself and produced more trees to shade him from the prying eyes of the enemy. He knew there was a time coming, the sooner the better, when the earth would, indeed, open itself, but at that time it would devour, not produce. Josh longed for the day when the islands would flee and the mountains would crumble, for that meant his heavenly deliverance was about to come.

Josh ran out of trees at the high school. Beyond the tree line was a small patch of open grass, then the football field. Josh scanned around, looking and listening for signs of life, but there were none, and so he ventured out into the clearing, and onto the field.

He looked around, trying to absorb as much of his surroundings as possible. Night was in full effect, and none of the field lights were on, and so the entire grounds were very dark. He actually felt a little scared. He knew better than to expect ghosts or zombies, but even still the deep dark was fundamentally scary to him.

He had no sleeping bag or family to comfort him; he was alone, hunted, and enveloped by darkness.

He stepped across the field, not exactly slowly but not running. His mind wandered. Though he never played football in high school, or even watched a football game for that matter, he had still clung to the idea that Seth would grow to be an athlete, to catch the Hail Mary throw and run it into the end zone for the game-winning touchdown, to be remembered in the annals of high school fame for all time. Josh would then throw him a party, and watch the drama unfold as the half dozen girls who were all interested in Seth would passive-aggressively vie for his attention, all while pretending they were friends with one another.

Josh began to live this game-winning moment. He visualized the ball coming at him, and jumped up to grab it. He clutched the imaginary pigskin to his chest and ran in slow motion down the field. He heard the cheers as the imaginary crowd chanted his name: *Seth! Seth! Seth!* He was his own son now, living vicariously through an experience neither of them would ever have.

Here came the linebacker from the opposing team! The man was big as a mountain, and Josh looked around for an alternative route to the end zone. He felt the electricity in the absent crowd as they watched the seconds count down on the clock, ticking toward a victory for the visiting team. All their hopes rested on his ability to get to the goal.

He sidestepped the mountain man, and chuckled as the enemy tripped over himself and went crashing to the ground, tearing up a patch of turf that the groundskeeper would have to painstakingly reseed and care for. But none of that mattered now! Josh saw a clear path down the remaining twenty yards and dashed in slow motion toward it. All the people watching him in his imagination collectively held their breath.

Oh no! Out of nowhere the skinny kid on the other team was barreling down on him! Josh envisioned himself, in the persona of his son, running as fast as he could but even still going more slowly than the skinny kid, who Josh dubbed Flash. Each yard passed by at a snail's pace. Near the very goal line, Flash jumped forward and grabbed Josh's feet, pulling him to the ground. The home team fans all rose to their feet, in disbelief of coming so close to victory, and all the while the clock ticked down, *tick, tick, tick.* But wait! As Josh hit the ground, he reached out his arms, and as his journey toward the end zone came to a halt, the ball was held firmly in his hands, successfully over the goal line.

A roar like the trumpet of God erupted from the bleachers. *Seth! Seth! Seth!* they all chanted. Josh saw confetti fall from the sky to shower him in his victory, as the hulking opposing team disappeared into their locker room with their tails tucked between their legs. Josh climbed to his feet and did a victory dance. He swayed out his knees, he spiked the imaginary ball to the ground, and did a jig he would have been embarrassed to have any real person witness. For a moment, for this fleeting moment in time, Josh was not being hunted like a criminal. His family was not in danger. Hundreds of thousands of people around the world were not being slaughtered like animals in underground camps constructed with taxpayer dollars. Right now, Josh/Seth was the local hero who had just achieved a victory worth retiring his jersey number. The imaginary NFL scout who had watched the game approached the imaginary coach to try to speak with him about offering a scholarship. Josh cared not if his imagination got all the football details correct. Everything was right with the world.

But alas, the realization came to him that the real Seth, the one who would never get the chance to be a high school athlete even if he had desired, was at home, huddled in the darkness and wondering if his father would actually come home to spend one last Christmas with him. Josh pulled himself together and, waving a final time at his adoring fans in his mind, moved on.

He walked across the high school campus toward the main entrance. This would ultimately lead to the road, where he was heading. He didn't dare travel along the open road, of course, but he could stay hidden in the brush alongside, and this would allow him to escape the prying eyes of any Babylonian soldier who might be looking.

The journey was uneventful for some time as he walked along the road leading him to a stretch of open field that had been purchased by the county as landfill space right before the economic collapse. No one had ever begun to convert it into a workable landfill, so now it was simply vacant. Josh liked this. Despite his vulnerability, he felt safe here. Few people wanted anything to do with a landfill, even an inactive one. He felt it to be unlikely that a soldier would wander into here.

Yet, he heard weeping. It was soft at first, and he barely noticed it, but as he kept walking the sound became louder until it was unmistakable. It was so dark that he could not see the source of the noise, but he could pinpoint the direction from which it came, and went immediately on the alert. After a minute of traveling indirectly toward the sound, he could make out a figure in the near distance, seeming to be huddled over someone else on the ground.

Josh saw a small mound of dirt nearby, and crouched down behind it. He peered over the top of the mound, and simply watched. The weeping sounded female to Josh, and he convinced himself that he could make out a woman's long hair. She did nothing but weep. She did not talk or yell. She never even moved. She just knelt there, crying over a body.

Josh felt a need to go and comfort this woman, to tell her of the day when He who was the resurrection and the life would call with the voice of the archangel and the living would be reunited with the dead. But he knew the prophecies well enough to know that it would not only be God's people who met suffering and persecution in the end. Babylon was so evil that it would hunt and kill its own people for little to no reason. The fact that this body had been dumped in the middle of ground designated for waste meant nothing in terms of the loyalties of the people involved. Even now, confronting this woman could mean certain death.

He fought the urge to approach her, and eventually continued his journey, leaving her behind to mourn.

The rest of the journey passed without further encounter, and eventually he reached the river. His right ankle continued to throb, and the realization that he still had to do the entire journey in reverse weighed heavily on his heart. But he had come for a purpose, and so he set his heart to accomplish that purpose. As he felt his way through the dark toward the sounds of running water, he prayed for strength and guidance.

Chapter XIII

On his knees at the edge of the river, Josh fumbled with his backpack, trying to open it to be filled with water. He cursed himself for not figuring this out before he had left the house. He had had the bag for several days! Yet it never crossed his mind that it might be tricky to figure out the mechanisms of the bag in the middle of the night while being hunted. He knelt there for several minutes trying one thing after another until he found the right valve to press to allow water into the inner bag. Even still, the fill rate was slow, and he had to partially immerse the bag in the river.

Just as his spirits were beginning to lift, as he passed what he reasoned to be the halfway point of the bag's capacity, he heard a sound that shot chills up his spine and that shook his very core. His blood turned to ice at this noise: a whining noise, like an engine that doesn't revolve, like a transmission that doesn't shift, a constant whine of gears and energy sounding the alarm of death. He had heard this sound before. Everyone alive had. For many, it was the last sound ever heard.

He looked so intently into the sky with such quickness that he nearly lost control of the bag, and had to re-concentrate on the task at hand to keep his bag from floating away down river. He caught himself thanking the Lord that the river was running at such a low capacity, for at full volume the current would have likely torn it from his hands. But once the bag was secured again in his grasp, he resumed his vigil toward the sky. The whine must be coming from somewhere.

To his horror, he saw it coming right at him. This was the noise that came from the drones, surveillance weapons in the sky that had been introduced by the United States military before it had sworn allegiance to Babylon. At the time, they were simply unmanned reconnaissance machines slightly smaller than the size of a man, designed to spy on enemy territory without risk to American lives if shot down. But once Babylon took control, these machines were quickly retrofitted to include ammunition, and now these flying craft were the most dreaded killing machines on earth. By the time they were heard, it was too late to hide. By the time they saw their victim, it was too late to escape.

When Josh saw one flying in his direction, he became so scared that he instinctively called out to his God in his mind. 'This is it,' he told himself. 'You won't see your family again tonight.' In a futile panic, he pulled the bag from the river, dumped it on the dry ground, and fled. He knew the drone must have seen him already, yet sheer instinct took over and he ran. He didn't even know in which direction he was running, or toward what. He simply ran, and hoped. The bag, never sealed, now lay spilling out the water that had been so difficult to get in there in the first place. All was lost. All was hopeless.

Yet, to Josh's amazement, the drone flew right over his head and continued on in the direction it was flying without seeming to take notice of him. This was so unusual that he didn't even register his safety at first, and only gradually slowed his pace to realize his life was not yet over.

But once this realization hit him, he wasted no time. If the drone passed him by, that meant it was on a mission, and the drones' missions never lasted long. Safety was fleeting, at best. He doubled back toward his bag, now nearly empty again, and resumed filling it.

Each second lasted a lifetime. His heart pounded in his ears. His entire body felt warm, then hot, as the blood surged through his veins like fire from heaven coming to scorch the earth. His vision became cloudy as his blood pressure rose, and he was breathing as if just having run a marathon. His hands shook so badly that the bag filled more slowly even than it should, as it sloshed around in the shallow water. Every few seconds, separated by what seemed like a decade, Josh looked again toward the sky for new signs of flying death. Each heartbeat echoed so loudly in his ears that he did not trust his own ability to hear the drone if it returned.

Finally the bag was full, or at least full enough by his standards. He then turned his attention to the plastic bottles that he had also brought, and filled them to capacity. When everything was secure, he pulled the bag onto his back and turned around to journey back home.

Josh's entire body sagged under the weight of all the water, and from the fatigue of the journey. His ankle began to throb again, and he was conscious of the pain there for the first time since hearing the drone. The journey ahead of him seemed absolutely unbearable. 'Lord,' he cried silently, 'give me strength.'

But he was knocked to the ground by a massive explosion coming from his right. The explosion was far enough away, over the treetops, that he could not see what was going on or who the target was, yet it was still powerful enough to topple him over. As he fell, he landed on his left knee, which twisted. He cried out in pain, but thankfully the explosion was so loud that he could barely hear himself, and worried not about others hearing him. With a hurting right ankle and left knee, the temptation to give up was enormous. Death seemed better to him than a long and painful trek home.

But a promise from above flashed through his mind, and his strength was renewed: 'God is faithful, and He will not let you be tested beyond your strength, but with the testing He will also provide the way out so that you may be able to endure it.' Josh claimed this promise and immediately he felt a resolve in his innermost being to get home, to see his family again, and to bring them this bounty of fresh water.

From his distant right, the conflict continued. The sky was alight with the burning remains of whatever had been exploded, and through the crackling of distant flames Josh heard the whining of the drone again. Now, though, he heard the additional sound of weapon fire from the drone, which was able to shoot concentrated bursts of plasma, more energy than matter, to devour its victims from the inside with flame. Josh likened the sound of this horrible weapon with that of laser beams in science-fiction movies. He only wished that he was living in fiction.

From the distance, "Run! Don't stop! Go, go, go!" This was followed by that noise, like fireworks racing through the sky but never exploding, molten hot plasma searing through the air to devour whatever it touched. Josh tried to tune this out. He knew better than to think these poor people would survive this attack. No one ever survived a drone attack.

Sure enough, the distant victims ended their struggle. A plasma bullet found its target, which was evidenced by the shrill firing noise followed by a loud flaming sound, like brush going up all at once. This meant that the bullet had struck body mass and ignited it. The man or woman at the receiving end of the drone's horror would be completely engulfed and turned to ash within a minute. He or she was likely already dead, and certainly would be wishing for death if it had not come already.

Josh heard cries from others who witnessed this horror, but all too soon they, too, were struck by the drone's weapons, and all fell silent except for the continuing crackle of deathly fire.

But this didn't surprise Josh. He had seen and heard this before. Rather, he swallowed his fear and contempt and kept moving forward. He knew the days of the drones' reign of terror would soon be over. He longed for the day when the blessed hope would be realized, when the Lord Himself would descend from heaven with a shout, with the voice of the archangel, and with the trump of God: and the dead in Christ, which Josh prayed included the poor souls burned alive just now on the far side of the trees, would rise first.

He had not traveled a half mile before he heard the tell-tale *thup-thup-thup* of an approaching helicopter. He slowed only marginally, because the sound was in the same direction as the drone warfare, and he knew Babylon often followed a drone attack with real people to clean up the mess. He did not figure they would be searching for him, but rather putting out the fire they had caused, and removing all evidence of their evil.

Yet another helicopter approached also, from the other direction, and, like the drone, passed right over his head. Josh instinctively covered his head from the force of the wind. As he looked, once the helicopter had passed him over, he saw it shine a large spotlight on the ground in the near distance. Illuminated by this light, he saw a half dozen people, ranging in age from, he guessed, mid-sixties to early teens, suddenly stop dead in their tracks and look fearfully at the helicopter, which was now hovering over them. The first copter joined them, and several armed men descended on ropes from the flying machines.

Josh knew danger was near and he kept moving away. He found shelter in a small ditch and stopped to watch what was going on. He could see the uniforms of the soldiers as they encircled the small family of victims. Each man was dressed in a dark purple outfit like army fatigues without the camouflage but with a scarlet covering over their chests which, to Josh, vaguely resembled a human heart. On each arm was a scarlet band emblazoned with a large cross, shining bright yellow like the sun. These men were hunting and killing in the name of his Lord and Savior, and it simply made him sick. As the soldiers raised their weapons at their victims, Josh turned away and continued his journey home. He knew what was coming.

A tear fell from his eye as he heard the inevitable gunfire, rapidly repeating clips of ammo being unnecessarily emptied into now lifeless bodies as if the threat they posed was so large that death must be redundantly administered to each one. In his mind was permanently branded the promise made two thousand years ago: "For then shall be great tribulation, such as was not since the beginning of the world to this time, no, nor ever shall be."

As he ran home, desperate to see his wife and children, he found himself wishing that this was one promise that God failed to keep.

Chapter XIV

Josh was a firm nonbeliever in coincidence. He had seen God operate too many times in his life to doubt that everything that happened did so at the permission of the Lord. He found that God often arranged the details of life cyclically, allowing His children to succeed at their past failures and using past events to prepare for future ones. Whenever Josh was tempted to call something a coincidence, he instead paid very close attention to the circumstances therein, so he might possibly see what God was up to.

In light of this, he was not surprised at all to find himself heading back into trouble at the same point he had encountered trouble during the first leg of the journey: at the remains of the fort he had built with his son, in the distant backyard of his former home.

To Josh's amazement, all had been quiet after the massacre near the river. The screams of the fallen echoed in his head, and more than once he cried out for understanding as to why he should be lucky enough to survive, and not them. Though he knew, and kept reminding himself, that the victims' slumber would be short, and in many ways they were better off in the sleep of the dead than continuing to live through the world's demise, he still could not shake the idea that he was luckier than they for no reason. He knew better than to consider that he was more "worthy" of divine protection than anyone else. He knew there was no prayer that could be uttered, no church service that could be attended, no good work that could be performed to earn grace in the eyes of God. These popular misconceptions were taught by Babylon, even before it took over the world. Yet if he was equal, no better or worse, than those whom he had seen slain, then why was he allowed to live when they were not?

This mystery confounded his mind and kept him occupied along his journey. He barely noticed the long miles he traveled, or the various pains and fatigue that coursed through his body. The weight on his back seemed small compared to the weight on his mind.

And before he reached any kind of conclusion to this great mystery, there it was again, the pile of stones that commemorated a time long since past, a time of happiness and optimism with his young son.

He knew he should keep on walking by but he just couldn't. He felt the calling to go back to the house, the same calling that had drawn him there earlier that evening. Without a clear understanding why, and while condemning himself for doing so, he turned and walked toward the home that had so nearly been his downfall. Each step he took brought more pain to his right ankle. His very body was protesting the decision to go there. Yet he went anyway.

It wasn't long before he exited the cover of the trees. Before him stood the house, but this time there were lights on inside. People were home. Real danger was present.

'Stop!' his mind cried. 'What are you doing? Go home!'

But he just could not. He was being drawn there by a force bigger than himself.

He walked through the back yard that used to be his, and approached the house. The moon above shone on him directly; no trees or clouds stood as a barrier between him and the lesser light that reflected the sun's illumination. He could be clearly seen from all directions. He was a moving target, and he was not moving quickly.

In the corner of the family room, the room visible through the windows at the back of the home, the room adjacent to the living room with the human skulls on the fireplace mantle, was a lit Christmas tree. It stood about six feet tall, and was adorned with all sorts of ornaments around the entire girth of the tree, even at the back which could not be seen from the family room itself, but only from the outside, where Josh was standing. Garland of red and purple snaked around the tree from the bottom to the top. Tinsel of gold and silver hung freely from the branches. Josh felt like this tree was mocking him. Facing him only, at the back of the tree, was an ornament with a family photo on it: two parents and two children embracing, with the caption "Merry Christmas." Like before, Josh felt hatred toward these people. He and his loved ones huddled together in a dark attic every night, scared that there may not come a morning for them, yet these people prospered at the suffering of others like him.

Josh caught himself. He was feeling hate, and had been hateful often that night. Yet his Lord called out for the forgiveness of the very men who crucified Him. The voice of his Savior called to him, "'But I say to you, love your enemies, bless those who curse you, do good to those who hate you, and pray for those who spitefully use you and persecute you. Therefore you shall be perfect, just as your Father in heaven is perfect.'" Josh knew that the burning sensation in his gut, which cried out for vengeance and blood against these people, was sin. It all came from the spot in his heart where God should be, but wasn't at that moment. He closed his eyes and offered a silent prayer. 'Lord,' he began, 'thank you for dying so that I may not have to. Help me to be empty of myself. You have already lived your perfect life for me. I am claiming that life as my own, by faith. Fulfill in me what you have already done.'

Peace settled over him. The cry for blood was quenched. He felt stronger than before, and more able to deal with whatever had drawn him to this place twice that night.

At the top of the tree inside the house was an angel looking down on the tree with love, as if the perky needles contained within them the newborn King. Everything looked like he remembered 'normal' being, except for the hated purple intermixed with the normal holiday colors, betraying the evil loyalties of the people inside.

The doorbell rang! This startled Josh but he quickly remembered that he was in the back yard, and no one was able to see him. He watched as a lone man, the same one Josh had seen in the ornament on the tree, emerged from the living room, where those terrible skulls were, and walked over to the front door. The man had on a purple shirt and an armband with a bright yellow cross on it, like the soldiers had at the massacre earlier. He stood over six feet tall by Josh's estimation, and was bald. He opened the door and in poured a small group of other people. They looked so normal.

Three adults came inside, a man and two women, and in tow were three children. The other man was slightly overweight and also going bald, though he retained more hair than the first. The women looked similar to each other, standing about Angelica's height with short hair cut just below their ears. Josh guessed they were sisters. The youngest child was asleep in the second man's arms. Josh remembered that tonight was Christmas Eve. He imagined that this group was returning from midnight service. They had been praying to the enemy, using the name of his God. While they were at church, thanking this 'holy' institution for its promises to restore order to the world, other members of the organization itself had hunted down and exterminated innocent people near the river.

One of the women came in and kissed the man from the ornament, and Josh recognized the woman from the ornament too. It was then that Josh noticed that all the people, even the children, were wearing the scarlet armbands with the bright yellow crosses on them. Maybe this had become mandatory for all those who pledged allegiance to the enemy. Maybe Babylon was running out of people to kill, and had to distinguish its friends from its enemies.

The entire group came into the family room, outside of which Josh was standing directly, but the man's wife first closed the front door. Strangely, she did not close it all the way. Josh hid from direct sight of those in the family room, still watching the people inside. The same woman took the sleeping child from the other man's arms, and moved to walk upstairs, with the other children following.

The people remaining downstairs moved to the center of the room as if preparing for something. They moved furniture around to clear a space. The man who had just arrived began to light candles. The man dressed in purple, who had been at home, grabbed a crucifix, about a foot high, off a nearby shelf and placed it on top of the television, which was in front of the area that was being prepared. Josh wondered for what, exactly, it was being prepared.

The woman returned from upstairs, and the others seemed glad that she was finally there. The man in purple moved to the far corner of the room, the opposite corner to where the Christmas tree stood, and that is when Josh noticed a sheet or some similar covering draped over a large figure, about six feet tall. His insides froze with the anticipation that the sheet might be concealing a prisoner, or a body. When the man pulled the sheet off, Josh realized his fears were unfounded, but new fears sprang up in their place. Under the sheet was a statue of an owl, standing as tall as a man, peering with open eyes down into the center of the room, where all the other people were now kneeling in a circle. The man in purple joined them. The others began removing all their clothes.

Like a ton of bricks, Josh realized he was about to witness a sacrifice, probably human. He did not know from where this sudden knowledge came, but he recognized that the large owl had nothing to do with Jesus despite the crucifix on the television, and everything to do with the evil institution that bore His name. As Josh's God required sacrifice to atone for sins, first typified through animals and finally through Christ the Lamb of God, so too did the enemy require sacrifice, but for a different purpose. Sacrifice for God was to redeem fallen humanity. Sacrifice for the devil was for no reason except evil.

Josh knew something must be done. The front door was still slightly ajar, and he now knew why. On the other side of it was someone who, without Josh's intervention, would find him- or herself in the middle of that circle soon, with the stone cold eyes of the owl looking down on his or her final moments. This is why Josh had been led here. He was to save this person.

Josh immediately got to his feet and ran to the front of the building. He felt no pain in either leg. He felt no fatigue at all. He barely noticed the pounds of water hanging from his back. His supernatural strength stood in stark contrast to his desire for death just a short time before.

Then Josh saw him, a man, bound and lying on the front doorstep, clear for anyone to see. He stopped dead in his tracks and, for a moment, could not move. The two men locked eyes.

The sacrificial man was on his stomach, hog-tied with his arms and legs pulled backward in the air and tied together. A piece of duct tape covered his mouth, which in turn seemed permanently opened, as if a sock or other object was shoved inside.

This man moved his eyes, the only part of him that was mobile. He did not know who Josh was, or what his intentions were. He was clearly scared.

Josh stood there stupidly, until an invisible hand seemed to shove him forward, and a silent instruction resounded in his mind, *GO GET HIM!* Without another moment's hesitation, Josh shed the pounds of water from his back and darted forward toward the prisoner. To his left, as he passed the windows at the front of his house, he saw those terrible skulls on the fireplace mantle, holding the stockings in place. The room was brightly illuminated this time, and there was no mistaking what they were: evidence of evil; evidence that other rituals like this one had not been interrupted in the past.

Josh reached the man and realized he had no tools with him at all. He had no knife with which to cut the ropes binding the man's hands and feet. He whispered to the man, "I'm not here to hurt you. Hold on, I'll try to set you free." But still, there was nothing with which to free him. Josh looked around frantically. He patted his pockets as if he would have accidentally stashed a blade there without knowing. He felt so suddenly hopeless.

He remembered the source of all hope, but powerful doubt flooded his mind. How could God intervene here? Where was there room for the Lord to come to the rescue?

But Josh subdued this doubt. He had seen too much evidence throughout his life to become a doubter now. He felt as if he had been led here for this purpose. He had not set out to accomplish this task on his own, so it was not his responsibility to solve the problem on his own either. He bowed his head, closed his eyes, folded his hands, and said in a whisper, "Lord, help. Please."

Immediately he lifted his head. He felt like he would find the answer in the water bag somehow. That didn't make sense, he reasoned. He knew there was no knife in the water bag. But he ran back to it anyway, unwilling to ignore the response he had gotten.

The prisoner on the front stoop made a noise, barely audible through the object in his mouth and the tape covering it, but Josh heard it. The man was scared of being left alone again. Josh recognized this but said nothing. Now was not the time for reassurances. Time was of the essence.

He heard a low chanting coming from inside the house, and felt his insides turn cold. At the water bag, he picked it up off the ground, and desperately searched through all the pockets he could find. He opened the main flap and ran his hand over the inner waterproof bag. He found nothing. His mind was racing.

"Lord, help," he repeated. "I don't see the answer!" He immediately turned his head to the right, for a reason he could not fully understand, and there, beneath the bush against the house, he thought he saw an object. It looked like a rock, but Josh moved to it anyway. Through his mind raced possibilities laced with doubt. *Am I supposed to use a rock to cut the ropes? Will that work?* Then, like an evil temptation, *Am I supposed to use the rock to put the man out of his misery?*

Josh grabbed the item, which was, indeed, a rock, and picked it up to figure out what to do with it. But as he lifted the rock, he noticed there was something under it! In the sheer amazement that comes only as a result of watching divine intervention unfold, he again stood there stupidly, unable to fully comprehend what he now saw. Laying there in the dirt, completely covered by a barely visible rock until just now, was a box cutter, buried in the earth except for its very tip.

Josh unearthed this treasure, and verified it had a working blade. He then ran back to the man, and went straight to work. He cut with tremendous violence and with such disregard to safety that later he marveled that he had not cut either himself or the other man. As he sawed away, he felt certain that the murderers inside would hear him or interrupt him in some way. He demanded of himself that these thoughts be suppressed. He would not have been brought this far only to fail. Failure was not an option.

After a seeming eternity, Josh finally cut all the way through, and the ropes fell from the other man's hands and feet. He fell onto his side as the blood suddenly returned to his limbs. His eyes closed in relief.

Josh knelt down and grabbed one end of the tape. He whispered, "This might hurt. Do not scream." He ripped the tape off the man's mouth with great force, and saw his face contract with pain. There was a clear red mark where the tape had been, and this mark was surely to get worse as it swelled. Josh saw that it was cloth of some kind, but not a sock, that had been stuffed in the man's mouth. He saw the man try to grab it but his coordination was off, as his arms and fingers were still numb. Josh grabbed it and pulled it out. He saw it was a piece of a shirt, a sleeve with a portion of the shoulder. To Josh's horror, he saw that it was stained red with what he could only imagine was blood. He did not imagine the blood belonged to this man.

Suppressing a gag of sickness, he said to the man, "Get up now. I know it's hard but we have to leave now." The man fumbled around as he tried to gain his balance and footing, but it was taking too long. Josh, without thinking, grabbed the man around his chest under his arms and lifted him into the air, carrying him away from the front door and back to where the water bag still lay on the ground.

Josh released the man onto his own feet, and he shook and wobbled but managed to stay upright. Josh looked him right in the eye and asked, "Can you walk?"

The man looked back at him, his eyes wide open in amazement. He said, slowly, as if dreaming, "Yes, I – I think so."

"How far do you have to go?"

"I don't know where I am."

"You're on Maybury Lane in –"

"Maybury," repeated the freed prisoner. "Yes, I know where that is. I don't have far. Maybe a mile."

"I can't travel with you," said Josh, realizing again that he was on a journey of his own, and had a family at home who were worried about him.

"I understand."

Josh pulled one of the bottles of water from a pocket in the water bag and handed it to the man. "I'm sorry I can't give you more. The rest is for my family."

The man nodded, still looking Josh straight in the eye. He simply could not believe what had happened in the last few minutes.

Josh stood there as well, unwilling to break the eye contact. But as the chanting from inside died down, he resolved to move. "I have to go," he said to the man. "God be with you." He moved past the man while slinging the water bag onto his back, and moved back toward the rear of the house, to return to the woods.

Before he had taken two steps, the man said, "Wait." Josh turned around to look at him again, for the last time. "Thank you," he said. "My name is Peter."

"Go home, Peter," said Josh. "I'm Josh. God willing, we will see each other soon, under better circumstances." He turned around again and headed back on his own journey.

He ran as swiftly as possible, though the pain and fatigue had returned to him, back to the rock fort in the woods. When he saw these rocks, he stopped to rest and recover. What had just happened? He had turned into some kind of superman back there! He had always read about adrenaline rushes in life-or-death situations, but had never experienced such a thing firsthand. He felt proud of himself, but also exhausted. He realized he was crying.

This man, who had in a single night seen death in so many different forms, who had been injured and hunted, who had saved the life of a stranger at a place he used to call home, knelt down on the ground and wept. He lowered his face to the ground not out of reverence or thankfulness, but out of sheer exhaustion, both physical and emotional. He wept for the state of the world. He wept for those who had chosen death over life. He wept even for those who were now worshipping a stone owl out of misguided loyalty to evil wisdom. He felt there was nothing to do now except to cry. If, as the wise man had said so long ago, 'To every thing there is a season, and a time to every purpose under the heaven,' then now was the time for weeping. All thoughts of danger, and even salvation, were gone from his mind now as he poured out his soul into the ground. Each tear that fell from his face felt like sweet release. He cared not for the noise he must be making. Now was the time to purge the evil he had witnessed from his life.

After several minutes, the tears ceased, and Josh caught his breath. He raised himself up and looked around, and determined that he was still alone. He climbed to his feet, strapped the bag to his back, and continued home. Right now, there was nothing he wanted more than to embrace his family. Nothing, that is, except to be delivered from this world.

Chapter XV

Josh finally made it back to his housing complex, and stood at the last position of shelter before dashing to his home in plain view, available for all to see if they were looking at that moment. He estimated the time to be well after midnight, maybe 2AM or later, so he hoped that any potential predators would be asleep. He certainly hoped that the world's children were asleep in their beds, with visions of sugarplums dancing in their heads. Hopefully there was still enough innocence left in the world for that, though after all he'd seen that night he found it hard to believe it could be so.

He looked ahead at the few hundred feet that remained between himself and the loving arms of his wife, and a nervous energy exploded in his gut. He could not shake the feeling that his adventure would not end the way he hoped. He saw this last stretch of open space as wrought with peril somehow, even though he could see no signs of conscious life anywhere.

He saw, in his mind, his darling Phoebe's face light up at the prospect of so much water all at once, but this thought was crowded by the idea that somehow he would not get to see her react that way. He tried as best he could to shake this nagging doubt, this sense of dread, but it would not leave him.

Terrible thoughts flooded his mind. Maybe the house had been invaded in his absence. Maybe there was an ambush waiting for him. Maybe there would be an insurmountable barricade between here and the house. Of course even if this wasn't so, the water he carried on his back was still finite. Before the world fell apart, he would not have considered it a large amount of water at all! Maybe his beautiful daughter would be disappointed that he wasn't able to bring home more. Maybe he would have to make this terrible journey again tomorrow.

The bottom line, however, was that he had to exercise a certain amount of faith right now and get home. Standing here in his doubt would accomplish nothing. Eventually the sun would rise. He had to go.

So he went. He took a step into the open, and when he wasn't instantly bombed to death he took another step. Gaining confidence, he walked faster, and faster still. He tried to run but his knee and ankle just hurt too much, so he settled for a brisk walk.

He went into the complex, past the first row of houses, into the open courtyard, and past the front of his home. He felt relieved. He was almost there. He walked around the side of the Cain home, now with curtains drawn, and headed toward the back door, where his journey would finally come to an end. He turned the corner, and was approaching the back door, when it happened.

He heard a rustling behind him, and a voice. "Hey. Stop."

Josh froze. After all he'd witnessed, he just could not believe he had been caught right here, right at his home. His mind raced. Had they gone inside? Did they know his family was there? Were they still alive?

Anger welled up inside him. He was so mad at himself. He knew, he just *knew* not to leave the woods! He should have stayed there until that feeling of dread passed. He knew better!

Then he got mad at God. Why would the Lord have sent him on this arduous journey only to be captured at its end? Couldn't he have become Babylon's victim without having to be injured all night first? Yes, he had saved that man Peter. But was Peter's life more important than his own? Where was Josh's miraculous rescue?

He turned around. If, per chance, his family had not yet been disturbed by this intruder, then he did not want to give away their presence. He would take the punishment for them all. He just hoped they would understand why he didn't come home.

Breathing heavily, and managing only barely to keep his angst and anger inside, he turned around with his hands extended out to his side, to show that he was not armed or dangerous. He didn't say a word.

He saw a woman there. She stood with her shoulders hunched, but Josh could not tell much more about her in the darkness. The moonlight revealed that her clothes were bundled in layers against her skin, and might be torn, but he just couldn't be sure.

Neither of them said anything for a few moments. Josh was determined not to give her anything with which to condemn him to her superiors. He fought the urge to curse her, and kept quiet.

Finally, she said, "Who are you?" Josh did not answer. "I said, who are you?" she repeated.

Josh heard her voice quiver. It was then that he noticed there was no purple band on her arm, no bright yellow cross demonstrating her loyalty. Even still, that meant nothing. He had not seen those bands on anyone except military until earlier that night.

"Why aren't you saying anything?" she demanded. "Are you dumb?"

Still, he said nothing.

She walked up to him and looked him right in the eyes. She had an odor. It was not bad. She did not smell like filth, but rather she had to her the smell of someone living off nature. He guessed she had not seen shelter in some time. When she spoke, he smelled stale breath, like dehydration. Maybe she was after his water.

She said slowly, "I've been watching you for awhile." Then she added, "Your family, too."

Josh felt like his heart stopped. She knew about Angelica and the kids.

He broke his silence, and asked, "Who are you?"

Now it was her turn to keep silent.

Josh spoke again, "What do you want from me?"

The woman's face relaxed, ever so slightly. She broke eye contact, and looked at the ground, as if ashamed. She said softly, "My name is Ruth. I don't think you're one of the bad guys."

Josh was stunned. What was going on?

Maybe it was a ruse. He wasn't ready to trust her yet.

"Then who do you think I am?" he asked her.

Ruth broke down. "Mister, I don't know anything. But everything is so crazy everywhere and you don't look like the bad guys. You sneak around like you're afraid of them too, like me."

Josh still had a hard time believing she posed no threat. His questions continued. "When was the last time you ate something?"

"It's been a long time since I had anything normal," she answered. "Mostly I eat whatever's around, sometimes bugs, anything I can find."

"Where did you come from?"

"I used to live in Tea Ridge," she answered, which was in the next county north. "I've been on the run since they destroyed our home." She paused before admitting, "I don't even know where I am now."

"You're about twenty miles from home," Josh said. "Who destroyed your place?"

"The bad guys," Ruth answered. The exasperation showed on her face, even in the darkness. "God, I don't even know who they are anymore. The military. The Christians. I don't know. Them."

"Real Christians don't behave that way," said Josh. "God doesn't behave that way."

Immediately her eyes met Josh's again and he could see her fear, as if she was not expecting him to say this, couldn't process it logically, and didn't know how to respond.

She said simply, "Please don't hurt me." She began to back away.

"Ruth," he said gently. She stopped moving away. "Ruth, I'm not going to hurt you." Josh was suddenly aware that they were still outside, visible to anyone who could be watching. That they were still alive meant that she was either a terrific evil actor, or that there was no present danger. But that could change.

He reached out and grabbed her hand, which she gave him reluctantly. He looked directly at her and asked her in as straightforward a manner as he knew how, "Are you one of them? Are you trying to trap me?"

Josh could see her eyes open wide in amazement at this, but all she said was, "No. I couldn't do something like that." The two of them stood silently in the darkness, sizing each other up. She added, "That's why they're after me now. That's why my family got killed. It's why I ran away."

Josh offered a silent prayer. 'Lord, protect me. Honor what I am about to do, for if it were not for you, I would not be doing it.'

"Come inside," he said. "It's not safe out here."

She said, "Thank you," and followed him through the broken back door.

The odor inside wasn't pleasant. Apparently someone had had to use the toilet bucket since he left. He quickly emptied it outside while Ruth waited inside. He used some of the water in the remaining water bottle to rinse it.

Back inside, the conversation resumed.

"You said you have been watching my family. Tell me what you've seen."

Ruth was visibly uncomfortable. "I know you have a girlfriend, or a wife," she answered. "She comes outside sometimes."

"That's right," Josh confirmed. "And she won't be expecting me to bring home a visitor. Most people would not be friendly to us."

She paused before saying, "I'm not going to hurt you. I don't know what else to say."

"We have very limited food here. Limited everything, in fact. We can't board you."

Ruth stated simply, "I understand," though even in the darkness Josh could see disappointment on her face as she looked away from him and toward the floor.

"Do you also understand that if we find out you're lying, that we can't let you leave here? Ever?" Josh was surprised at his own words, but he realized he meant them. Nothing could compromise the safety of his family.

Uncomfortable, Ruth said, "Maybe I should go."

"You can't do that either," said Josh. "You know we're here now. All by itself, that poses a threat to us."

Ruth began to stammer in exasperation, "I don't know what to do! Everything was just fine, everything was okay, we were happy, and then out of nowhere everything just fell apart, like the whole world changed overnight and suddenly I was all alone and homeless and everyone wants to kill me just for being alive!" She began to cry. "I'm so hungry, and so tired, and I'm so scared all the time, and nothing makes any sense anymore, and I didn't even do anything wrong! I just want things to go back to the way they were, when things made sense and everything was okay. And now everyone is out to get everyone else and I'm like a criminal and the government is killing people and America sucks and I thought Jesus was supposed to love people and I didn't do anything wrong!"

Josh's heart just melted hearing this. He was convinced. The raw emotion pouring out of this poor young woman was too real, too deep, to have its origin in Babylon. He wasn't sure how exactly he would convince his wife and kids that she posed no threat, but he knew he must. Here was a child of his God in need of comfort and shelter, and it was his duty, his privilege, to provide what he could.

"Come upstairs," he said. "Let me introduce you to my family."

She wiped her eyes and followed him.

Josh led her into his son's room. He saw her look around at the remains of a little boy's room with posters of superheroes adorning the walls and action figures littering the ground. Her gaze came to rest on one of the posters and she said simply, "I wish the superheroes were coming to save the world now."

Josh smiled as he moved to the closet and began knocking on the wall for he knew that Jesus, the most powerful hero in the universe, really was coming to save the world very shortly. *Knock*, pause, *knock*, pause, *knock knock*, he tapped against the wall. This was a pre-agreed knock between him and his wife that advised that Josh was not alone, but everything was okay anyway.

It was a few moments before anything happened, and Josh wondered if Angelica didn't believe his knock, or had maybe forgotten what it meant. But eventually the portal to the attic opened, and a rope was lowered down.

Angelica poked her head through the opening. It was still dark, but Josh could see the mixture of relief and concern that was on her face. She said, "I'm so glad you're home. What's going on?"

Josh replied simply, "We have company."

Chapter XVI

Josh and Ruth climbed up into the attic, which was nearly pitch dark. The children were asleep and had been for a few hours. Angelica had nodded off herself.

Angelica seemed to understand immediately that the presence of a new person was a big deal, and that the night had just taken a turn that required attention. She got out three candles and lit them. Phoebe stirred but didn't wake up. Seth remained as unconscious as before.

Josh didn't want to wake his children but knew he must. When they were awake, each of the children knew right away that something important was happening. They had not seen anyone but their parents for months, and no one outside their church family for longer than that. No one but the immediate family had ever been into the attic, or even knew it was there. The very existence of this woman in their lives was an amazing turn of events.

Josh gave them as much back story as he knew about Ruth, but he had more questions than answers. He reassured his family that he believed she posed no threat. There was also a small celebration about the gathering of several gallons of water, some of which was portioned out among the family and Ruth now. Once the water was distributed, however, Josh wasted no time.

"Ruth," he began, "tell me what the world is like right now. How are things different from six months ago?"

Ruth told them how the only thing that had changed was the brutality of the Babylon government. There were still devastating storms somewhere in the world every week or more. Babylon boasted of itself as the only glue holding together a planet in crisis, and continued to promise an improvement if every person alive would bow down in restful obedience on the first day of every week, and offer worship to their global ruler. When the conditions of the world failed to improve, they vilified one group of people after another, and the groups kept coming. Ruth believed every person on earth would be killed before anything got better, and the terrible soldiers of Babylon seemed to be in no hurry to stop killing.

Ruth said that the food conditions had not improved. Babylon had set up some farms in various areas of the world but the crop cycles had been so thoroughly decimated that they were predicting a full calendar year before food would become readily available again. In addition, the food that was available now, scarce as it was, was available only as it was funneled through and released by Babylon, so often the cost was too high for common people to afford. The authorities had been known to turn away starving people who came to the very storehouses, if they did not have the funds to purchase the food. They claimed there was not enough food to go around, so some means must be used to determine who gets the food and who does not. Not surprisingly, Babylon's selection method was monetary. When questioned about the inhumane nature of starving people to death over economy, the authorities replied that this had been done during famines all through history, and that it was, after all, evolution. The fittest people during this crisis were the ones with money, so they would be the ones to survive, and usher humanity into the next phase of its development.

Josh could hardly keep still. He had studied in earnest, in his school years, the unique adaptive skills possessed by life on earth.

He had always seen a beauty in the gift God gave His creatures to be able to change in order to survive in a world constantly decaying in sin. He was amazed, now and always, that the tiny idea of a species adapting to its environment could morph and change and grow as if itself were a living being; could turn into, in many ways, a religious belief system called "evolution" whose fundamentalists rivaled any other groups'; and could now have become a literal weapon against God's people, while bearing the name of his Christ. As if his God would work in such a way as to promote the elite at the expense of the poor! Yet these terrible men were preying on the ignorance of the masses, and convincing them that it was God's will to weed out the weak from the strong. What a massive, sickening lie.

When Ruth ran out of current events, she paused. Josh broke the silence by asking, delicately, "How did you come to be on their bad side?"

Ruth did not answer right away. She breathed heavily for a few seconds, as if mustering the courage to speak. Eventually, she said, "My younger brother was born blind. We filed for a Disability Exception with the local Christian office," Josh cringed at this term, "so they wouldn't take him away for being weak. They told us they would protect and support Timmy, my brother, if we continued to be loyal to them. So we agreed."

"Real Christians don't act that way," said Angelica.

"I told her that outside," advised her husband.

Ruth seemed not to know how to respond to that, so she continued right on with her story. "Timmy joined a school for blind kids, but it was far away."

Josh knew about these schools. Babylon had decided that there were simply too many human beings to sustain life on earth, and that the severe weather was not only a direct response of the earth's overpopulation, but also a judgment from God against weakness. To solve two problems at once, they issued a decree that all physically handicapped people from every corner of the globe be captured and imprisoned for study. They would be scrutinized, operated on, experimented on, maimed, tested, and tortured in the name of science so the authorities could determine what about them had caused them to be weaker, so this could be eliminated from future generations. Babylon had sold this program to the world in terms of how much more food would now be available per person for those remaining after this genetic cleansing was complete.

Loyalist families were able to petition the government for the Disability Exceptions, called DEs for short, which Ruth had mentioned; but these were not always granted and, as Ruth was about to tell them, the system was designed to track the disabled, not protect them.

"The school held a party one week on Salvation Day so the DE kids could get to know each other and stuff," Ruth explained. "We got a special permit to drive there without going to church first. There was lots of, like, propaganda at the party, with slogans from the Christians saying they were like a loving Savior allowing the DE kids to grow into functioning members of society. There was lots of food, somehow. Everyone was really happy."

Her story continued. There was a buffet-style dinner, which had become all but extinct after the farms burned, and a worship service was arranged to happen on the grounds at the school for everyone to participate in.

Ruth's family, however, had decided to go home first. They lived a significant distance away, and Ruth's mother had a phobia of traveling in the dark. Since it was after dark already once the buffet was concluded, she insisted they go home and attend the late worship service near their house. They all agreed this was a good idea.

But on the way home the left front tire went flat. Ruth's father knew how to handle such a thing, and carried a jack and a spare in the car. The tire was fully changed and the family was back on the road with no injury or major inconvenience. However, they were delayed.

When they got home, they discovered the worship service had already begun. A quick calculation revealed that they would likely miss the Communion portion of the service even if they were to leave right then. As a family, they agreed that the service was not worth attending if Communion was missed, and that they would go to service the following day to catch up.

But the following day never came. At the first light of dawn, the soldiers had broken into their home and the invasion had begun. Ruth's bedroom was on the lower level of the house, next to the furnace closet, and when she heard the noise she hid behind the furnace. She never expected to escape detection. She didn't pray for deliverance. She simply sat there and wept silently and hoped it wouldn't hurt too much when they found her. They just never found her.

The screaming stopped after just a few minutes but the noise did not. For about an hour, there were noises of violence coming from the home, as furniture was destroyed, dishes were broken, bookshelves were overturned and the house was reduced to rubbish. Then everything went quiet.

Too quiet.

Ruth gathered her nerve and emerged from behind the furnace. She went out from the furnace room into her bedroom, and grabbed the handle of her bedroom door to enter into the rest of the house. But the handle was warm.

She opened the door anyway and was met with tremendous heat. The house was on fire! The fire was about fifteen feet away from her, but it blocked her only exit from the home. She panicked. Adding to this, she also saw her mother's dead body, filled with holes and covered in blood. Her neck had been twisted around, clearly fracturing if not severing her spine. Next to her mother's body was that of her brother. The top of his head, beginning at the eyes that had been shut to light forever, was bashed in.

But Ruth did not have time to wallow in horror at what she saw, for she needed to escape now! The fire was spreading and she knew it would not stop until it had consumed the entire home.

Her bedroom, being on the ground floor, had a window through which she could climb out, but this window would not open. Ruth had been placed in this downstairs bedroom to keep her away from the rest of the family, with whom she did not often get along. Out of fear that she would run away in the middle of the night, her window was sealed closed. Her parents thought this action might save her life someday, but here it was contributing to her death.

Ruth grabbed the heaviest item she could find at that moment, her stereo, and hurled it at the window. The window did not break, but the stereo did. Then she took the small nightstand from the side of her bed and smashed it against the window. The window still remained unbroken, but thankfully so did the stand. Again and again she beat the glass until it cracked, then broke. Immediately she felt the difference in temperature as the heat of the fire escaped into the chilly morning. She used the nightstand to knock out as many glass shards as she could, then climbed out the window. She sustained cuts to her hands and legs but made it out safely otherwise. She had been homeless ever since.

"Let me see your hands," said Angelica. Ruth presented her palms, and Angelica saw the scars of the improperly healed cuts. "You poor child."

Ruth was only a teenager, though Josh only realized this now, in the attic, as she was illuminated by candlelight. Her story implied her youth, and now he saw how her face still bore the smoothness of skin that was present before age took over. He saw that the bags under her eyes were from weariness, not age. He didn't imagine she was a day over sixteen.

Everyone sat in silence after this. Ruth seemed reluctant to say anything further. The kids kept quiet. Finally Josh asked, "Do you have any questions for us?"

Ruth was looking down at the floor, but when spoken to she lifted her stare and gazed right into Josh's eyes. Sincerely, she asked, "What in the world is going on?"

Josh took his time and chose his words carefully. The answer to this question involved a lot of unlearning on Ruth's part, a delicate undertaking for anyone. He said finally, "I want to tell you the story of the biggest conflict the universe has ever experienced. It involves you, me, and all of us. Your whole life is in this story, and what is still to come. You'll see things the way they really are."

She looked straight at him, not sure what to think. "I want to trust you," she said.

Josh smiled and said simply, without breaking eye contact with Ruth, "Seth, get the Bibles, please."

Chapter XVII

Josh started as early as he could think of: page 1.

"The first verse of the first chapter of the entire set of Scriptures begins with the simple phrase, 'In the beginning God...'" Josh stated. "The rest of the verse, chapter, book, and sixty-five books that follow tell the story of all the things God has done and will do."

Josh pointed out what he believed to be a common misconception. The first two verses state: 'In the beginning God created the heaven and the earth. And the earth was without form, and void; and darkness was upon the face of the deep. And the Spirit of God moved upon the face of the waters.' Only then, only after the undefined period when the earth had nothing in it or on it, did God begin the seven-day week of Creation. God's creation *of* the earth, and God's creation *on* the earth, were two separate events.

"Therefore," he concluded, "there must have been some period of time between those two events. Right? Turn to Psalm 8:5. What does it say?"

It took Ruth some time to locate the book of Psalms, but the family patiently waited for her to consult the table of contents and find the appropriate passage. She read, "'For you have made him a little lower than the angels, and you have crowned him with glory and honor.'" She paused. "Who is 'him?'"

"Good question," answered Josh. "Verse four tells you that this passage is talking about mankind. It says that humans are made similar in nature to the angels, but not the same. The Bible repeats this idea in a different place, too.[4] But tell me, Ruth. If man was made in relation to angels, then which came first, the human or the angel?"

She thought about this for a while because it seemed to her like a strange question. But logically she answered, "The angels came first, I guess."

"Angels, therefore, occupied that time when the earth was here but had nothing on it. Why is that important? Turn to Genesis chapter 3."

Josh demonstrated that in the earth's initial perfection after the Creation, in God's perfect garden, in mankind's intended eternal home, there was already a deceiver. The devil was already there, in the form of a serpent, to lure the human family into ruin. Paradise had already been broken somewhere else in the universe, and the war had been brought to earth.

Seth read from his Bible at his father's request. "'Now the serpent was more crafty than any other wild animal that the Lord God had made.'"

Josh continued in summary, "This serpent then tempts the first woman into rejecting what God had told her not to do, and after she listens to this snake and breaks God's command she then convinces her husband to do the same. Because of this, the earth is then plunged into sin and decay, because sin is the transgression of God's law."

Ruth looked skeptical. "A talking snake?" she asked. "Seriously?"

Josh smiled patiently. "Why does that trouble you?"

---

4   Hebrews 2:7, 9

Ruth was quiet for a moment. She answered slowly, as if afraid there was some big piece of the puzzle she was missing. "Because snakes don't talk."

"First of all," Josh began, "the Bible has several stories of animals speaking and behaving in abnormal ways as a result of divine influence, and the devil is a divine creature, so he would definitely be able to cause something like this. Second, do you believe that the government right now has really been blessed by God and is acting for the good of the planet?"

"No," she answered.

"Remember when that strange storm happened in Washington and there was that fire from the sky that no one could figure out?" Ruth nodded. "What happened after that?"

"The entire world went crazy," she answered.

"Everyone suddenly believed that the church really was divine like they claimed to be, right? And they took charge of the whole world. Because when people see things they can't explain, they tend to automatically assume that the force behind it is God, even though the Bible is quite clear that the devil can imitate many of the things God is able to do. That's what happened in Washington, and that's what happened in the Garden of Eden. Honestly, if you saw a talking snake one day, wouldn't you do what it said?"

Ruth wanted to deny this, but she knew that, indeed, she probably would listen to such a thing, simply because it would be so out of the ordinary.

Josh continued. "So the first people break God's rules and are thrown out of paradise and sentenced to eventually die, along with the entire human family all through time. I know that seems harsh," he said, in response to Ruth's alarmed look, "but God's law can't be changed, and when it is broken, death has to follow. That's the only way to maintain order in the universe. The Bible says plainly that the wages of sin is death."

Angelica jumped in here. "Do you think that God's law is important if He condemns to death those who violate it?"

"I think it makes God pretty narrow-minded," said Ruth.

"Yet look at what the end result has been of that tiny little mistake in the Garden," Angelica said. "All the death, the mayhem, the illness, the lying, the wars, the violence. Everything that makes this world so bad never would have happened if God's law was obeyed. That's why God has to strictly enforce His law, because to do otherwise leads to chaos and will eventually destroy the universe."

Ruth thought this over and responded with a simple, "Okay."

Angelica continued, "So what, then, happened to this serpent? How do you think God has dealt with this problem, and the devil specifically?"

Josh took over again here, and directed everyone to read Genesis 3:14-15, where they found the very first promise from God that a Savior would come. Josh explained that God promised right then, immediately after the first people made that fateful mistake, that a clear line of distinction will forever be drawn between God's people and the devil's, and that one day the controversy between them shall come to an end. The devil and his followers will receive a fatal blow to the head, and order will be restored to the universe. However, in the process, the promised Messiah will suffer as well.

"So therefore," concluded Josh, "each and every human life that has ever been lived has been part of this great controversy, and everybody's thoughts, actions, and decisions have been ultimately either for God or against Him. Even now, when the devil is using God's name, most people think they are following God but really they're not. The devil is very tricky that way."

"The serpent is more crafty than any other animal!" declared Phoebe, paraphrasing what Seth had read earlier. "He's very smart."

Ruth said nothing, so Josh took that to mean she was doing okay, and the Holy Spirit was helping her to understand. So he continued the lesson.

"But remember, the devil was already present at the world's beginning. So what happened? How did the devil come to exist in the first place? Turn to Ezekiel 28, and read starting in verse 12."

Ruth had put down her Bible while they had been talking and picked up a different one this time. She checked her contents and made it to the passage in question. When she got there, she read, ""'You were the model of perfection, full of wisdom and perfect in beauty. You were in Eden, the garden of God; every precious stone adorned you: ruby, topaz and emerald, chrysolite, onyx and jasper, sapphire, turquoise and beryl. Your settings and mountings were made of gold; on the day you were created they were prepared. You were anointed as a guardian cherub, for so I ordained you. You were on the holy mount of God; you walked among the fiery stones. You were blameless in your ways from the day you were created till wickedness was found in you.''"

Josh stopped her here. "Do you see what happened? God made a perfect angel who was more beautiful than you can imagine. He was perfect. He was a 'guardian cherub,' among the 'fiery stones.' God made him to serve the very throne of God in heaven, to be first among the angels, serving under only God Himself. But one day it went wrong, and something evil was born in this angel's heart."

Angelica saw by Ruth's expression that she was thinking all this over. She asked, "You okay so far?"

Ruth answered without making eye contact, still mulling it over. "That kind of makes sense. But why would that happen? Why would the angel get upset if everything was perfect?"

Josh smiled broadly, delighted at her questions. "Pick up the Bible next to you and read Isaiah 14, starting in verse 12."

Ruth obeyed but not without skepticism. As she picked up the other book, she asked, "Why can't I just read the one I had?"

Josh replied, "You can. But I noticed you've already read out of two different Bible translations, so I'm giving you a third one. Lots of people never study the Bible because there are so many translations, so they kind of think all the meaning has been lost. I want you to see that it doesn't really matter which version you use, because the message is the same in all of them. You're about to read out of something called the New King James Version. And you could read out of any of these other ones too and see the same ideas. Go ahead," he said, noting that she had found Isaiah.

Ruth read, "'How you are fallen from heaven, O Lucifer, son of the morning! How you are cut down to the ground, you who weakened the nations! For you have said in your heart: "I will ascend into heaven, I will exalt my throne above the stars of God; I will also sit on the mount of the congregation on the farthest sides of the north; I will ascend above the heights of the clouds, I will be like the Most High."'"

"Can you see what the problem was?" asked Josh, stopping her after that text.

Ruth kept her eyes on the page, re-reading the passage. "He wanted to become God?" she suggested.

"He wanted to become God," confirmed Josh. "That's exactly right. His sin was self-interest. Lucifer was not content in the role given to him, being subordinate to God, even though he was close to the very throne of the universe. He wanted the throne to be his own. He wanted to hold the Creator God as subject to himself!"

"Wow," said Ruth, despite herself.

"So total chaos ensued. Lucifer caused discord in heaven, and he stirred up grumblings and accusations against God. And the angels could do nothing against this! No one had ever questioned the sovereignty of God before! No one knew of any alternative to God's government of love. And eventually the first war ever seen broke out. Turn to Revelation chapter 12 and read verses 3 and 4. It's the very last book in the Bible."

Ruth read, "'And another sign appeared in heaven: behold, a great, fiery red dragon having seven heads and ten horns, and seven diadems on his heads. His tail drew a third of the stars of heaven and threw them to the earth. And the dragon stood before the woman who was ready to give birth, to devour her Child as soon as it was born.'"

"See how he's called a dragon here?" asked Josh. "Isn't a dragon a large serpent? The Bible uses the same imagery here as it did in Genesis. The talking serpent fooled the angels in heaven too, and a full third of them took his side and lost their place in heaven. And where does it say they went?"

Ruth replied, again still looking intently at the page, "Earth."

Josh summed up the whole controversy here by showing how Lucifer was reborn as Satan, the Accuser, whose goal was to corrupt all of God's creation into losing their favor with the Lord just as he had himself. And by this eternal temptation, by bringing an entire planet down to his corrupt level, he would show that God's government was flawed; His laws were too strict. No created being could follow them. By this accusation he would acquit himself of guilt and turn the universe against its Creator, and Satan would ascend to the throne.

"So the Bible reveals the entire history of the world as seen by the one who created it. It tells us plainly about the stories of Paradise Lost, and Paradise Regained, and the sixty-six books in between tell all about how God accomplished it. Each person, too, even you and me and all of us, have played a part in this whole thing, as we decide for ourselves whose set of laws we value more, God's or the devil's."

Josh continued to show how over the thousands of years that have come and gone, history has repeated over and over again the tale of how God's people, which are those who hear what God is saying and respond by giving their lives to Him, are persecuted and hunted for no reason larger than their loyalty to the Lord. It began with Cain's slaying of his brother Abel and ends, Josh demonstrated, in this attic space, and other such places of refuge around the world. The devil was trying his very best to purge the world of all God's people, and the persecution would not cease until Christ's second advent upon the earth. Therefore, the horror of each cramped, smelly, uncomfortable day hiding from the world was eclipsed by the knowledge that they had come one day closer to meeting their Savior and Redeemer face-to-face. Josh believed this event was very close. He believed today was the last Christmas the world would ever see.

"The last Christmas?" Ruth asked, alarmed. She wasn't even sure why it sounded alarming to her, since she wasn't looking forward to another year of the world being in this condition. Even so, it hadn't occurred to her that there might be some grand conclusion to this whole mess. "What do you think is going to happen?"

Phoebe answered without being asked, "But you are cast out, away from your grave, like loathsome carrion, clothed with the dead, those pierced by the sword, who go down to the stones of the pit, like a corpse trampled underfoot."

Josh said, "She is reading the rest of that passage you read in Isaiah earlier. The Bible talks about the destruction of Satan many times. Eventually God will win."

He showed Ruth how Revelation declares triumphantly that as a result of Satan's destruction, 'death and hell were cast into the lake of fire. This is the second death.' He who invented death would taste the fruit of his own labor. The world and the universe would be rid of all evil, and harmony would be restored after so very long. 'And God shall wipe away all tears from their eyes; and there shall be no more death, neither sorrow, nor crying, neither shall there be any more pain: for the former things are passed away.'

Ruth didn't really believe all the things she had been told so far, but she understood the story, and realized how the family viewed themselves. They had been living here, this small family of believers, hiding in the attic awaiting their final redemption and deliverance to a land where there will be no more death. It seemed far-fetched to her, and yet she admired the strength with which they seemed to believe it. In order to choose to live this way, she reasoned, they must have great faith that what they were saying was true.

Josh was done. The Bibles were closed. The family had answered Ruth's question about why the world was in its current condition, and she realized they were waiting for her to react in some way. But she had never heard anything like this before, and had no idea what the right thing was to say.

Chapter XVIII

The atmosphere in the attic was strangely warm and inviting. The soft candlelight glowed against the walls and flickered across the faces of everyone there. No person, adult or child, felt the weary effects of the late hour, and knowing that the sun was closer to rising again than to having set the night before had no impact upon them. Each was wide awake; each was present in the very moment they were in.

Ruth was still wondering what to say. The story sounded so cartoonish, she thought, and completely unable to be proven. Yet the words on the pages before her moved her heart like it had never been moved before. Each Biblical author told the same story, yet each man's writing was distinctly unique. She was surprised at the consistency between all the books, as if each one had a common author despite being written centuries apart on several different continents. She did not want to believe that she was part of a cosmic struggle much bigger than herself, yet this so simply and perfectly explained how the world had gone so irrationally mad so quickly. And, for the first time in as long as she could remember, even before losing her family to such traumatic violence, she felt hope. This would end someday, and end well, and, if these people were right in their hopes, end soon.

"Why would Satan attack using God's name?" asked Ruth, confused by this. Why would the harbingers of death declare the name of the very one they were fighting against?

Josh had them all turn to Paul's second letter to the Corinthian church, and read from the eleventh chapter. He answered Ruth, "'And no marvel; for Satan himself is transformed into an angel of light.' He knows he will be able to trick more people into following him if they think they are really following God instead."

Angelica added, "Look at Ephesians 6:12."

Each time the group turned to a different verse, Ruth was the last one to find it, because she had never before looked at a Bible, and didn't know how it was organized. She had to look at the table of contents to find the book first, and then narrow down her search to the chapter and verse. The family helped her by giving her clues, such as which Testament the book was in. Josh also added contextual information about the time periods in which each book was written, and its author, and purpose. Ruth felt an excitement growing in her gut as each verse seemed to unfold a new chapter in this description of the world in which she lived.

Angelica read, "'For we wrestle not against flesh and blood, but against principalities, against powers, against the rulers of the darkness of this world, against spiritual wickedness in high places.' So you, see, the real enemies aren't the people who hunt us. The real enemies are the fallen angels giving them power. And if we were to fight back, and kill these men and women, there would be more to take their place. This conflict won't ever end until Christ comes in victory."

Ruth asked, "Why does my book say something different?"

"Tell us what yours says," said Josh.

Ruth read, "'For our struggle is not against enemies of blood and flesh, but against the rulers, against the authorities, against the cosmic powers of this present darkness, against the spiritual forces of evil in the heavenly places.'"

"Is that so very different than what Angelica's said?" asked Josh.

Ruth considered this and replied, "No. No, it's not."

Angelica reiterated what Josh had explained earlier, that many people used the issue of the different translations of the Scriptures as evidence to discount them, arguing that in fact the true meanings had been lost in translation or edited away. But they needed only to read and compare for themselves to see how plainly untrue this was! Having several translations from which to read only broadened a person's chance of finding the truth within! If any person clung only to one version of the texts, then any ambiguous or unclear passage in that particular version would forever remain unclear, because different perspectives would be lost.

Of course, she continued, the texts could be reviewed in their original languages of Hebrew, Aramaic, and Greek, or at least could have been back when the internet was part of everyday life. But many people did not have a working knowledge of these languages, and so must instead accept by faith that the true meanings had been expressed by those who were capable of translating these original languages: the editors of each of the Bible translations.

Phoebe inserted her own wisdom here, to the surprise of Ruth, who couldn't believe such profundity could come from someone so young. Phoebe said, "God can do anything. He would only let us have what he wanted us to have."

Josh added, quoting the Scriptures, "'The words of the Lord are pure words, like silver tried in a furnace of earth, purified seven times. You shall keep them, O Lord, you shall preserve them from this generation forever.'"

Ruth was deeply conflicted here. She had approached this man, Josh, with an idea that she would find refuge from the terrors of religion, which had wrought such destruction upon her family and household. She envisioned a sanctuary of sorts, with a small band of freedom fighters who were plotting to overthrow the wicked Christian authorities to regain their freedom over the world. Yet instead, she sat huddled in a small attic being taught the very material she had already decided could lead only to evil, and these people were planning to do nothing at all except wait for a God who Ruth doubted even existed to show up and save the day. What had she gotten herself into?

But they all seemed so calm, so happy even, with the knowledge they clearly had that she did not, even if that knowledge was fictional. They had been living here, in this cramped space and squalor, for as long as she had been staking out their home, and she guessed much longer than that. Yet even the little children weren't complaining, as she already felt the temptation to do.

There was silence in the attic. Each member of the family was waiting with bated breath to see what Ruth would say next. She, in turn, was scared to open her mouth, scared that this strange moment would break, and that she would lose the glimmer of hope that burned inside her, to be replaced by the hopelessness that she had come to accept as reality. At any moment, these people could go crazy, crazier even than their Bible made them sound already. They would start talking about eternal damnation or the like, and Ruth would have to excuse herself and go back out to the world.

But Seth looked right at her and broke the silence by saying, "He really is coming to get us. He really is."

She was totally stunned. It was like he read her mind! Before she even knew what she was saying, she replied, "How do you know He hasn't come already and left you behind?"

Phoebe's attention was arrested immediately, and her gaze became so strong that Ruth felt as if she were boring a hole through her head. Ruth had to look away, and felt ashamed for asking.

But that's what they had said! Babylon, the Christians, they said over and over again that they were getting the world ready for the return of Jesus, purifying the world so to speak so that the evil left behind once He came and left again would be manageable. Or something like that. She had never really paid close attention, but she knew that someday all of "God's people" were supposed to disappear without a trace, and the world would plunge into chaos with those who remained. Yet she felt the world had already plunged into chaos.

Angelica reached out and gently touched Ruth's arm. She said softly, "Honey, once Christ comes back, there will be no one left here afterward. We're still here because He hasn't yet appeared in the clouds."

Appeared in the clouds. Those words struck somewhere deep in Ruth's heart, somewhere she didn't know existed, and she felt that strange hope again, though she didn't know why. She asked simply, "What does that mean?"

"When Jesus comes, it won't be a secret," said Josh. "Here," he offered, opening his Bible again, "let me show you."

Chapter XIX

Unlike during her first study, Ruth just sat and listened to the story Josh told. It was so radically different than anything she had heard before, that she could do nothing but sit enraptured. She followed along with the Bible in her hands as best she could, and to her surprise she did better than she thought she would.

Josh, then, told the story of the end of the world:

Until the day when Christ comes again, the world will spin as it always has from the beginning of Creation until the very last day. Each morning the sun will rise upon the scorched earth, and each evening night will come. Throughout time this celestial drama has lulled humanity into the belief that things will always go on as they always have, and that even the worst of conditions on earth will somehow correct themselves with time, like they always had before.

But one day God will conclude the divine drama between good and evil, and things will no longer go on as they always have.

In the very last days the global population will be largely devastated by disease, starvation, and persecution, yet the survivors will barely even notice the absence of the fallen. Babylon will claim dominion over what remains of the world, and the Holy

Spirit will be completely withdrawn from the earth, except as He dwells within the hearts of God's people. Aside from those few, every inclination of the minds and the hearts of all mankind will be only evil all the time.

But one day, God's final judgment will begin. In rapid succession, a series of terrible calamities will fall upon the earth.[5] Nearly everyone alive will be afflicted with sores that never heal. Then the sea waters will coagulate inexplicably, and become devoid of oxygen, and all life within them will die. Almost simultaneously, the fresh water around the world will coagulate as well, and marine life on earth will become a thing of the past.

A mass panic will break out everywhere as everyone suddenly realizes that there is no more water to drink anywhere. They will see their collective doom coming and know they are powerless to stop it.

Then it will get worse.

The sun will seem to expand in the sky. There will be nowhere to hide from the relentless heat. Already broken and painful bodies, overwhelmed with incurable sores and parched with thirst, will feel the weight of this heat as if the sun itself were pressing against the earth. No one will doubt what is happening or who is behind it, yet even then they will not repent to give glory to God.

As if emphasizing man's impotence to do anything about it, the earth will become full of darkness, yet the heat will remain. The sun will seem to go out. Massive confusion will reign. Civilization itself will crumble.

Babylon will try to reassure the imploding world that everything will be just fine if they continue to pledge their allegiance to it, but the devastating plagues on the world will convince the populace otherwise. Rapidly, global support for this church-state government system will dry up. The way will be prepared for the return of the one and only King,[6] and those who

---

5 The story of the final plagues can be found in Revelation chapter 16. The physical plagues described here are in verses 1-11.

6 The plague on Babylon is in Revelation 16:12.

had rejected Him will know, in light of the exposure of Babylon's heresy and falsehood, that they've made a fatal mistake.

Around the world, however, there will be a select few who will be immune from all this. This small group will remain largely absent from public view until the plagues begin. These people will claim to be God's true followers, and they will present themselves to a dying world free from painful sores, nourished inexplicably despite the lack of food and water, unfazed by the searing heat and unhindered by the palpable darkness. They will proclaim Babylon be based on lies, they will announce 'Babylon the great is fallen, is fallen,' and they will walk out into the world with no fear. Their strident assurance not in the world's system of religion but in the invisible God of Forever will be a driving factor in Babylon's demise.

But even still, after these devastating events, the world will keep spinning, as it always has.

After losing the support of the world's people, Babylon will reorganize to wage war against God Himself, and a new slew of evil miracles will be wrought by its hands. This will not win back the people's support, but nonetheless will have infinite universal implications, for this demonstration of evil power will be the battle of that great day of God Almighty, which will occur in the place called in the Hebrew tongue Armageddon. This will be the final battle waged in the unfolding of the Great Controversy between good and evil, between God and Satan, between the fallen angels and the rest of the universe.

And while the whole world watches, on that day which will start as every other day has ever started, there will be flashes of lightning, rumblings, peals of thunder and a severe earthquake, such as the earth has never seen.[7] The city that Babylon claims as its home will be divided into three parts, and all the earth's cities will be destroyed. During this great earthquake, the earth itself will seem to quit, to wear out like a garment as the islands and mountains alike will disappear.

---

7   The seventh and final plague is found in Revelation 16:17-21.

Yet despite this, the afflicted masses still will not turn back to God!

> 'From the sky huge hailstones of about a hundred pounds each [will fall] upon men. And they [will curse] God on account of the plague of hail, because the plague [is] so terrible.'

Though those who proclaimed the power and glory of Jehovah God will seem miraculously spared all of these calamities, the remaining will seem determined to curse Him who offers salvation. And so they will choose their own fate.

And as the world's populace, mired in evil and violence, will turn one final time against those who were spared the wrath of the plagues, the final event of this world's history will unfold. John recorded it in his vision, writing:

> 'I saw heaven standing open and there before me was a white horse, whose rider is called Faithful and True. With justice He judges and makes war. His eyes are like blazing fire, and on His head are many crowns. He has a name written on Him that no one knows but He Himself. He is dressed in a robe dipped in blood, and His name is the Word of God. The armies of heaven were following Him, riding on white horses and dressed in fine linen, white and clean. Out of His mouth comes a sharp sword with which to strike down the nations. "He will rule them with an iron scepter." He treads the winepress of the fury of the wrath of God Almighty. On His robe and on His thigh He has this name written: KING OF KINGS, AND LORD OF LORDS.'

How glorious it will be for those who had longed their entire lives for this moment! As each man and woman sealed by God will be assaulted for the final time, the skies will open and the voice of Him through whom all things were made will cry out to His people slumbering in the dust, and they will come triumphantly from their graves, wherever those graves might be. Christ's mighty army of heaven's angels will spread all around the world with the great sound of a divine trumpet, and they shall gather together His elect from the four winds, from one end of heaven to the other, helping the newly resurrected to understand what was happening, and where they were about to go.

Together with the risen dead, the persecuted few that are alive and remain shall be caught up together with them in the clouds, to meet the Lord in the air. As Christ will return on a cloud, so too will they who waited patiently for His return depart this fallen world on clouds.

As for those who had put their trust and faith in riches, in earthly power, in self-promotion and unfounded righteousness, they will be unable to stand in the presence of God, and they will be killed by the brightness of Christ's return. As God's faithful people will be delivered by the Lord's angelic shout, the wicked will be destroyed by the same divine sound.

And as the faithful will depart this world to ever be with the Lord, the world itself will be left in ruins.

The prophet Jeremiah records this amazing event so simply: 'The clamor shall resound to the ends of the earth, for the Lord has an indictment against the nations; He is entering into judgment with all flesh, and the guilty He will put to the sword, says the Lord.' And afterward, 'the slain of the Lord shall be at that day from one end of the earth even unto the other end of the earth: they shall not be lamented, neither gathered, nor buried; they shall be dung upon the ground.'

There will never have been any event like this ever seen in any corner of the universe from the beginning of time, nor ever will be again. All creatures great and small, in every unfallen world between heaven and earth and beyond, will gaze in awe as their Creator reclaims what He has made. Silence will descend over the universe as all unrepentant men and women return to the dust from which they came, and Satan will be left no one to deceive.

When the Redeemed of the Lord look back on their lonely planet, which will bear the scars of sin until God chooses to re-create upon it, they will see no one left behind. All men and women, great and small, will participate in Christ's triumphant return, whether they want to or not; whether they are ready for it or not; whether they survive it or not.

Chapter XX

This was pure madness! Ruth's mind raced with fury now, pulled in a thousand directions all at once. Nobody was flying around anywhere, the sky never rolled away, the sun could never grow! Unwittingly, Ruth had fallen into the company of crazies! Everywhere on earth things were as real as could be, as authentic as a bullet in the brain and a burned carcass could possibly be, and these maniacs were huddling together in a cold, empty attic reading fairy tales about the oceans turning into blood and some trumpet playing angels!

"You're all crazy," said Ruth, and Josh's chest fell in visible disappointment. "If God is coming to get us, then why hasn't He come already? Tell me that!" There was clear panic in her voice. Something was going on here. God's message was conflicting with something deep inside her. Ruth continued, "How can He let all this go on if He cares about it so much that He's coming to destroy the planet over it and fly all the good guys away into space?"

Immediately Phoebe said, "'First of all, you must understand that in the last days scoffers will come, scoffing and following their own evil desires. They will say, "Where is this 'coming' He promised? Ever since our fathers died, everything goes on as it has since the beginning of creation." But they deliberately forget that long ago by God's word the heavens existed and the earth was formed out of water and by water. By these waters also the world of that time was deluged and destroyed. By the same word the present heavens and earth are reserved for fire, being kept for the day of judgment and destruction of ungodly men.'"

While she was saying this, she was not reading from any text, and the plain truth of this startled everyone else in the room, even Ruth, who did not know that the young girl was quoting 2 Peter 3: 3-7 from memory. It was not lost on Ruth that these verses seemed to directly address her objection.

Phoebe continued, "'But do not forget this one thing, dear friends: With the Lord a day is like a thousand years, and a thousand years are like a day. The Lord is not slow in keeping His promise, as some understand slowness. He is patient with you, not wanting anyone to perish, but everyone to come to repentance.'"

"What does that mean?" interrupted Ruth. Why must God be patient with us? What did He want from us?

"It means that there are still people left who will decide they want to be on God's side," said Josh. "It means Jesus still has people left to call."

Phoebe went on, concluding. "'But the day of the Lord will come like a thief. The heavens will disappear with a roar; the elements will be destroyed by fire, and the earth and everything in it will be laid bare.'"

"How do you know all that?" Ruth asked Phoebe. To see anyone, especially such a young person, recite anything like that off the top of her head was impressive to Ruth, so much so that by default she nearly came to believe the validity of what the passage said.

With big eyes that demonstrated her sincerity, Phoebe answered, "I talk to God a lot."

Josh summarized. "Peter is telling us that God's plan is bigger than us. The way the world is right now was pre-determined a long time ago, and written down for us so we would be ready."

"Who's Peter?" Ruth asked, confused.

"Saint Peter," said Angelica, "as some churches call him. He wrote the book Phoebe was quoting."

"Daddy, I want more water," said Phoebe. Ruth was surprised by Phoebe's sudden dramatic shift from spiritual leader to little girl. "Can I have more water now, Daddy?"

Josh looked down at the floor and spoke with a quiet tone because he had to say, "No, honey, I'm sorry, but we have to drink this water slowly or it will run out."

But Ruth said, before even thinking about it, "I can get you more water."

Silence filled the room.

"Where?" asked Josh.

"From the library," said Ruth, plainly. Ruth had discovered the local library while exploring the neighborhood in the recent weeks. Phoebe sat straight up and smiled excitedly.

The parents, however, remained solemn.

"The library won't let us in," said Josh.

"They won't let you in, either, now that you're on the run," added Angelica.

This confused Ruth, but she said, "There is no one to keep us out. The library was raided about six weeks ago."

"How can we get water, then?" asked Angelica, surprised.

"Go in and take it?" suggested Ruth. "There's still running water there."

Angelica looked at her husband with a worried expression on her face. Ruth had shared this information as good news but it didn't seem to be going over that way. No one said anything for awhile.

Ruth broke the silence by asking, "Is everyone ok?" When no one responded, she added, "Did I say something wrong?"

Josh answered her. "I went to the library the day that we were hunted. It was the last day of my old life." He caught himself and corrected, "Our old lives."

"They hunted you at the library?" asked Ruth, shocked. 'They' had come to her old home. It seemed strange for 'them' to be so bold, to hunt in public.

Angelica said, "Honey, I think we'd rather not talk about that."

"No, no," interrupted Josh, "it's okay. They didn't come into the library. It was more subtle than that. But it ended with us living here," he motioned to the cramped quarters around them, "forever. Until this whole thing ends."

"Until Jesus comes back," summarized Ruth, not entirely believing it.

"Until Jesus comes back," confirmed Seth. "We can wait here for a little while because we're going to live forever with Him after that."

This did not sit well with Ruth. She was tolerating all the magic talk, she was even kind of interested in what they had taught her from the Bible, but she considered it plain madness to sit quietly in a little attic and expect everything to turn out just fine without doing anything. Worse still, these people were expecting the sky to open up and for God Himself to come raining down His anger on the bad people.

She got up. "Listen, thanks for everything, but I think I made a mistake coming here. I don't see myself sitting still until the world ends. I don't even want the world to end. So if you could just let me out, I promise to be careful when I leave the house."

She moved toward the attic opening as if to leave, but Josh stopped her.

"Let me tell you about the library," he said. "If you still want to leave after that, go ahead."

He had told her earlier that she couldn't leave because it was dangerous for them. This felt like a trick but Ruth sat down anyway. A million thoughts raced through her mind, not the least of which was that she didn't really want to go back outside in the cold.

Though part of her still wanted to flee from this place screaming, instead she quietly said, "Okay. I'm listening."

Chapter XXI

The attic had been finished for about three years before the family moved in for good, but it had been largely ignored for that time. Josh and Seth both poked their heads in from time to time but neither really made the space into their own. Josh could not stay in the space without working on it, because to do so brought to his mind the reasons why he had remodeled the attic in the first place. He figured he would eventually spend more time there than he cared to, out of necessity, so he was not in a hurry to stay there before that time came.

Over the three years between its completion and their habitation there, however, the family did furnish the space as best they could. Josh installed shelves on the walls. Non-perishable food was stocked there, as well as the propane torch and several spare bottles of gas. He brought up some chairs and a small folding table. He moved his collection of Bibles up there. He even hung a painting.

Josh insisted this happen because he had an idea that when the time came to move in, there would be little time to spare. It turned out he was right.

The family's entire lives changed within twenty-four hours.

The world had been several years into the global economic meltdown already when Babylon rose to power after the last great war, and though the Ragizzos were doing comparatively well financially, the parents saw the wisdom in cutting back expenses wherever possible. Both had cashed out their 401(k) and IRA plans, because neither expected to reach retirement age before the world was destroyed and recreated. They had withdrawn a hefty amount of their money from the banks and kept it, at Josh's suggestion, in the attic. They had left enough money in the bank to sustain their accounts, and thus not draw undue attention to themselves, but they lived primarily on the cash, and thus minimized their paper trail.

Part of this budgeting process was going to the library for everyone's reading materials. Libraries surged in popularity when the unemployment rate began going up, but largely fell into disrepair because the tax revenue plummeted. More and more, going to the library felt like a chore, because of the ever-increasing crowds, and the ever-decreasing quality of the materials there. But Josh tried to bring his family there every couple weeks or so anyway.

Meanwhile, Babylon eventually succeeded in its goal of world dominance. It had been trying for a long time, decades even, to write its mandate for a particular day of rest into the constitutions of the most influential nations of the world. Anyone familiar with the history of the most visible power at the head of Babylon knew that this was only a modern manifestation of a centuries-old agenda, and that the power had been much less subtle in the past about persecuting those who did not agree with its mandates.

In the modern world, however, Babylon succeeded through legislation. It began in Europe, when the Working Time Directive was written to include 'in principle' that this particular day of the week be a moratorium for all kinds of work, all across the continent. The language was modified several years later to remove the 'principle' and install a mandate. After the great war, the United States followed in this same vein with a constitutional amendment of its own. Then everyone else did too. The world became constitutionally required to rest on the first day of the week.

Josh knew this would happen. God had stated it thousands of years before. God used imagery in his prophecies for mankind to illustrate broad truths about the powers described therein. Many people and most churches used this symbolism as an excuse not to ever learn what it meant, and it was widely accepted even in Christian circles that there was no specific, correct meaning to this imagery, or that it was never meant to be understood by mankind in the first place. Therefore when the prophecies were fulfilled, many were caught unaware.

But Josh was not! He had learned as a child that there would be a governmental power that would masquerade as a church, which God described as a beast,[8] which would have 'seven heads and ten horns, and upon his horns ten crowns, and upon his heads the name of blasphemy.' The fact that this terrible power had more than one head meant that it would bear characteristics of several past persecuting powers that had hunted God's people throughout time.[9] But this beast would bear resemblance to one entity more visibly than the others, and it was this power that was most closely associated throughout time as spiritual Babylon. Even in Josh's current day, living in the attic, the term Babylon brought to mind one specific power over the others.

Who would that be?

God continued the description: 'And I saw one of his heads as it were wounded to death; and his deadly wound was healed.' This was an allusion to the past, and therefore to a pre-existence of this most visible power. It had ruled once before, and been killed. But

---

8   This term is used several times in Revelation 13:1-10, is referenced in v11-18, and appears again in chapter 17. All versions of the Bible contain this term.

9   Specifically, the imagery used in Revelation 13:2 is borrowed from Daniel chapter 7, and thereby we can understand that the beast described here includes characteristics of those from Daniel 7, namely (historical) Babylon, Medo-Persia, and Greece.

it had risen again, just like the Savior it counterfeited, the Savior it claimed to worship.

But it was the next passage that had always truly terrified Josh. It was the passage that let him know the tribulation at the end of time would not be easy, and must be taken seriously if he wanted to survive it.

> 'The whole world was astonished and followed the beast. Men worshipped the dragon because he had given authority to the beast, and they also worshipped the beast and asked, "Who is like the beast? Who can make war against him?"'

God promised here that the entire world would fall victim to this power, which was fueled not by God, but by the enemy, the *dragon*, who had deceived the first human parents, and would work to deceive humanity until the very end.

Babylon had succeeded in getting the United States to adopt its suggestion of shutting everything down on the first day of each week. But there was a time when this was not enforced, and Josh kept waiting for the announcement of the coming enforcement before taking drastic action with his family. He just never imagined that the world could move from 'suggestion' to 'mandate' with such little fanfare.

The day Josh went to the library for the last time was the day that enforcement began, and he didn't even know it. God's description of Babylon's relationship to the rest of the world continued, in the same Bible chapter. 'And all that dwell upon the earth shall worship him,' this terrible beast, 'whose names are not written in the book of life of the Lamb slain from the foundation of the world. If any man have an ear, let him hear.'

Josh had an ear.

He knew that he would absolutely not bow down in obedience to this power, no matter what it threatened. If those who chose to worship Babylon were, by God's own description, those whose names had not been recorded for salvation, then Josh knew he would rather face death than be obedient to the government. So when the 'suggestion' to rest and worship this beast on a particular day of the week came through the legislation, Josh promptly ignored it, and his family did the same. They ignored it for months, and nothing ever happened. Josh slipped into a false sense of safety.

Eventually, though, Josh knew something else would happen. The United States would stop 'suggesting' this mandated rest, and begin enforcing it. Here, in the country he knew and loved, the government 'exercised all the authority of the first beast on his behalf, and made the earth and its inhabitants worship the first beast, whose fatal wound had been healed.' Due to their alliance which began in the late twentieth century and continued throughout and after the last great war, his beloved USA would become the primary enforcer of Babylon's doctrine, and it would 'cause all who refused to worship the image to be killed. He also forced everyone, small and great, rich and poor, free and slave, to receive a mark on his right hand or on his forehead, so that no one could buy or sell unless he had the mark, which is the name of the beast or the number of his name.' There would be a way to distinguish the followers of this earthly power that claimed to be the sole provider of salvation, and those without that distinguishing factor would be singled out and removed from society, and ultimately killed.

Josh knew for as long as he could remember that this distinguishing characteristic would be the choice to worship the beast Babylon according to its own criteria. Babylon itself had claimed for centuries that it alone was responsible for changing the day of worship from the seventh to the first, thereby altering the fourth commandment. It claimed as proof of its authority to do such a thing that nearly all other Christian churches disregarded the plain command of the Bible and chose to follow its tradition instead. Babylon called this its mark. It eventually succeeded in mandating this mark through legislation to all the inhabitants of the world under penalty of imprisonment or worse. So as history unfolded to the astonishment of all the atheists and arrogant scholars who proclaimed that such a thing could never and would never happen, the entire planet earth was divided into two camps: those who followed Babylon's brand of worship out of fear, loyalty, or greed; and those who followed the commandments of God, even in the face of persecution and death.

Josh and his family failed to participate in this false worship. And people noticed.

When Josh headed to the library that day, he brought Phoebe with him. The libraries were obviously shut on Sundays, and his family often chose not to go there on Sabbath, especially as the frustration of going grew with the crowds. Josh had earned a chunk of vacation time and decided to cash in a week's worth, since it was summer, and his kids were not in school. That day was a Tuesday, and he was able to take Phoebe with him on his trip. He was excited for an afternoon of quality father-daughter time, and the weather was perfect. The two of them walked to the library, and planned to gather reading materials for a lazy day of reading and sunbathing at home. At the library, each gathered two books: one each for themselves, and one each to bring home to Seth and Angelica. Josh had picked up a DVD also, an old cartoon, for the family to enjoy that night.

Everything fell apart when the librarian would not check out the materials to him.

"Why not?" asked Josh when the woman behind the counter said he couldn't have the media he had chosen.

"I'm sorry, sir, your account has been blocked."

"Blocked by whom?" he demanded. "I don't owe any money here."

"No sir, you're right, you don't. But there has been a permanent block placed on your account. I'm afraid I have to confiscate your library card."

In that moment, standing there listening to the death sentence for the life he knew and loved, Josh felt an eternity pass. Everything seemed to move in slow motion. He felt his heart pounding in his chest, and feared to look down at his beautiful daughter's face, which he was sure would be wracked with disappointment and terror.

He immediately stopped arguing. He knew what this was about. "Someone" had blocked his account. It would be the same "someone" who noticed him missing from church. It would be Babylon. And all at once, Josh knew he was never coming back to the library ever again.

"That's okay, we'll just leave," said Josh, moving to leave.

"Sir, please give me your library card."

Josh looked at the building entrance, and suddenly there were security guards there. They were not advancing upon him, but they were looking right at him. He made a decision right then that this was not one of the moments in life to fight for what was right. Rather, this was a moment to be quiet and get through it.

He turned back to the woman behind the counter, and slipped her his card. It was the last time he ever had a library card. It would be the last time he read through books that were not his own until he could read through the books in heaven with his Savior.

He moved slowly toward the door, each step seeming like a mile. His face was red hot, flush with the knowledge that every eye in the building was on him. He gripped Phoebe's hand tightly in his own as he walked past the two guards at the door, expecting them to detain him and take away his daughter. But nothing happened. He walked successfully out the door, and began the walk home.

On the way, Phoebe finally spoke. She was confused. She had been taught for as long as she could remember that the day would come when her family wouldn't be welcome in the world, but in her youthful outlook she never really thought it would happen. Even now, she was mostly just confused why she couldn't check out the books she wanted. She felt embarrassed. And she was angry.

Josh did the best he could to calm her down along the way but it was a losing battle from the start, and when they did reach the house Phoebe immediately told everyone else what had happened. Josh didn't need to open his mouth.

Josh knew exactly what needed to be done. He had rehearsed it a million times in his head, and the time had finally come to execute it.

He went upstairs to Seth's room and opened the attic. Then he went into the hallway closet and removed the family's luggage set, which consisted of several suitcases that fit inside one another, so the entire set took up no more room than the biggest of its bags. He brought it downstairs and out to the garage, where he loaded the entire set, each bag empty except for the smaller bag inside it, into the trunk of the car. By this time, they only owned one car. They had sold the other one several months before in an effort to simplify and reduce all paper trails.

Angelica knew what was happening as soon as Phoebe told the story. When she saw her husband bring the unpacked luggage outside to the car, all doubt was removed.

She instructed Seth to grab his backpack and fill it with some food, enough for everyone to make it to that coming night. She also told Phoebe to check the attic and make sure everything she wanted was up there. When Seth produced the bag, filled with snacks and water bottles, she told him the same. Then she went to the attic to check for herself.

Within an hour of Josh and Phoebe arriving home, the family was ready to leave again. Everyone knew what was about to happen, as they tied up their loose ends before moving forever into the tiny attic space. Seth cried silently. Phoebe was quite angry. But there they were, all four of them, driving to their car's final resting place.

As they pulled out of the garage, Josh saw that his neighbor on the opposite side of the Cain home was standing in his own garage with the door open, working on one of his own cars. Josh made a point to stop and wave to this man, and to say that the family was going on a trip, and would be back in a few days. After waving goodbye to this man, who had been their friendly neighbor for so many years, Josh prayed that it would be the final time they ever met except, hopefully, in heaven.

There was a small lake on the outskirts of town, geographically closer to their home than the river, but no one ever went there. The lake had become heavily polluted over the years, and was no longer in public use. Children used to play there, but no more. Families used to swim there, but no more. The concentration of pollutants was so high that a fence was erected around the lake at a hundred foot perimeter. The lack of rain in recent years had drained the water level, which only meant that the pollution was more concentrated in the water that remained. It was to this lake that Josh drove his family.

There was no natural opening to the fence, so Josh had to create his own. In the car's trunk was a large pair of bolt cutters, put there for this very purpose. Josh drove to a remote location, got out, and cut an opening in the fence large enough to drive through. He was worried that someone might see him, but there was no way around that. And he hoped that the foul smell of the water, pungent even from the distance of the fence perimeter, kept bystanders away. Once a large enough patch was cut in the fence, he pulled it back to allow the car to pass through. The edges of the fence scraped against his vehicle, and he cringed at the damage being caused to this machine that he had bought so long ago, the first car he ever owned outright.

Ten minutes later, after the appropriate amount of hand wringing and fond memories about the car, Josh put it in neutral, and pushed it into the lake. He had left the windows open a little, to let the air inside escape. The last thing he wanted was for the car to float! He had let most of the air out of the tires for the same reason, and left the trunk ajar.

To the amazement of the entire family, it took several minutes for the car to sink below the water's surface.

They all passed out through the fence the same way they came in, and walked out of range of the smell of the lake. Then they rested. Though they had a long journey ahead of them to get home again, the parents had decided among themselves long ago when first planning this whole thing that they would venture outside the safety of the attic only under the cover of darkness. After all, they weren't famous, they weren't rich, they kept to themselves most of the time, and yet they had been targeted by Babylon anyway. There was just no telling who was watching, or when.

So the family camped out until sunset, eating the food that Seth had brought, and trying their best to pretend that everything was normal. Angelica talked about how fun it would be to live in the attic, like they were on a spaceship traveling to a distant planet. After that they sang songs to God. The children each recounted their favorite memories from the previous year: Seth's had been when an artist for a favorite comic book of his had visited a local store to sign autographs, and signed one for him (that comic book was among Seth's belongings that had been moved to the attic for safekeeping); Phoebe's had been when they rode the miniature train at a park in a neighboring town. Eventually, the sun descended behind the horizon, and they began their journey home.

This was before Babylon had really starting persecuting in force. It was before, even, there was an inkling that there would be persecution at all. Though the family did not walk out in the open, even still their journey was much less perilous than Josh's journey to and from the river would be on the night he met Ruth. It took a long while, and each of the children was tired and a bit crabby when they got home, but they did make it. They went around the back of their home and through the back door, after checking to ensure that no one was watching. They wanted to give the impression that they had left and never come back.

Inside the house, the temptation was huge to delay moving into the attic at least until the morning, and maybe beyond that. Despite the library incident, there was a feeling like they were overreacting just a little bit, and that even now they had not come to a point of no return with the world. After Seth began whining about sleeping in his own bed that night, and Angelica's patience began to wear thin over the issue, Josh was ready to concede this point and postpone the attic move.

It was Phoebe who gave them all a reality check.

As the days and months would progress, Phoebe would increasingly become the spiritual leader of the house, not because she knew the most about the Scriptures or even talked the most about God, but because she just seemed to know what was important at any given moment. That night, after their return from the lake, she demonstrated this role for the first time. She just would not give in to the temptation to relax and make the move the following day, or the day after. She insisted, then insisted again, and insisted right up until they were all settled in their secret room, that they could not, must not pretend that everything was okay. They had committed to their plan, and now they must finish executing it. When no one else seemed willing to join her in the attic, she marched right into Seth's room and moved herself in.

Begrudgingly, the family followed suit. Josh noted that the space still retained the smell of fresh paint, even three years after he had turned the walls blue.

Seth hated the attic and wasn't afraid to say so. He said so until they settled in for the night. Thankfully, sleep finally came to him, and then to them all.

But not for long! Before the sun rose again, they were woken by the sounds of violence in their house. It began with a loud BANG, as the back door was forever torn off its hinges. There was crashing, and men's voices. Orders were being yelled, and soldiers shouted their responses. Plates and electronics came crashing down. Furniture was toppled over. Downstairs, where the family had been living just a day before, where they had been considering sleeping that night, downstairs in their very home, the enemy was present as a roaring lion looking for someone to devour.

Phoebe was the first to speak, asking, "Daddy what's happening?" but her mother shushed her. Both children escaped into their mother's arms. Josh was astonished. He never would have imagined, never in a million years, that the government would move in so quickly. How could it have gotten so bad so fast? Everything was just fine the day before!

Seth was in tears again, as he had been for most of the day. Each time a new round of crashing floated through the floors and into their ears, the family collectively had to repress the tremendous feelings of injustice and rage that welled up inside them. Their home, their personal space, was being violated with force, and no one was there to help.

This ransacking went on for what seemed like eternity but eventually the invaders moved upstairs. The threat to the family's safety became quite real to them all at that point. The soldiers had finished wreaking havoc to the common living spaces. Now each person's private space must also be torn apart.

Unfortunately for the family, they could hear quite well from their position in the attic, and they were able to hear the things said by the soldiers. They said terrible things, using profanities and harsh language that Josh wished with all his might that his children didn't have to hear. A couple of these men entered Seth's room to tear it apart, and they could be heard from the hiding space as if they were in the attic themselves.

"I don't get these terrorists," said one of them as he overturned the bed and tore open the mattress with a knife. Seth cringed at this ripping noise. "It's like they want the plan to fail. Like everything isn't bad enough."

"Shut up and do your job," responded a second man, who was chopping up the desk in Seth's room with what Josh could only imagine was a fire axe, based on the destruction he saw later on. "None of the subversives deserve any better. Let 'em go hide off in the woods somewhere without all their stuff."

"Superman," observed the first man, looking at a poster on the wall which, for some reason, he left hanging there untouched.

"There ain't no superman coming to help you, kid," he said, as if addressing Seth directly. For no reason, he continued to verbally abuse Seth, often with swearing.

The second man finished demolishing the desk and moved to the dresser drawers, emptying out their contents one drawer at a time and looking through the ensuing piles. "You think this would look good on Bart?" he asked the first man, evidently holding up one of Seth's shirts.

"Whatever. You don't want to give your kid something from these freaks. Everything's got bad juju on it, or worse. It's all corrupted. Let it all go to hell with them."

"Hell?" questioned the second man. "You really believe in that stuff?"

"Well yeah," responded the first man, sounding surprised. "They sure ain't going to heaven, or else they'd do what the church says. They gotta go somewhere. What should we do with all this junk?" This man was indicating the pile of toys in Seth's closet. He was now directly below the secret entrance to the attic. Everyone upstairs was scared to death.

"Just leave it. It'll all burn anyway. And I don't believe in hell."

"Yeah?" asked the first man, still standing directly below the hiding family. "Then what happens to everyone who God doesn't want in heaven?" There was a clear note of skepticism in his voice. He was asking in order to ridicule his comrade's belief system, not enlighten his own.

"I don't believe in God. Never have. Never met Him."

This seemed to genuinely surprise the first man. "What are you doing all this for, then? Why do you come to church every week?"

"I don't go, I end up on the receiving end of what we're doing now. And I want the world to get better again. These guys are in charge now. I'm just playing along till something else happens."

"That's … ridiculous," scolded the first man, fumbling for words and clearly upset by his companion's statement. This was followed by a loud crashing noise: he had smashed the full length mirror on the closet sliding door. The noise was so violent and unexpected that Phoebe let out a short cry of fright, and Josh was sure they would be found. But the men seemed not to notice. Thankfully, her cry was lost amid the shattered glass. "Don't let the priest hear you say that. He'll report you to the general. Or worse."

"I don't think so," said the second man. "I think all they want is attention. And power. I keep showing up and making them feel important, they'll leave me alone. Look at this!" He was now holding a pair of Seth's underpants. "Superheroes on his underwear! What is this kid, five?"

"Probably has daddy issues," said the first man, finally walking away from the closet. Disgusted, he concluded, "I'm glad these people are gone. Hope they're dead."

"There's nothing important here," said the second man. "Let's get out of here before the burn starts." Then they left. A few minutes later, the sounds of violence moved back downstairs.

Josh could barely think straight. He was furious at this intrusion. He was protective of his son's belongings and honor, and deeply offended to the point of violence if circumstances were different. He was terrified that he would have gone to all this trouble to hide his family and cut themselves off from the world, only to be burned alive in their own hiding place. He had no idea what to do. They couldn't leave where they were now or they would be arrested, or likely worse, maybe even executed on the spot. But to stay meant burning alive like animals trapped in an oven.

Once the soldiers had gone back downstairs, Seth said, a little louder than he should have, "I hate them, Dad. I hate them and want them to die."

And Josh, not feeling compassionate at all in that moment, agreed. "Me too, son. But be quiet now."

Angelica was in silent tears, and Josh's heart just broke to see his wife in that state and be helpless to do anything about it. He noticed Phoebe was crying too. Everything had gone to pieces. There was nothing good in this moment. Their dignity had been stolen along with their possessions. Their living space had been violated. These men, these strangers, maligned them for no reason. His and his family's spirits were broken. Every fiber of his being cried out at the unjustness of this moment, and he felt as if his God were far away.

At that moment, the words of the prophet Amos came to his mind, and he recalled the warning from the Lord about this time in history: 'In all the squares there shall be wailing; and in all the streets they shall say, "Alas! alas!" They shall call the farmers to mourning, and those skilled in lamentation, to wailing.' Everywhere on earth would feel this terrible persecution before the end came, and Josh felt a strange comfort in knowing this, that all of God's people would be put to the ultimate test, not just himself and his loved ones. 'The day of the Lord is darkness, and not light. As if a man did flee from a lion, and a bear met him; or went into the house, and leaned his hand on the wall, and a serpent bit him.' Nowhere would be safe. Even the safe places would become desolate. 'Will not the day of the Lord be darkness, not light – pitch-dark, without a ray of brightness?'

As Josh considered this silently, he came to realize the sounds of violence had departed. There was silence, except for his own heavy breathing, and the quiet sobs of his family. He couldn't be sure, but he imagined that a fire in the home would make a noise of some kind.

And all at once, a peace that he knew from experience could only come from the Lord came upon him. More words of Amos seemed imprinted upon his mind: 'In that day I will restore David's fallen tent. I will repair its broken places, restore its ruins, and build it as it used to be.' This global terror would pass, and God would be victorious with His people. Josh looked at his family and saw that their breathing had returned to normal, and their tears had been stopped. The grace of the Lord had come upon them all in that moment.

No one left the attic to check for fire or to see what had become of their once lovely home. Sure enough, as the night wore on, they remained alive and no fire consumed them.

From that night on, the family lived primarily in the attic. The parents both knew that there would be others around the world, even other faithful followers like themselves, who would deal with this tribulation differently. They knew there would be some who would engage the governing powers at their own game, taking their arguments against Babylon's reign to what passed for legal courts these days. They knew there would be some who stood their ground and fought. They knew some would flee, to brave the wilderness. But they chose to hide, both for their own sakes, and those of their children. If their plan did not work, then they would perish, to slumber and await Christ's triumphant return. But for better or worse this was the path they had chosen, and they trusted in the Lord to see them through it.

They longed very much to be part of the group described in Revelation, those 'which came out of great tribulation, and have washed their robes, and made them white in the blood of the Lamb. Therefore are they before the throne of God, and serve Him day and night in His temple: and He that sitteth on the throne shall dwell among them.' All this trial was worth the reward, for the promise of the Lord was worth more than any money could ever buy: 'They shall hunger no more, neither thirst any more; neither shall the sun light on them, nor any heat. For the Lamb which is in the midst of the throne shall feed them, and shall lead them unto living fountains of waters: and God shall wipe away all tears from their eyes.'

Chapter XXII

Ruth had not left. She had sat for the story, and when it was over she still sat, silently watching the family. Several minutes went by. Josh felt compelled to speak but refrained.

Eventually Angelica concluded by saying, "That's the end, Ruth. We've been here ever since."

Carefully and deliberately, Ruth said, "You prepared for this." It wasn't quite a question or a statement, but rather an observation.

Angelica responded, "We did."

"Because you knew this was coming."

Again the mother said, "We did."

"How could you know this was coming?" Ruth asked.

This time Josh answered. "Because God said so. And God doesn't lie."

There was another pause, then Ruth admitted, "This is very hard for me to hear. I feel like one of them," motioning outside, indicating Babylon, "talking about these things."

"God knew you would struggle," said Josh. "In Matthew's gospel, Jesus tells us about the end times, saying, "'For there shall arise false Christs, and false prophets, and shall [show] great signs and wonders; insomuch that, if it were possible, they shall deceive the very elect. Behold, I have told you before.'" He's warned us about this time and how hard it is to determine truth from lies for millennia. He knew all the way back then that you would struggle with this tonight."

"How could he know that?" she asked.

Phoebe, who had shed silent tears as her father related the story of her family's persecution, said in her unique profound way, "Jesus is the Alpha and the Omega, the Beginning and the End, who is and who was and who is to come, the Almighty. He exists outside of time."

"He is the only one who exists outside of time," added her brother.

"But then how do you know you're right, if there's so much deception everywhere?" demanded Ruth. "Maybe you just think you're right, like they do."

"Maybe," admitted Josh. "I can't prove to you otherwise. But our salvation doesn't depend on who we are. It depends on Jesus. It's up to Him. And John tells us in his gospel that Jesus is the very Word of God. So the only thing that matters at all is this," he said, indicating his Bible, "God's Word."

Angelica clarified, "You can only tell what is true by checking it against God's Word. That's the only way. That's the way it's always been, all through time. God tells us that plainly, somewhere in the book of Isaiah. He says to check all things against the law and the testimony, what we call the Bible, and if they speak not according to this word, it is because there is no light in them."

"Isaiah 8:20," advised her husband.

"Thank you, Josh," said Angelica, a little annoyed that he always had to be the know-it-all, but secretly thankful for his wisdom. "So, honey, we just try to be as faithful as we can to the Word of God. You can choose to disbelieve it, but then ask yourself what it is you really do believe."

"But they believe the Bible too, don't they?" asked Ruth, meaning Babylon. "So how do you know you're interpreting it right?"

"Actually they don't really believe the Scriptures," Angelica answered. "That group has claimed authority over the Scriptures for centuries. They put greater weight on their own teachings and traditions. They claim the Scriptures give them that power."

Ruth seemed shocked at this, but Josh added, "It's true. They don't even deny it. They never have."

"But then," Ruth began, but stopped. Could all this be true? She proceeded slowly, as if considering each word. "If they act against the Bible, then according to the Bible they have no light."

"'There is no light in them,'" confirmed Angelica. "That's right."

"So my family has gone to hell."

This surprised everyone in the room.

A bewildered Josh asked simply, "What?"

"You've been telling me since I got here that these people are against God. You said that the devil gives them their power. So they can't be going to heaven, right? And when my family was killed, they belonged to that group. So they must be in hell."

Still stunned, Josh stammered out, "I never meant to give you that impression."

"What other impression can I have?" she asked.

"First of all," began Seth, "people don't go anywhere when they die, except to sleep to wait for Jesus to come. And hell doesn't exist. Not the way you think."

Josh knew that Seth felt strongly about this issue. He had been taught the Bible's truths about death and heaven and hell from his birth but ran into trouble about his beliefs when he went to school. There, he met and became friends with several kids who identified themselves as Christians, but who had all sorts of strange ideas about these things. They all contradicted what he had been taught, and often they even contradicted each other. This had caused him a great deal of stress at school, Josh remembered sadly, and he became a perpetual outsider for holding to his beliefs. He was ostracized by the very people he wanted to most closely identify with, his fellow brothers and sisters in Christ. He had a very lonely childhood.

"So," began Ruth, absorbing this, "my family is nowhere?"

"'For the living know that they will die, but the dead know nothing, and they have no more reward, for the memory of them is forgotten. Also their love, their hatred, and their envy have now perished. Nevermore will they have a share in anything done under the sun,'" said Josh. He continued, "'Whatever your hand finds to do, do it with your might; for there is no work or device or knowledge or wisdom in the grave where you are going.' That's from Ecclesiastes 9, in the Old Testament. Even in the New Testament, when the apostle Stephen is stoned to death in Acts chapter 7, it says he 'fell asleep.' Nowhere in the entire Bible does it say that there is a part of the human that continues on after death. In fact," he exclaimed, excited that this opportunity had arisen, "the idea that the dead aren't really dead but are continuing on somehow was Satan's very first lie in the garden! When Eve tells him what God had commanded about the forbidden tree, and that they would die if they disobeyed, you know what Satan's answer was?"

"What?"

"'Ye shall not surely die.' The devil has been telling that lie since the beginning."

"Also, Ruth," offered Angelica, "consider this. If Jesus is coming back and His deceased people will rise again to meet Him in the air, like we talked about before, then think about what they must go through if they're already in heaven. First, they would have to exist in so-called paradise watching their loved ones still get sick and die and struggle down here, but then they would have to get called out of heaven, back into their graves, only to be resurrected again with a new body which I guess they didn't have the first time they were in heaven, then go back to heaven again. Does that make any sense?"

"It doesn't make any sense," said Ruth. "I never really understood going to heaven when you die. It always seemed like everyone who died was going to 'a better place,' no matter who they were or how they lived. And I never quite got how Christians who spent so much time talking about how bad people went to hell to burn forever could also just assume everyone went to heaven when they actually died."

"That's very wise," said Josh, impressed. He was relieved that Ruth seemed to accept this so well. He couldn't even count the number of times he had taught this Bible truth to others and had them reject it. People seemed to really like the idea that their enemies went to burn forever, and that their friends went home to Jesus immediately.

"But then there is no hell?" asked Ruth.

Josh saw an opportunity here. "People say all these things about heaven and hell because they don't really know what the Bible says about heaven and hell, so they make stuff up that sounds good. Then they teach it to others, who teach it to others, and so on. That's why the Word is the only thing that matters. Everything else is just make-believe." He made a motion to the Bibles, which were now closed on the floor as the group was talking. "So do you want to see what the Word says about all this?"

Visions of her family bounced around in Ruth's mind. She missed them so very much. She was still not convinced about all the things she had heard from this family that night but, she admitted to herself, they had the only set of explanations for a world gone mad that made any kind of sense at all. Therefore, in a way she never would have envisioned herself responding until that very night, she answered Josh's question with a simple, "Okay."

Chapter XXIII

Before the study began, Angelica offered as much comfort as she could. "All my family and friends I used to know before I met Josh and learned all these things ultimately fell in with Babylon when they rose to power. I don't know if any of them are alive or dead, and I don't know how God will deal with the decisions they've made. So I share a lot of your concern, Ruth. But I also trust that God will do the fairest thing possible, and I know He wants them to be in heaven even more than I do, and that He'll do anything possible to get them there."

Ruth paused for a moment and said, quietly, "Thank you."

Josh was a little nervous about this lesson. He had taught it several times to many groups of people and the reactions were always mixed. Even within his own church there were members who refused to see the topic the way he did. But since Ruth had asked, and since it was a topic of greatest importance and one that he and his family felt strongly about, he undertook the task and prayed that it would turn out the way he hoped. "Open to Revelation chapter nineteen," he said.

When everyone had found the proper place, they read verses eleven through sixteen, which they had read before when learning about Christ's return to earth. This passage told the story of His descent from heaven to rescue His people and wage war against

His enemies. Even though it had been just a short time since she had read this exact same passage, Ruth felt amazed by it all over again.

This time, however, the family kept reading. Josh read aloud verses seventeen through twenty-one. This passage told the story of Christ's return from the perspective of those on earth who did not want Him to come. "'The kings of the earth, and their armies, gathered together to make war against Him who sat on the horse and against His army,'" read Josh, in verse nineteen. "You see, there will be lots of people on earth who don't want Jesus to come back, and they'll fight to keep Him away."

"Why would they do that?" asked Ruth.

"Not everyone is hiding away in an attic," answered Josh. "There are men and women who are very rich and powerful right now, and living in as much luxury as possible. They won't want to give that up." The passage concluded by describing how Christ's enemies would be slain, and how the earth would be made desolate as a result.

The family continued to read the story into chapter twenty, verses one through three. In this short passage, Satan was left prisoner on the desolate earth for a thousand years. God's people had been taken to heaven, and the wicked lay all around the earth, dead and unburied since no one was left to bury them. "'But after these things he must be released for a little while,'" read Josh, concluding the passage.

"Why would he be released?" asked Ruth.

Josh liked that she had so many questions. From a purely human standpoint, it truly didn't make sense that the author of confusion and death would be released from his prison. Ruth questioning this told him that she was paying attention.

"Hang in there, Ruth," answered Josh. "The Bible will explain itself. Why don't you read the next passage, through verse six?"

Ruth read about how, for the same thousand years during which Satan was a prisoner on the barren earth, all of God's people were in heaven judging and reigning with Christ. But she didn't really understand it. "What are they judging?" she asked. "And why does it say, 'The rest of the dead did not come to life until the thousand years were ended'?"

"Think about this," suggested Josh. "When you get to heaven, what if your parents really aren't there, like you fear? Would you want to know why?"

"Of course," she said, solemnly.

"How about the people who killed your family? What if they are in heaven and your family is not? Would you want to know why?"

"Of course!" she nearly shouted. "That's not fair!"

"It certainly doesn't seem fair to us," Josh agreed. "So God gives us a thousand years to look over the books of everyone's lives, to see the choices they made and the motives behind their actions. Now consider this: if that scenario is true, where the people you love are absent but the people you hate are there in heaven with you, as you look through the record of everyone's lives to see why God made the choices He did to save some and not others, whose choices are you really judging?"

Ruth thought long and hard about this. No matter what the people did while they were still alive, it was ultimately up to God whether or not to raise them up and bring them to heaven. So if she was in charge of judging why some made it and some did not, then she was really judging, "God," she said. "God's choices, I guess."

"Exactly," affirmed Josh. "God brings us to heaven to allow us to judge for ourselves whether or not He was correct in the decisions He made. That's why He has to raise the rest of the dead eventually, and release Satan. The controversy isn't over yet. But before He takes the final steps to resolve the problem and make everything right again, He allows us to make sure we agree with what He has already done, and what He is about to do. God has nothing to hide from us."

"Wow," said Ruth, without even realizing it.

"And you can ask Him anything you want!" added Seth, excited about this.

"Where does it say that?" asked Ruth, looking at the page.

Josh chuckled. "It doesn't say that, specifically. But it does say we will reign there with Christ. He won't be hidden from us anymore. And," he added, remembering another point, "if you read the first part of chapter nineteen, before this story began, you would read about the 'Marriage Supper of the Lamb,' when Jesus marries each person He redeemed from earth, including you and me. We will be eternally married to God, forever and ever! If you have a question for Him, you can just ask!"

"I wanna be married to God!" said Phoebe with excitement.

With a smile, Angelica agreed. "Me too, honey."

"Me too," said Josh. "So should we read how it ends?"

They all agreed.

Together, they read verses seven through ten, which told of a great and final battle between good and evil, as the resurrected wicked surrounded the camp of the saints and the beloved city in which they now lived. God's people were safely in their new heavenly home with free access to the tree of life but they were attacked by the unrepentant sinners who wanted the very thing they had rejected during their first life on earth: immortality. Satan, who now had people to deceive again as he had during all of earth's history, was freed from his prison of solitude and went right back to his ways of evil and destruction. But God would not allow His people to suffer harm, and so He rained fire on the wicked and devoured them all, including the devil. Evil was erased from the universe forever.

Josh could tell by Ruth's furrowed brow and look of concentration that she had several questions about what she had just read. He attempted to answer her questions before she had a chance to ask them.

"Revelation does a lot of interesting things in the way it is written," said Josh. "Two of its literary structures converge here, and you have to understand them for the rest of the story to make sense. So, please read for me verses eleven and twelve."

Ruth obeyed. "'Then I saw a great white throne and Him who was seated on it. Earth and sky fled from His presence, and there was no place for them. And I saw the dead, great and small, standing before the throne, and books were opened. Another book was opened, which is the book of life. The dead were judged according to what they had done as recorded in the books.'"

"So where is this part of the story taking place?" asked Josh.

Ruth read it again and pondered it. There were dead people who were alive again, judging out of God's books, standing before God's throne. "I guess in heaven?" she said.

"You guess right," said Josh. "But we already saw the judgment in heaven back in verse four. And right before, in verse nine, God's people are back on earth being attacked by Satan. So can you see how the story is not written chronologically? It told the story up to a certain point, then kind of backed up and is telling it again."

Angelica added, "So this judgment and the one from verse four are the same thing. God is telling the story twice."

"Why?" asked Ruth.

Josh answered, "The book of Revelation is just written that way, starting in chapter twelve. It tells the story from the beginning of time all the way through almost the very end, all in chapter twelve. Then it back up, starting in chapter thirteen, and tells the story again, but it starts earlier than the previous story ended, and gives more detail. It happens again in chapter fourteen verse six. It happens several more times as well. Right here, when suddenly we're back in heaven judging, it happens again. I call it a 'progressive revelation' literary structure. And unless you really understand it, then this entire passage is quite confusing."

"No kidding," said Ruth.

"But if you do understand what's happening, it's actually quite clear. See? Verses eleven and twelve are the judgment. Verse thirteen is the second resurrection, where the wicked people are brought back to life to be judged by those who had been looking at the books for a thousand years. And verse fourteen, when they acknowledge their guilt before God, before the saints, before the entire universe, they are destroyed forever."

"Wow," was all Ruth could find to say.

Angelica added something here. "Psalm 22:29 says, 'All those who go down to the dust shall bow before Him, even he who cannot keep himself alive.' The Bible says that every single person shall kneel before God when they recognize that He truly is the author of the universe. Right here, in Revelation, right before they are destroyed forever, is when that happens. It's the only time it can happen, when all the wicked are together at once, accepting their eternal fate."

"That's..." began Ruth, but couldn't find the words to end. Eventually she said, "amazing, I guess."

"I think so!" stated Josh, excited. "But that's not the end! The best part is still to come! It continues in chapter twenty-one, and the story kind of takes a small step backward again. This is where we see the city of heaven and all the saints inside it returning to earth after the thousand years. Do you want to read it?"

Ruth began at the beginning of the chapter. "'Then I saw a new heaven and a new earth, for the first heaven and the first earth had passed away, and there was no longer any sea. I saw the Holy City, the new Jerusalem, coming down out of heaven from God, prepared as a bride beautifully dressed for her husband. And I heard a loud voice from the throne saying, "Now the dwelling of God is with men, and He will live with them. They will be His people, and God Himself will be with them and be their God. He will wipe every tear from their eyes. There will be no more death or mourning or crying or pain, for the old order of things has passed away." He who was seated on the throne said, "I am making everything new!" Then He said, "Write this down, for these words are trustworthy and true." He said to me: "It is done. I am the Alpha and the Omega, the Beginning and the End. To him who is thirsty I will give to drink without cost from the spring of the water of life. He who overcomes will inherit all this, and I will be his God and he will be my son.""''"

"You can stop there," advised Josh. "Isn't that beautiful?"

The words danced around in Ruth's mind like the most tantalizing dream she had ever had: 'There will be no more death or mourning or crying or pain, for the old order of things has passed away.' But she said nothing. Josh knew her head must be spinning.

Ruth spent some quiet moments thinking over everything. Her eyes darted back and forth across the page as she re-read the passages over and over. She seemed to grow more troubled as the moments wore on, and eventually she said plainly, "Why do you think evil will be destroyed when it says the bad guys will be tortured forever?"

Josh was hoping she would agree about the story's beauty, and was more than a little disappointed that she got hung up where so many other people did: on a single word. But he had been down this road before, enough times to be able to mask his disappointment. He answered, "I assume you mean chapter twenty verse ten, which reads 'The devil, who deceived them, was cast into the lake of fire and brimstone where the beast and the false prophet are. And they will be tormented day and night forever and ever.' Right?"

Ruth nodded. Josh was encouraged to see that her heart didn't truly seem to be in her objection. Nonetheless, it was a question that deserved an answer.

"Alright," he began. "First, look at the previous verse. It's talking about the humans now, those raised in the second resurrection, the unrepentant sinners. It says, 'They went up on the breadth of the earth and surrounded the camp of the saints and the beloved city. And fire came down from God out of heaven and devoured them.' So you need to understand that the Bible is very clear that at least for the human sinners, there is a definite end. 'Devoured' means consumed until it is no more. Anyone who believes in an eternal hell where human sinners burn for all time is simply not reading correctly. Okay so far?"

She nodded again without saying anything.

Josh continued. "So the only real problem is this torment 'forever and ever' for the devil and Babylon. But consider two things. First, the Bible sometimes uses the word 'forever' to mean something like 'as long as it lasts without interruption.' Like when Jonah was in the belly of the fish for three days, but he then describes the ordeal as lasting 'forever.' God uses this term Himself, also, like when He says His anger will burn against His people 'forever' in Jeremiah 17:4, when in reality it lasted only seventy years. 'Forever' in the Bible often means that when something begins, it cannot be interrupted until it ends. I think that is what it means here, that the devil will endure torment until it is over, and cannot be interrupted. But if you turn to Ezekiel 28:18-19, I'll show you the real evidence why I think this."

Everyone turned in their Bibles to this passage, but Ruth continued to say nothing. Josh realized she was being abnormally silent but he didn't know why or what to do about it. So he continued on.

"We looked at part of this passage earlier. It's a prophecy of Satan, telling us who he used to be and how he went sideways. But we never finished it. Starting in verse eighteen, it reads, 'You defiled your sanctuaries by the multitude of your iniquities, by the iniquity of your trading; therefore I brought fire from your midst; it devoured you, and I turned you to ashes upon the earth in the sight of all who saw you. All who knew you among the peoples are astonished at you; you have become a horror, and shall be no more forever.' So this is pretty clear, right? Just like all the human sinners, he is devoured by fire and turned to ashes. It even says this will happen in the sight of the remaining people. We will get to watch it happen."

Josh was hoping for some kind of response. Ruth didn't look upset but she didn't seem happy either. He tried prompting her to speak by asking, "Do you have any other questions?" But she simply shook her head, no.

He had never dumped this much Bible knowledge on a person all at once before. It was not an effective way to share the Scriptures with someone, and he knew from experience it would be much better to share a little at a time, and allow the student to digest it. But things were different now. The world no longer afforded the old method of doing things. Therefore, despite the many times he had taught the Bible and led others to Christ, he felt as if he were doing it for the first time. He had no idea what to expect.

To break the silence, Josh said, "Remember I said there were two literary structures going on at the same time in that whole passage? The progressive revelation is just one of them. The whole thing is also written in a chiastic structure, which means the beginning and the end counterpoint each other, and the story progresses into the middle with matching themes until the center, which doesn't have a counterpoint at all. The middle is the primary focus of the entire story."

Ruth looked up at him but still said nothing.

Josh continued, "So you see how the whole thing started with Christ descending from heaven when He comes back, and ends with the New Jerusalem descending from heaven after the thousand years? Then it tells us how Christ's enemies are slain at His return, and toward the end of the story His resurrected enemies are slain again, forever. After that we see Satan being imprisoned for a thousand years, and he gets released from his prison when the thousand years are over. So the beginning and the end of the story all match each other. And right in the middle is the judgment. So we are able to understand just by the way it is written that the reason God goes to all this trouble and drama is to allow Himself to be judged by His people before He takes that final step of destroying the wicked. Even though He can do whatever He wants at any time, He still allows us to give Him permission first."

Ruth continued in her silence, and Josh became quite nervous, so he kept on talking to try to cover it up. "Can you see how the two literary structures depend on one another? If the story was told chronologically, then the judgment would end, the city would descend, the wicked would be resurrected, then attack the city, then be destroyed. But that would not form a chiastic structure! So God purposefully tells the story out of sequence in order to emphasize the thousand year judgment in heaven!"

"Wow," said Seth, clearly learning something for the first time.

But Ruth stayed silent still. If Josh could peer into her mind, he would see a war raging, and no clear idea at all as to what to say.

Some time went on without anyone saying anything. Josh felt like he had said too much already and didn't want to make it any worse than it already was. He desired for Ruth to feel at ease, to know the peace that comes only from God, and yet she appeared to have shut down right in front of him. He looked quickly at his wife, whose expression of concern told him she didn't know how to proceed either. With each passing moment Josh felt the urge to say something but the moment would pass without finding the right words.

The silence thus continued, and continued still.

Chapter XXIV

Thankfully, Phoebe eventually said, "I'm thirsty."

By this time, several hours had gone by since Ruth had arrived. The minutes ticked by one at a time and no one seemed to notice, right up until the end when Ruth had fallen strangely silent. But there they were, after a night of action and theology, and to Josh's surprise he looked up through the small skylight in the roof and saw the beginning of dawn. It was officially Christmas. Children all around were waking up to presents. Songs of joy were ringing through the land. Even the Ragizzos, in their cramped space, felt joyful. The joy of Christmas could permeate even a desperate hideout.

Josh felt uneasy doling out any of the prize pack of water he had gathered the night before, but offered a quick prayer of thanks to the Lord and acted in faith, opening up the water sack and pouring its contents into the various cups the family had in the attic. The Lord would continue to provide water for them, somehow, maybe at the library, and maybe somewhere else. Right now, he wanted his beautiful daughter to have the best Christmas gift he could think of: quenched thirst.

Soon after, the topic of food came up, and Angelica moved to prepare another round of pasta, delighted to use fresh water for boiling instead of the congealing water from previous pasta dishes. No one seemed terribly excited about sauce-less pasta for Christmas breakfast, but no one wanted to be hungry, either.

Ruth felt strangely disconnected from everything around her, as if she were just a little bit distant. It was as if her perception slowed, like she was lagging behind in space-time by just a fraction of a moment. She tried to focus on what was happening at that moment but couldn't. Her mind kept jumping backward to the few hours that had just passed.

In Ruth's mind, a battle was being waged. She had given religion no more than an afterthought all throughout her life. When Babylon took over, she saw it as just another form of government. When they attacked, she saw it as evil. Every fiber in her entire being wanted to reject what the family had taught her, yet her mind just would not let go of it. For the first time, religious ideas made sense to her. These ideas, in turn, helped her to understand the very world she lived in.

Specifically, her mind reeled with the ideas of a rain of hellfire that would destroy the wicked and burn out. Never in her life had she ever heard such a thing before. She wanted to fear this idea. She wanted to hate it. She wanted to use it as yet another reason to disbelieve what she had heard all night long. Yet she couldn't. It just made so much sense to her. God would prove once and for all that nothing could ever make the wicked repent, and then destroy them for the benefit of those who remain so they could live forever in a world without death. She actually saw it as an act of love.

But what about her family? She never did get an answer about that. Wouldn't they be condemned to this punishment, since they pledged loyalty to a group that was so clearly in opposition to God? Yet that group had murdered them all. She realized she would not get an answer that night, or at all unless the story was true and she was able to look through the books herself. The war raged on and on in her mind. The very universe was battling for her loyalty.

Her inner tension did not resolve itself, but she was aware that Angelica was about to cook food, and Ruth felt compelled to make an offer to the family that had shown her such kindness. "Wait, I want to give you something," she announced to the family, then convinced Josh to let her leave the attic for what she promised would be a short time. There was a small amount of lecturing on the dangers of ever leaving the attic, especially as the sun was dawning, but Ruth was insistent, and stated emphatically that there was little danger, and that the reward would be well worth it. And so Ruth was released into the house.

Within two minutes she returned with a dozen eggs in a carton.

In response to the many questions that rose from the family, she told the story of how the local government supermarket had mysteriously caught fire about a week prior, and once the fire was extinguished the store was simply shut down. She had gone into the abandoned store a day later, and found that some groceries had not been damaged in the fire. Among them were the eggs, which remained essentially refrigerated despite the lack of power since it was, after all, December, and the temperature was low. So she had swiped the eggs along with a few other things. Because she had spent most of her time since then staking out this house, she had hidden the eggs behind a bush in the small backyard a couple days ago, where they had gone undisturbed since then. She now shared these eggs with her new family.

How delightful it was to eat these eggs! It had been so many months since the family had gotten to have this previously mundane breakfast food. Yet now, despite the hundreds of eggs they had each consumed in their lives previously, these eggs seemed like manna from heaven, like divine sustenance in a desert land.

While they ate Ruth stated, "I'll bring you some pasta sauce too if there is any left at the store."

Everyone agreed this was an excellent idea.

Josh looked at his family, which he now felt included this woman Ruth even though they had all just met her, and felt peace from God. He was exhausted; he had been awake for over twenty-four hours, and been through a grueling physical endeavor for many hours the night before. Yet he was keenly aware that this was the best Christmas he could remember and maybe the best Christmas of all time. They each had everything they wanted: good, warm food; relative safety and comfort; good company and good conversation. In that moment, at a small celebration of the final Christmas the world would ever see, everything was perfect.

When the meal was over, the extent of Josh's exhaustion really set in. The pain in his knee and ankle returned worse than ever, as if he had run out of energy to keep the throbbing down. Every muscle in his body seemed to scream in weariness. He could barely keep his eyes open. His belly, usually angry with hunger, was silent. He felt the world slipping away in a haze of satisfaction.

To fix the problem of now having five people but only four sleeping bags, Angelica volunteered to use her one bag as a blanket for herself and her husband, and therefore Ruth could have Josh's bag in which to sleep. Josh was too tired to argue this, and the arrangements were made. He then nestled into his new sleeping situation and hovered ever so delicately on the edge of unconsciousness while life resumed around him.

The kids had found some way to entertain themselves while Angelica began to ask about the adventure to the river and back. Josh kept his eyes closed but found it easy to retell his adventures, or at least a milder version to spare some of the more horrible details from his family's ears. But he went through it as much as his weary mind could remember, including his two trips to their former home.

His children were not ignorant of what was going on in the world, not even of the horrors perpetuated by Babylon and its institutions. They knew people were dying and being hunted. They knew that many of their friends had disappeared at the hands of the religious government. They had even heard the stories of strange ritual sacrifices in the Lord's name. Josh was not afraid to recount these details in their presence.

Even still, he omitted the most gruesome details, like the skulls on the mantelpiece holding up the Christmas stockings. He failed to tell of the large unarmed family brutally gunned down in his eyesight. He could not see the benefit to sharing these things, and his mind did not wish to dwell upon them in its weakened state.

But he did mention the old fort in the woods, to Seth's delight. He listened in his half-conscious state as Seth recounted his dim memories of this fort to Ruth, who was also only half awake. Josh felt good that his son had these memories, despite his young age at the time.

Josh then told the story of his return to that house on the way back from the river. He told how he did not know why he made that choice, to return there for no reason, yet upon doing so he was able to rescue a man from the Loyalists who now lived there.

This aroused some excitement from the rest of the family as they quizzed him about it. Even Ruth asked a question or two about it, though she remained sleepily dazed. Josh told of how he had wanted to cut the man's restraints but had no tool to do so, until he was able to find one in the dirt in front of the house. Then, with the tool, he was able to –

"Where did you find it?" interrupted Seth, leaning forward toward his father with sudden interest.

Josh paused to think. It had all happened so fast, and his mind was so bleary right now. He had to concentrate. He had to wake up just a little bit. The details swam around his brain until they formed a concrete picture. "Um," he began, not wanting to get it wrong, "I was at the front corner near the fireplace, and I had this idea to look under a rock right there below the window. It was under the rock. I saw a blade and dug it up."

"Was it a box cutter?" asked Seth meekly.

"Yes," Josh answered, already losing track of his thought. "Yes, I think it was. So I used that knife and, um," he stumbled over what he was saying as drowsiness crowded his thoughts, "freed the man."

But his wife had caught the strange tone of her son's question, and she interrogated him about it. "Seth, honey, why did you ask that?"

"I dunno."

"I think you do know," she insisted. "Why did you ask if the knife was a box cutter?"

"Just cuz," Seth answered, seeming a bit afraid.

This barely registered to Josh or Ruth, both of whom drifted farther away into sleep each moment.

Angelica got serious, "Seth, do you have something you want to tell me?"

Despite having no idea what was going on, Phoebe piped up, "Yeah, is there something you want to tell us?"

"Well," began Seth, uncomfortable for some reason, "it's because maybe, when we used to live there, maybe I might have buried something by the front window."

She asked him directly, "Did you bury a box cutter under a rock by the front window?"

Seth looked away from his mother's eyes and answered, "Yes."

Josh and Ruth both heard that loud and clear.

Ruth seemed to wake up very quickly. "Wait. What?"

Seth was still looking at the floor, as if ashamed of his role in this. "Mommy told me to throw it away but I buried it instead."

"Honey, I'm sure I told you to put it away, not throw it away," she said. "How do you even remember that?"

"I dunno," he said, still looking at the floor. "I just do."

Josh was clearing the cobwebs from his mind but had a vague recollection of a box cutter mysteriously going missing at around that same time. He had looked all over for it, even asked his wife if she had seen it, but it was never found, and no one ever put the clues together. Apparently Seth, not wanting to dispose of the treasure he had found, had buried it for later use. Then it never got unburied.

"How did you know it was there?" asked Ruth, stunned at this amazing coincidence.

"I – I didn't," Josh replied. "Seth, did you ever tell me you buried the box cutter there?"

Seth shook his head, no.

"And you didn't either?" he asked, addressing his wife.

"I thought he put it back in the tool box," said Angelica.

The whole attic was in stunned silence. Josh and Ruth had both sat up from their resting positions, and all of them sat facing each other. Seth was rocking back and forth with nervous energy. Phoebe wore a big smile and was flipping through a Bible.

"How did you know it was there?" demanded Ruth again, sounding a little freaked out.

"I don't know," said Josh. "I have no idea. It was just there."

"'"The wind blows wherever it pleases. You hear its sound, but you cannot tell where it comes from or where it is going. So it is with everyone born of the Spirit,"'" said Phoebe. She was reading from John's gospel, which she had opened in front of her.

Josh closed his eyes. It made perfect sense. "God. Of course."

But Ruth was having trouble. "What do you mean, 'of course'? You're saying God showed you that knife?"

"God knew Seth put it there," stated Phoebe. "God told Daddy."

"God caused Seth to put it there in the first place," realized Josh. "So I could free that man tonight."

Ruth was still in disbelief. "God put a knife there like ten years ago just for tonight? You know how crazy that sounds?"

But Angelica realized she had a part in it too. "God kept me from putting it away. Why wouldn't I put it away? Why would I have my four year old put it away?"

Ruth was powerfully affected by this. "I don't understand! How can that happen?"

"It just does," said Josh, feeling incredibly humbled by his part in such a large picture. "God uses all circumstances at all times to His greater purpose and good. Of course God arranged this whole thing. God made us move to that house just so Seth could put that knife there. God has been working to save that man's life for years, since before we ever lived there. Since before Seth was born."

"That's the way God is!" exclaimed Phoebe, excited.

Reality was spinning like a vortex inside Ruth's mind. She had been affected by all the stories she had heard that night from the Bible. She had watched these strangers living their lives in faith that the words on the pages were true. She had even admitted that such a story might be true, and that she might find it attractive. But it had not been real, not really real, until this. That very night, the night she met these people, God had worked to complete something He set in motion a long time ago, and He had done it through His people, these very people. This was not a story from the other side of the world, or a story in a book, or from another point in time. This was happening right now. It had just happened. This random man was somewhere out there now, alive because God had intervened. And these people seemed amazed, but not really surprised.

"That's the way God is," Phoebe repeated. "He's just that way."

And this was it. To Ruth, the unfolding of this story had broken her, and to hear such strong but simple words of faith from this young girl cemented that brokenness. Amid all the strife in the world, amid all the death and torture and chaos, the God of the universe had reached down and saved someone. She felt so inadequate to even hear of such a God. What kind of omnipotent being could be interested in her? How could she ever measure up to such amazing power and kindness?

She suddenly had tears forming in her eyes. She had never thought that tonight would go this way. She never even dreamed this could be possible, let alone that she would find it. She stammered out as best she could, "This God, your God. Can He be my God too?"

"He's everybody's God," said Angelica. "He died for you too. He loves you like you're the only person who ever lived."

The tears fell from her eyes as Ruth declared, without even realizing it, "Then your God is my God, and I will go where you go, because He is with you."

"Daddy!" cried Phoebe, excited again. She was holding up her Bible, and pointing to the page. Josh took the Bible from his daughter's hand and looked at what she was pointing to. She had opened to the book of Ruth, which they had studied only the prior Sabbath. The lesson was fresh in Phoebe's mind.

Josh situated himself to read the passage his daughter had indicated. He began, "This is from the book of Ruth." Their own Ruth was surprised to hear of a book that shared her namesake. "It's when Ruth refuses to leave her mother-in-law, deciding instead to adopt a new life and leave her old life behind. She says to her mother-in-law Naomi, "'Don't urge me to leave you or to turn back from you. Where you go I will go, and where you stay I will stay. Your people will be my people and your God my God.'" Wow."

"That's what you just said," remarked Seth to Ruth.

But Ruth had no words to respond. She had never felt like this before. She felt like the universe itself was coming together to care for her in a way she never thought possible. She felt lifted up in her solitude. She felt strength in her body despite the intense weariness. Most of all, she felt a certain peace that defied all understanding, as she sat there in this small attic space and cried.

As the minutes ticked by, she simply wept. God had caused her to come into these people's lives at the very instant she needed in order to find Him. Overwhelmed by the idea of an Almighty God arranging events in order to reach her, she had no choice but to cry. Each tear that fell from her face seemed like a weight being lifted from her soul that she didn't even realize was there before.

She felt relieved, and for the first time in her life she understood what it meant to feel free.

Angelica began to hum a song from church that came into her mind while Ruth wept. No words were needed in this moment. The rest of the family each recognized the tune and, one at a time, joined her in humming it. For a minute, to everyone present there, reality seemed to freeze around them, and the perfect moment of melody and divinity was the only thing they desired. When the tune ended, the family fell silent but Ruth continued in her tears.

Chapter XXV

Tuesday came and went, as did Wednesday, and Thursday and Friday. Despite the addition of another person to their family, the day-to-day routines remained largely the same. Ruth volunteered to share the responsibilities of gathering food and water with Josh, to allow him to stay at home with his family more. As she had claimed, water was available at the library and pasta sauce at the store, and suddenly everyone seemed so very optimistic about everything. It seemed like Christmas never ended, and each new day brought them a new abundance of sustenance. Phoebe felt like she was already in heaven.

The days were not idly spent. Ruth was suddenly on fire with questions about everything. The family spent most of its time engaged in Bible studies on every topic they could think of. Josh found this task exhilarating, and not a little challenging. There were certain verses and stories that he knew by heart, but mostly in the past he had relied on an extensive series of notes, books, and electronic study guides created by himself and others that were saved on his computer. But these days his library had been destroyed, and there was no longer any power to the home, so any and all hopes of using a computer for any purpose were long gone. Instead, Josh now had to rely entirely on the Holy Spirit to guide him through the Scriptures to where he needed to go, to help his new sister in Christ to better know her Lord.

Ruth found it a little strange at first when she awoke to find the rest of the family on their knees or faces in prayer. She had never witnessed anything like that before. Of course, she had seen television and movies of large groups of Catholics and Muslims worshipping in unison, or smaller groups of Protestants and Jews worshipping together if not in unison, but she had never seen a family of individuals each approaching God through prayer in their own, individual ways outside of a worship setting. It had never occurred to her before that God could exist outside of church, or that people would choose to commune with Him at home.

Despite this, and in fact because of it, Ruth felt like each day, even each new hour brought her a new perspective on the world. She began to hope, despite herself, that at any given moment the sky would open up and Christ Jesus would descend from heaven with His divine shout. She began to hope for a reunion with her family, whom she allowed herself to miss for the first time since their execution. The aching loneliness had dispelled.

The day after Christmas, Angelica had told her that the family would be going to church that Friday night, which Ruth found exceedingly strange. Going out for any reason at all was dangerous, so she simply did not understand why they would all voluntarily go out at the same time to join other people who were also hunted by the government. It seemed like lunacy. It seemed suicidal. It seemed exciting!

But Ruth caught herself, and before she could ask what the purpose could possibly be in taking such a large risk, she instead asked, "Why Friday night?" She was expecting them to say 'Sunday.' She had never heard of any other day of worship for Christians.

This, of course, prompted a Scripture lesson on the Sabbath.

"It's really quite simple," said Josh, opening his Bible. "I'll show it to you in four verses. Turn to Genesis chapter 1."

Angelica added words of reason to Josh's explanation. "Honey," she said, addressing Ruth, "what Josh means it that the principle of the Sabbath is very straightforward, and can be demonstrated in the four verses he's about to show you. But really we could spend all day, and all tomorrow and so on, learning about God's Sabbath. It's very important."

Ruth, no longer a skeptic, understood the gravity that Angelica was trying to convey, and diligently opened to the first chapter of Genesis, eager to learn more.

"You'll see that chapter 1 recounts the story of creation, how God made everything on earth. On the first day, He created light. On the second, He made the atmosphere. On the third, He made land and plants. On the fourth, He cleared the skies so we could see the sun, moon, and stars and use them to tell time. On the fifth…"

"Wait, what?" she asked. Though she had never believed it, she had always thought that God created the sun and moon during the creation period. But Josh had just described it in a different way. "What do you mean He cleared the skies?"

"Read verses, um," Josh began, looking for the correct place, "14 through 18. Tell me what yours says."

Ruth read, "'And God said, "Let there be lights in the dome of the sky to separate the day from the night; and let them be for signs and for seasons and for days and years, and let them be lights in the dome of the sky to give light upon the earth." And it was so. God made the two great lights – the greater light to rule the day and the lesser light to rule the night – and the stars. God set them in the dome of the sky to give light upon the earth, to rule over the day and over the night, and to separate the light from the darkness. And God saw that it was good.'"

"So what does that mean to you?" asked Josh.

Hesitant, Ruth answered, "That God made the sun and moon and stars?"

"Listen to how God describes this. He tells it from the perspective of the earth. He didn't necessarily make those things on that day. He simply made them visible from earth on that day. I mean, I guess they could have been created at that time, I'm not saying that's wrong, but I wonder what the earth was orbiting around before then, or how there was evening and morning for the first three days without the sun. I will definitely ask God about it when we all get to heaven. Mine says, '"Let there be lights in the firmament of the heaven to divide the day from the night."'"

"But what does that mean?" asked Ruth. "We could always see the sun from the earth. The moon, too."

Josh paused before he answered her. "How do you know the sun was always visible from earth? Were you there?"

Ruth had never considered this. "No," she answered. "But we can see it now. Are you saying the sky was different then?"

"I'm not saying anything. God says it was different then. Did you know that in the beginning it never rained?"

And there it was, that familiar seed of skepticism in Ruth's mind.

"Look at chapter 2" Josh continued quickly, "verses 5 and 6. It's telling a larger story here, but look about halfway through verse 5. What does it say?"

Ruth scanned and read, "'For the Lord God had not caused it to rain upon the earth, and there was no one to till the ground; but a stream would rise from the earth, and water the whole face of the ground.'"

"See?" said Josh. "Mine reads, 'There went up a mist from the earth, and watered the whole face of the ground.' The Hebrew word here is pronounced 'ade,' and it means an enveloping fog. God watered the earth with worldwide dew each morning."

Even Angelica seemed impressed here. "How do you know that?" she asked him.

"I don't really know," he admitted. "It's just one of those things that stuck with me over the years. It's not a hard word. 'Ade.' But let me show you when it changed! Check out Genesis 7!"

They all turned there together to read.

"Ruth, why don't you read verses 11 and 12 for us?"

185

She did so. "'In the six hundredth year of Noah's life, in the second month, on the seventeenth day of the month, on that day all the fountains of the great deep burst forth, and the windows of the heavens were opened. The rain fell on the earth forty days and forty nights.'"

"'The windows of the heavens were opened,' and it rained! No wonder no one believed Noah the whole time he tried to get people to listen! They thought he was mad! Rain had never fallen and the earth was watered by harmless dew. No flooding had ever taken place anywhere. But the earth then spewed water from beneath and above at the same time, and everything was destroyed. And it's rained like we know it ever since."

Ruth considered this. Because the planet produced rain now, because in fact whole sciences were built around rain and the atmosphere, Ruth had never been introduced to the idea that rain did not exist here until after mankind did. Such a concept must be fictional, she immediately felt in her heart, because it is so contrary to the way we can see nature actually working! But then Ruth saw, in that moment of self-realization, that to assume that nature has always been the way it is now was just that: an assumption. She was learning over and over not to make assumptions about God.

"So," continued Josh, "you'd think that the people would get scared that the flood was coming back the next time the rain came down, right?"

Again, this was another logical conclusion that Ruth had not considered.

"Therefore you'd think God would give them some kind of way to know that it was just normal rain, and not a world-ending inundation. Do you know what He did?"

Ruth seemed to enjoy this, though she and everyone else in the attic understood that of course she didn't know what God did. She was learning every word for the first time.

"Go to chapter 9, verses 12 through 15. When you get there, please read it for us."

Ruth flipped a few pages, found the verses in question, and read. "'God said, "This is the sign of the covenant that I make between me and you and every living creature that is with you, for all future generations: I have set my bow in the clouds, and it shall be a sign of the covenant between me and the earth. When I bring clouds over the earth and the bow is seen in the clouds, I will remember my covenant that is between me and you and every living creature of all flesh; and the waters shall never again become a flood to destroy all flesh."'"

"So what are we talking about?" prompted Josh.

Ruth paused, then answered, "A rainbow?"

"A rainbow!" cried Josh. "That's right!"

"Calm down, Josh," advised his wife. "We're all right here, don't yell."

"I like it when Daddy gets excited," offered Phoebe.

"Me too," laughed Ruth. She liked that rainbows were God's reminder that He would not flood the whole earth again. "Thanks for showing me that."

"You're welcome," said Josh. He paused, then, "Why were we talking about this?"

"You were showing me how the sky used to be different. Because of creation."

"Ah, yes!" he answered. "Okay, go back to chapter 1." As they flipped backward, he chuckled and said, "It's easy to get sidetracked in God's Word."

"Amen," said his wife.

"Amen," repeated Seth, a little sarcastically.

"So," Josh began, resuming the actual lesson they had set out to learn, "on the fifth day God made the birds and the fish, and on the sixth He made the animals on the ground, including the only rational animal, mankind. So what did He do on the seventh day?"

Ruth didn't quite understand the question. "Or the eighth, or the ninth?"

"Good point! But how many days are there in a week?"

"Seven."

"Why is that?" Josh asked.

Ruth gave no answer at first. She asked, "What do you mean?"

"Well," he began, "each time the sun sets, we have a day. Each time the moon goes around the earth, we have a month. Each time the earth goes around the sun, we have a year. But what celestial event dictates a seven-day week?"

Ruth answered, "None?"

"None! That's right. So why does the entire world work on a seven day week if there is no celestial reason?"

Ruth began to see it. She answered, "Because of creation."

"Bingo. It's amazing that the world at large has fallen away from an understanding that God is the author and creator of all things. We live our weekly lives according to the schedule He gave us at the very beginning of time!"

"Okay, so what did God do on the seventh day?" asked Ruth.

"Read it for yourself. Genesis 2: 1-3."

She read, "'Thus the heavens and the earth were finished, and all their multitude. And on the seventh day God finished the work that He had done, and He rested on the seventh day from all the work that He had done. So God blessed the seventh day and hallowed it, because on it God rested from all the work that He had done in creation.'" She looked up, processing this information. "So God rested," she stated, as if expecting confirmation.

"So God rested. That's right. And He established it as a memorial to His creative work. Look at Exodus chapter 20."

The entire family flipped to the book of Exodus. Josh asked Ruth to read the fourth commandment when she found the proper text. She read, "'Remember the Sabbath day, and keep it holy. Six days you shall labor and do all your work. But the seventh day is a Sabbath to the Lord your God; you shall not do any work – you, your son or your daughter, your male or female slave, your livestock, or the alien resident in your towns. For in six days the Lord made heaven and earth, the sea, and all that is in them, but rested the seventh day; therefore the Lord blessed the Sabbath day and consecrated it."'"

"So God asks us to partake in His holy rest on His holy day. The seventh day."

"How do you know which is the seventh day?" asked Ruth.

Angelica piped in and teased her husband, "I knew you couldn't do it in just four verses."

"Quiet, you!" he teased back. "There are a few ways we can know. First, look at the calendar. Which is the seventh day?"

Of course, there was no calendar in the attic. But Ruth didn't need one to be able to answer, "Saturday."

Josh answered, "There you are. Saturday."

"But in Mexico Sunday is the seventh day," said Ruth.

"Smart girl! Germany too, and others. That's right. So we need more proof. Have you ever met any Jewish people?"

"No," she answered truthfully.

"Alright, um, then did you ever pay attention to what Babylon said when they invaded Israel?"

"You mean the Christians?" asked Ruth, genuinely.

"Honey, we're the Christians," said Angelica. "The government just uses our name. Christ doesn't kill people who disagree with Him."

"Yes, I mean them," said Josh. "What justification did they give the world for doing that?"

Ruth thought hard about this. She hadn't really paid much attention at the time. The world was filled with so much war that she hadn't thought it was any different from the countless other conflicts. "Something about not obeying the law. It was like some day of the week they had a problem with."

"It was the Sabbath they had a problem with!" said Josh, getting excited again. "Did you go to church on Saturday when you were part of the government system with your family?"

"No."

"Why not?"

"They said to go on a different day."

"And what happens if you don't go on that day?"

Ruth kept silent. In her mind raced the horrors of what this family had faced because they refused to do what the government said. She saw also the horror of the last day of her own family's lives, and the brutal end they all met because they failed to go just once.

Seeing Ruth's discomfort, Josh kept talking. "Well Israel did not adopt the government's day. Most Jews refused around the whole world. Babylon invaded because Israel kept the Sabbath. And what day is the Sabbath?"

"Saturday," Ruth answered.

"Saturday. It's always been Saturday. In fact technically it's sundown Friday to sundown Saturday. In order for the Jews to have mixed up which day of the week is the Sabbath, every Jewish person in the world would have had to fall asleep at the same exact time, and sleep for more than a day, and all wake up at the same time and not realize what happened, or else there would be a bunch of different Jewish groups each claiming a different day. The existence of Jewish culture is, all by itself, a testament to the Sabbath."

"Wow," was all Ruth had to say.

"And if that's not enough for you, then go to Mark 16, verses 1 and 2."

They all turned to that passage, and Ruth read it. "'When the Sabbath was over, Mary Magdalene, and Mary the mother of James, and Salome bought spices, so that they might go and anoint Him. And very early on the first day of the week, when the sun had risen, they went to the tomb.'"

"What day of the week did Jesus rise from the dead?" asked Josh.

"Sunday," answered Ruth triumphantly. "Even I know that."

"Everyone knows that!" said Josh. "That's just about the only thing that all Christians have always agreed on. Sunday is resurrection day, the first day of the week. So if Sunday is the day after the Sabbath, then what day is the Sabbath?"

"Saturday."

"Saturday. Exactly." Josh was feeling really good. He enjoyed sharing such a simple Biblical truth with people. So many people missed it. "Since you're in the New Testament already, go to Matthew 5."

When they were there, Josh read verses 17 through 19. "Jesus says to His followers, "'Think not that I am come to destroy the law, or the prophets: I am not come to destroy, but to fulfill. For verily I say unto you, till heaven and earth pass, one jot or one tittle shall in no wise pass from the law, till all be fulfilled. Whosoever therefore shall break one of these least commandments, and shall teach men so, he shall be called the least in the kingdom of heaven: but whosoever shall do and teach them, the same shall be called great in the kingdom of heaven."' So what does that mean?"

"What's a 'tittle?'" snickered Seth, having fun at the expense of the ancient language of the King James translation.

Phoebe answered her father. She said, "God never changes."

"But we keep changing," said Ruth. "The Christians don't ... I mean, the government doesn't meet on Sabbath."

"That's right," said Josh. "They say Jesus changed the Sabbath day when He rose on Sunday. But what does Jesus say Himself, right here in this verse?"

Phoebe answered again, simply but profoundly, "God never changes."

"And God's law never changes," added Angelica.

"Wow," said Ruth again. She had gone through life thinking that mankind had progressed beyond what religion and the Bible had to say, and in fact that somehow humanity had changed enough to make the Bible obsolete. But the Bible itself said that God would never change, no matter how much we did. His truth would always be true. And now the world was paying the ultimate price for its rebellion against His truth.

"I have one more for you. Go to Exodus 31."

Dutifully, they all turned to this chapter.

"Ruth, can you read for us verses 12 and 13? This was written by Moses to the baby nation of Israel after they fled from captivity in Egypt."

"Okay. 'The Lord said to Moses: You yourself are to speak to the Israelites: "You shall keep my Sabbaths, for this is a sign between me and you throughout your generations, given in order that you may know that I, the Lord, sanctify you.""""

"Also verses 16 and 17?"

""""Therefore the Israelites shall keep the Sabbath, observing the Sabbath throughout their generations, as a perpetual covenant. It is a sign forever between me and the people of Israel that in six days the Lord made heaven and earth, and on the seventh day He rested, and was refreshed.""""

"So Sabbath points backward to creation, and exists as a reminder to us and to the world that we are God's people."

And Ruth was convinced. It was tempting to consider all days the same, but if those who kept a different day spent their lives hunting and killing everyone else, and those who kept the day set apart by God were able to survive against all odds and give their God glory amid discomfort and persecution, then Ruth was willing to believe that somehow, in a way only God could understand, obeying His instruction to worship on His holy day made a difference. She felt renewed by this knowledge. She felt closer to God than she had at the beginning of the study. She wanted to know more, and more, and more.

The family spoke again about heading to church on Friday night. They told her that in the past, when the world was better off, they had met on Saturday morning for church, but since the persecution began they had decided to meet in large groups only under the cover of darkness. Sabbath began at sunset Friday so the meeting this week would be Friday night.

This coming Sabbath, Ruth would celebrate the very last Christmas on earth with her brethren in Christ.

Chapter XXVI

It was about an hour until sunset on Friday the 28th of December, and the sky was already dimming in anticipation of the night to come. Phoebe and Seth were both visibly excited. Phoebe, especially, was finding it difficult to stay still. Even though the day of Christmas had already passed, both the children knew the Bible well enough to know that Christ was not born at the end of December, and that this date had been chosen by the church several hundred years after Christ's ministry in order to unify the Christians with the pagans so that the failing Roman empire could be salvaged. Prior, it had been a celebration of the rebirth of the sun god, since it was at this time of year that the days began to lengthen again. Therefore, the children found the fellowship at church on Sabbath to be more exciting than the Christmas celebration on the calendar day of the 25th. Four years ago Seth had dubbed the Sabbath after the 25th as "the seventh day of Christmas." His church, all observers of the seventh-day Sabbath, had adopted his clever title for their celebration of the birth of Christ.

Josh was the only one who had been to church in a long while. He had gone the week before to collect the water bag from Pastor Benny, but even before that he had managed to get to the church with relative regularity. His family, at his insistence for their own safety, had not come to worship in several months.

Because of this, Josh was also the only one who had any real idea what to expect at the service. Though their church had traditionally celebrated "the seventh day of Christmas," obviously the world was in a much different state now than it had been in the past. The rest of the family had no idea what to expect. All Josh had told them was that Benny wanted to get as many members as were left together for a special worship on that day.

Ruth, of course, had a completely open mind and no preconceptions about what would occur. She was tempted to think that the service would be somehow just like it had been with Babylon, but she refused to believe that was true.

As the minutes ticked by, the sky grew darker and darker still, and eventually the Sabbath was upon them. It was the last holy day of the calendar year.

Ruth remained full of questions about everything, and she had no trouble at all keeping up conversation with the family as they tried to while away the time until it was dark enough outside to leave. As the sun dropped beneath the horizon, Ruth asked, "How long have you known Benny?"

Angelica answered, "He was assigned to our church about five years ago, when our previous pastor was sent to New York to minister there. He came from Arizona, so none of us knew him before then. He's been with us ever since."

This surprised Ruth. She was expecting them to say that they had joined his church, not the other way around. "So you've been at the church longer than he has?"

"At this particular church, yes. But the larger body of the church exists all around the world, and Benny has been a pastor for a long time."

"How was it different before he came?"

"It was kind of the same," she answered. "The church is made up of its members, under the spiritual guidance of the pastor. Benny is very energetic, and he was good for the young people, and he's very knowledgeable of the Scriptures. He's been very good for us during these hard times. But the flavor of the church didn't change much when he came."

Ruth pondered this, but didn't have long to do so before Josh commanded everyone's attention. The time was coming when they would leave the house.

"I cannot stress enough," he began, after advising them all that the trip that night was of deathly importance, "the most important thing is to be quiet. If they find us, they will catch us. You understand?" He was addressing them all at once. Assorted murmurs returned to him in agreement, but not from his daughter. "You understand, sweetie?" he asked her directly. She simply nodded silently.

He continued. "Everyone follow my lead out there. Ruth, stay close to me." Ruth also had recent experience maneuvering outdoors without being detected. "Any questions?"

The family remained quiet, and resolute.

Josh said, "Then let's go."

"Dad?" said Seth. "We should have prayer first."

"Thank you, son, you're right. Let's pray." The small group nudged a little closer together and bowed their heads. "Merciful Father, thank you for the opportunity to go and fellowship with our brethren who also await your return. We give you glory and honor tonight as we enter into your special day. We trust in the rest you have for us, and we place our lives in your hands, Lord, so we might best see your mighty power to save. Help us turn whatever we do to your glory, and help us come one step closer to your kingdom, that we might come home soon. In your name, Amen."

"Amen," came a chorus of answers from the family.

Then they left.

Chapter XXVII

The trip was uneventful. They each had to decide how many layers of clothes to wear to be both bundled up against the chilly air yet also flexible enough to move quickly. They had taken a good long time before exiting the house through the back door, and again before darting through the open courtyard area in front of the house. They made it to the woods, to the creek, and along the creek bed until they had to deviate in order to come to the church grove. They encountered no one. They heard nothing.

Josh experienced the notable exception to this uneventful journey. He had seen something along the way that his family had not, and he had fought the desire to share with others his horror, choosing instead not to spread the horror unnecessarily.

He had seen a corpse.

As best he could tell, it used to be a woman, but her body was badly mangled. She had been left dangling in a tree, almost as if she had been tossed away there like garbage, like an afterthought. He saw her limbs and neck moved in ways that surely indicated broken bones beneath her intact skin. He saw large wounds everywhere there was exposed flesh: some were distinctly trauma wounds; some were evidence of wildlife scavenging.

Josh saw this woman when the moonlight glinted off something and caught his eye. He told his family to stay put while he investigated something, and moved off toward the tree.

When he realized what he was looking at, he knew immediately that he could not tell his family what he had found. It was too horrible for the children and he could see no benefit to burdening the women with this discovery. He was ready to leave her there and return to his family when he saw what had caught his eye in the first place.

There was a small golden chain with a crucifix on it, tied to this woman's left ankle. The chain itself had been knotted so as not to fall off. The bottom of the cross itself had been jammed into the woman's fleshy calf, and the bottom of the feet of that idol figure of his Savior were sticking into her wound. The whole thing was revolting. It was as if these monsters were literally claiming this victim in the name of Christ.

He paused for a moment and offered a silent prayer. 'Have mercy on her, O Lord. You died for her too. Remember her when you come into your kingdom, victorious.'

When he got back to his family, he said he had not found anything, and they moved on to finish their journey.

At the clearing for the church grounds, they waited. Josh quietly instructed them about the 5-minute rule to watch for spies or soldiers. They settled in and began this vigil. Each minute seemed like an eternity for everyone there.

Phoebe was excited to get back to church, where she had not been for so long. She had always enjoyed church. She liked the upbeat mood of everyone there. She felt close to God there. She enjoyed all the singing and the celebration of the world yet to come. She had been back to the church once or twice since it had been ransacked by the military, and she knew that it would look violated and overturned on the inside, but from the outside perspective she had now, looking at the building from a short distance, it looked as peaceful as it had ever been. Her mind wandered during those long minutes, as she remembered the countless praise songs, baptisms, sermons and potluck lunches she had witnessed there. She remembered fondly the older women who always paid her so much attention, and told stories of when they were younger at that same church. She remembered the classes held there each Sabbath, which she could remember attending for as long as she had memories. When the five minutes were up, she was sad to return to the reality of danger and persecution. Her mind had gone on to the mystery of heaven and being reunited with these people again.

Seth felt a twinge of guilt in his heart, looking at his church now with darkness spilling out the windows. Inside there was no light, nor laughter. Inside seemed empty though he knew there would be people there as scared as he was. They, like his father, had known enough to pay attention to all the pastor's sermons about the end times, and had loved God enough to be ready. As he looked with sadness at the building that was looted because of what it stood for, a loyalty to the God of heaven over the men of earth, he remembered the many Sabbaths he had resented coming here, or fallen asleep during the message, or both. He remembered the baptisms during which he always felt boredom, and wished he was home playing video games. He remembered Pastor Benny, and at this moment Seth could recall only fond memories. Seth's heart cried out to the Lord for forgiveness. He was sorry for his selfishness. He desperately desired for God to be with him now. When the five minutes were up for Seth, he felt humbled before Jehovah, yet strengthened by Him. He felt ready for the task ahead.

Ruth had been full of awe and wonder for a few days, and that didn't stop now. She took stock in her life waiting there silently for the minutes to pass, and it was not lost on her that even just one week prior she would have envisioned herself dying before trying to sneak into a church for worship. The very fact that she was here with these loving people, risking her safety to join with others to worship the very God that the enemy itself claimed to worship, seemed so incredible that she felt invincible. Logic had ceased to exist, and only faith remained. If the enemy showed up now, their bullets would pass right through her. She had stopped feeling scared. She had learned to be free. When the five minutes were up for her, she delighted in the challenge before them. She was glad to have yet another reason to praise God.

For Angelica, this moment was all about her kids. Each of them had been born into this drama. They had no choice but to experience this in some way. She and Josh had always been convinced beyond doubt that Babylon would rise to power some day, and had never raised their kids to know anything else. So here, in this present moment waiting to see any signs of life either hostile or benevolent, she felt both proud of her children for being wise enough to follow their invisible God, and sorry for them that they had to live through the consequences of their good choices. No pre-teen should ever have to bear witness to the horror of fully ripe sin. No child should even comprehend what life is like outside the healing and graceful hand of God. When the five minutes were up for Angelica, she prayed that her children might be among those who are alive and remain at Christ's return. She asked God to take her own life, if someone's life must be taken, and to spare her children.

For Josh, these long minutes were spent in heavy surveillance of the surrounding area. He listened for every noise and watched for every movement. He felt a protective role for the people he was with, and envisioned God feeling this way about all His people. He did not want to let them down. He was nervous, but he reflected on all the times in his life when he had been aware of the motions of God directing him, and those memories were vivid, and numerous. He reviewed them each in his mind to remind himself that he was never alone, and that through his Christ he could do anything. He asked for mercy on himself, and forgiveness for his pride. He pleaded silently with the Father that all his, Josh's, impulses might be subdued so that only divinity shone through his words and actions. Only this way would he lead his group to safety. Only by God's mighty hand would they live to see another day, and to worship again. When the five minutes were up for Josh, he felt like he needed another fifteen seconds to be ready, and fifteen seconds beyond that, and fifteen more. Catching his weakness and casting it to his God, he said to his family, "Okay, let's go. Move fast. Follow me."

Across the clearing they hurried, Josh first and Ruth pulling up the rear. As was always true during these periods of vulnerability, the actual distance seemed multiplied, and time seemed to slow. Josh saw his legs move as if in a dream, slow like frozen molasses. He imagined he saw government agents at the top of every tree in view, and around every corner. Each time his foot fell to the earth, the *crunch* of the leaves or ground beneath him sounded like gunfire in his ears. His heartbeat rose faster than it should. The noise of his breathing came to drown out everything else.

But sure enough, the party of five eventually made it to the front door. The glass door had not been replaced, and the empty skeleton of the once proud glass panes gazed at them like a toothless grin. He held the door open a little and motioned for the others to go inside. When all four had entered, he followed.

As he closed the door behind him and entered into the sanctuary area to look for Benny and anyone else who had arrived, he thought he had successfully executed their trip to the church. No one had been injured, no one died, and there were no signs of anyone having seen them. God had delivered them. They were victorious.

As Josh walked away from the door, he failed to see that in the distance, at the top of a small hill a thousand feet away, was a small platoon of Babylon's soldiers watching them. They had seen all five of them leave the woods and dash across the clearing, then enter one at a time into the darkened church.

One of the men among this brigade pressed a button on the side of his radio, and said into it, "We have confirmed five more entered the building. Waiting on your order to go." He then set his radio back into its place on his belt, and picked up his automatic rifle.

Chapter XXVIII

Tom was second in command of his unit that night, watching the terrorists sneak into the abandoned church one small group at a time. He heard his commanding officer radio back to base that another group had just arrived, then saw him pick up his rifle and check to make sure it was loaded and ready to fire. It wouldn't be long now, and they would advance.

Tom took this job before the enforcement began. He was a recent graduate from a masters program with an enormous pile of debt behind him. He had gone through undergraduate school and immediately on to the graduate program in his field of study, which was European history. His life choices had been about trying to have the least responsibility he could possibly take on. His choice of major was because he found the subject easy, and kind of interesting. He absorbed history well, and read quickly. He enjoyed interacting with the historical figures better, generally speaking, than interacting with his present day fellow man. It was certainly easier for him than majoring in calculus or business or physics. And the only thing he was really interested in was auto repair! Toward the end of his education, he strongly regretted not simply going to trade school in the first place and spending his days getting dirty with cars.

At the end of his undergraduate career, the idea of actually paying back his student loans was disagreeable to him because it would require him to find full time work and take on some responsibility or other to make his payments each month. So he gathered up all the necessary application forms, took the necessary tests, and committed himself to another three years in school, during which he could simply defer the existing loans while taking on new ones. He was confused when he received a letter in the mail from his loan company offering to let him pay the interest during the deferment, and he could not understand why they were presenting this option to him as if it were a privilege. He did not understand the concept of compounding interest until he graduated from his masters program, and realized how much larger the loans were now than they were when he had deferred them in the first place. As he looked at the mountain of paperwork and repayment terms being presented to him, he realized with dread that there was simply no way on earth that he could pay back what he had borrowed, short of winning the lottery.

Because of this, it was an easy choice when Babylon offered a job in its military wing. It was prepared to pay down the debt loads of anyone who pledged loyalty to it at a very high repayment percentage per year. Whatever the debt load, Babylon did not seem scared by it. It promised any debt, no matter the size, would be paid off in fifteen years on its dime, provided the debtor remained in active military duty for that entire time. Tom weighed his options and took stock of his life. Around him, the world was falling apart rapidly, and although the various world governments kept promising to fix everything with their taxes and financial policies, he just didn't believe it. He knew he would be lucky to find any job at all, let alone one within the major he had been studying for nearly a decade, and even if he found one he would be a slave to his bills for his entire life. With Babylon, he was promised a debt-free life in a decade and a half, and free transportation around the country and the world wherever his services were needed. The new world government had not yet begun its full military campaigns, and Tom honestly thought it never would. So he signed up.

He had an amazing moment of horrific realization when he was mobilized and put into active duty, to hunt and exterminate his fellow citizens.

Now here he was, perched atop a hillside getting ready to slaughter people he had never met, on the orders of people he had never met, who belonged to an organization he barely believed in. His loyalty to Babylon ended with its financial promise to him.

He recalled with tremendous self-loathing the various and numerous people he had been forced to murder during his tenure with the religious government. The first one had been like a punch to his groin, and he had been sick for several days afterward. He had seriously considered quitting and taking back the financial burden of the debt, and had even convinced himself to do it, but when he presented the idea to his commanding officer he was advised never to mention such a thing ever again, unless he desired to count himself among the enemies of the state. Babylon would not let anyone go, once it got its evil claws around a person's life.

After the first murder, there had been so many more that he had lost track. He hadn't had a full, restful night's sleep since that time. Whenever he closed his eyes, he saw the countless horrified faces awaiting their death before him. The victims' expressions always bore the agony of death after the bullets did their work, but even this was warped in his mind, and the parade of corpses that was permanently burned into the backs of his eyelids reflected expressions of anger, malice, hatred, and loathing. He saw these dead faces reflecting the emotions he had toward himself.

Tom had lost all his friends. He had grown estranged from his family. He was close to no one in his platoon. Every single day he wondered if killing himself would be a better alternative. The only thing that stopped him was Babylon's promise to the world that suicide would land them directly in hell, to burn forever in God's unending wrath. Tom was not a religious man, but he deduced that if God was mad enough to cause His servants in Babylon to hunt and exterminate His enemies, then he, Tom, wanted nothing to do with this God's eternal wrath in fire. It was bad enough here on earth.

The officer in charge got a message over the radio, and Tom overhead it. The static crackle of the walkie-talkie made Tom chuckle a bit. He was living in the 21st century, when he had been promised flying cars, jetpacks, and world peace. Yet the orders to exterminate benign families were coming through a children's toy, filled with static.

The radio crackled: 'Stand down, hold your position. Mobilize in thirty. Be ready to advance in sixty. Copy?'

"Copy," answered the officer. He then stood up and addressed the dozen men with him. "Orders just came in. We are standing down for a half hour, gentlemen. I want every one of you locked, loaded and ready by then. We're advancing in one hour. You!" he shouted at the rear guard of three men, "I want you three watching the back of the building. If anyone sneaks out the back or if you see any breach in the perimeter, we're moving in ahead of schedule to contain the threat. Report back to me with any movement at all. Got it?"

"Sir, yes sir!" they answered in unison.

When the officer settled back down to his original position and looked through his binoculars for any more worshippers coming to the church, Tom asked a question. It wasn't out of bravery; Tom had become so apathetic toward life that he simply didn't care if his question brought about consequences. "Father?" he asked his commanding officer, using the terminology of Babylon's priesthood, as instructed. "What have these people done to deserve this?"

"Who knows?" was the reply. The officer didn't even look away from the binoculars. "Does it matter? You want your pay, don't you? You like eating? Not being in prison?"

"Yes," Tom answered.

"Then shut up and do what you're told."

This was just about the only answer Tom ever got from anyone about anything. So he did just that. He sat back and rested as much as possible, knowing in advance that the sleep that would eventually come that night would be haunted not only by the faces of his past victims, but would have several new faces added to them. He resigned himself to this terrible fact, and his only thought, repeated as if on an infinite loop, was his strong desire to die.

Chapter XXIX

"Welcome to the seventh day of Christmas!" was Benny's response when Josh introduced him to Ruth, the new addition to their family. Benny was dressed in a suit, which was his common Sabbath attire before the church was ransacked. He listened with intense interest to how the previous few days had gone, and interrupted the stories only to utter a quiet "Praise God" or "Thank you Jesus" in response to one point or another.

There were several others already at the church when the Ragizzos arrived. They had been the fourth family to show up, and Benny was expecting at least one more small group. The other families totaled ten people in number. Josh had not seen this many people in the church since Babylon began its enforcement. He didn't even know that this many were still alive.

The church looked almost the same as it had a week before when Josh had come for the water bag, except that Benny had tidied up a bit. He was feeling bold that day, and was not hiding in the secret room behind the library, but rather was gathering everyone at the rear corner of the main sanctuary. There was no electricity, but Benny had set out and lit a couple dozen candles, and the church had a warm, soft glow to it that Josh really liked. It reminded him of how he pictured heaven as a boy. He felt safe here, and in the presence of his Lord.

Against the back wall stood a small pine tree that had been recently cut. It was not placed in a stand or in water, and the stump appeared to be cut crudely. Benny had fashioned a way to perch a candle at the top of the tree and two other candles on the branches, and although Josh's first thought was one of fire safety, he recognized instead that the tree catching fire was among the least dangerous things that could happen. But the tree itself would have been a strange sight in the church even before the world went mad. Benny had an aversion to Christmas trees.

"Pastor," said Josh to Benny privately. "What's up with the tree? And Jeremiah 10?" he asked, reminding the pastor of the Scriptural reason why he had shunned Christmas trees in the past.[10]

Benny answered in a way that demonstrated the effort he put into the decision to have the tree there. "I know, I know. I almost didn't get it. But it's pretty simple, right? And no one here is expecting Santa to show up. And I thought it would help everyone feel comfortable." He paused. "Do you think I did the right thing?"

"I don't know," responded Josh, who had a Christmas tree in his home every year until this one, when he could not get one anymore. "I guess God thinks it's okay if He let you get it here."

"I hope so," said the pastor.

Twenty chairs had been set up in a small half-circle around the tree, but no one was sitting in them yet. Everyone continued to make small talk. Phoebe was on the receiving end of a number of compliments about how tall she had grown, and how pretty she was. Ruth was shocked over and over again at how loving and inviting each of these people were toward her, as if she had

---

10 Jeremiah 10:2-4 KJV reads: "Thus saith the Lord, Learn not the way of the heathen, and be not dismayed at the signs of heaven; for the heathen are dismayed at them. For the customs of the people are vain: for one cutteth a tree out of the forest, the work of the hands of the workman, with the axe. They deck it with silver and with gold; they fasten it with nails and with hammers, that it move not."

known them forever. Angelica and Seth both felt calm in the soft flickering candlelight, and neither felt the least bit afraid.

A few minutes later, the final family of three arrived. They quietly appeared at the broken door, huddled and slightly shivering in the cold December air like they all had been, and came in to join the rest. There were two women and a man.

They entered and greeted everyone else with normal pleasantries, but one of the women was visibly excited, and Benny picked up on it immediately.

"Sister Dana," he addressed the excited woman. "You look on top of the world tonight. Has the Lord been especially good to you?"

"Oh, pastor, yes!" she cried, relieved to be able to get it off her chest. "The most amazing thing happened to me a few days ago. My brother came back to life!"

This, of course, took everyone quite by surprise, even Benny. The woman who had arrived with Dana clarified. "What my sister means," she began, "is that we thought Peter had died but he came home to us on Christmas morning!"

This caught Josh's attention.

Dana continued, "It was so amazing! He came home right before dawn and we were still sleeping and I thought that Babylon had come to get us but it was Peter instead! I couldn't believe it even after I saw him! I felt like Lazarus had come out of his tomb!"[11]

This evoked a chuckle, but not from Josh.

"So what happened?" prompted the pastor.

Dana's sister told the story, since Dana was too excited to speak calmly. "He had left the house on Sunday to go get food even though we all knew it was a bad idea. But we hadn't found anything on Friday and we didn't go out on Sabbath so we were hungry and he went. But then he didn't come back, and when Monday came and went and he still wasn't there we thought he'd been captured."

---

11 This story is found in the eleventh chapter of John's gospel.

"He was captured," added the man with them.

"Thank you, Jeremy," said Benny. "Susan, please continue."

"So yeah it turns out he got captured," said Susan, "and we never would have known it except he came home on Tuesday morning! He was pretty badly banged up but all in one piece and breathing, so it was a true miracle from God."

"How did he get free?" asked another woman in the congregation.

"He said they took him to a house all tied up but someone else showed up out of the darkness and freed him, then disappeared back into the night."

"Sounds crazy, right?" asked Dana, still excited. "But I have to believe it because he's home again, back from the dead!"

"You should believe it," said Josh, and everyone turned in unison to look at him. "I'm the one who freed him."

There was total silence in the church.

Josh's family all looked at each other. They had just put all the pieces together themselves.

"I had gone to the river that night to get some water," said Josh, "and on my way home for some reason I stopped at my old house. While I was there a bunch of Loyalists showed up and they had a sacrifice with them. It was Peter. He was bound and gagged and they just left him on the front step while they got ready to kill him. Somehow I found a knife and I was able to free him." Josh was speaking slowly. He could hardly believe his own story. He felt as if his words were leaving his mouth independently of his will to speak.

"Josh," stated Dana, putting it together in her own mind. "You're Josh."

Josh's family and Dana's never knew each other very well before the rise of Babylon, and afterward they had never really crossed paths. Dana realized just then that her brother's hero Josh was the same man she had seen at worship for so many years. She felt like a fool for not realizing it before.

"I put the knife there!" added Seth excitedly, and then as an afterthought, "When I was four."

Again, total silence reigned in the church. Ruth just could not believe that the amazing work of God that had triggered her conversion had actually gotten more divinely astounding than it already was. She felt weak in the knees. She felt too dirty to be in the presence of something so pure.

"Why didn't he come tonight?" asked Josh.

Susan answered, "You know he was never a member here. He said he didn't feel right coming."

"But that doesn't mean anything!" stated Josh. "Ruth isn't a member either, but here she is!"

"That's true," said Ruth, confirming.

"I know, I told him that," said Susan. "He also didn't want to go outside again, after what he went through. And he was hurt pretty bad. I don't know exactly why he didn't come. Maybe all of those reasons."

"Well tell him I said hi," said Josh, "and I'm looking forward to seeing him again."

At Seth's urging, Angelica filled everyone else in on the details of the box cutter incident when Seth was four years old, and how that same knife had been used to free Peter so many years later. Nothing but stunned silence followed.

Benny dropped to his knees and began to pray without inviting anyone else to join him, but once they saw what he was doing, they all joined him anyway.

"Lord," he began, "thank you so much for being so faithful in such an amazing way. Thank you for strengthening us in our time of need, and providing for us in a way only you can. Please bless our brother Peter as you continue to reveal yourself to him. Heal his body and his mind according to your perfect will. You are so amazing, and we praise your name tonight. Amen."

The congregation echoed in unison with an "Amen" in response.

Once back on their feet, Dana walked silently to Josh and hugged him. In their embrace, Josh felt her tears soak into his shirt. He accepted her silent weeping as gratitude, and said simply, "Praise God."

Chapter XXX

With the arrival of the final family, the congregation numbered nineteen. Once the commotion had died down, the pastor asked everyone to sit down around the tree, and they complied.

After they had quietly sung a short song that somehow everyone knew by heart except Ruth, the pastor began his sermon.

"Brothers and sisters," he began, addressing everyone, "the sun has gone down and the Lord has blessed us again with His holy time. Let's remember to give Him thanks for the breath in our lungs and the ability to rejoice in yet another wonderful Sabbath. We've come together tonight despite the danger and difficulty, to celebrate the birth of our Lord and Savior, Jesus Christ. Open your Bibles to Matthew's gospel, chapter 2."

Though no one had actually brought any Bibles, Benny had provided a small stack of them that had not been destroyed in the raid. They were all the same translation, the New International Version.

As everyone turned their pages, Benny continued. "We know that we've been saved by grace through faith in the sacrifice made for us at Calvary's cross, when Christ died in place of us, and freed us from the bondage of sin. But we celebrate the Savior's birth because without His birth, he could not have had a death, and we would be no better off than this world. So, Christine," he said, indicating a woman in the group, "could you read for us verses 1 and 2, and also verses 9 through 11?"

The woman Christine read, "'After Jesus was born in Bethlehem in Judea, during the time of King Herod, magi from the east came to Jerusalem and asked, "Where is the one who has been born king of the Jews? We saw His star in the east and have come to worship Him."' Then verse nine, 'After they had heard the king, they went on their way, and the star they had seen in the east went ahead of them until it stopped over the place where the child was. When they saw the star, they were overjoyed. On coming to the house, they saw the child with His mother Mary, and they bowed down and worshipped Him. Then they opened their treasures and presented Him with gifts of gold and of incense and of myrrh.' Is that good?"

"That's fine, Christine, thank you," said Benny. "So can anyone tell me how many of these magi, or wise men, there were who came to see the baby Jesus?"

Ruth, knowing the answer, volunteered excitedly, "There were three of them!"

Benny cocked his head toward her and smiled, saying, "Are you sure? Does anyone else have a guess?"

Phoebe answered, "We don't know how many there were. We think three because that's how many gifts they brought."

"Very good!" cried Benny. "You're a very smart little girl! That's right, the Scriptures don't tell us precisely how many of them there were. But thank you, Ruth, for giving the answer you did, because that helps to illustrate my larger point."

Ruth settled back in her chair and smiled sheepishly.

"Now," continued the pastor, "turn to Luke 2:8 and someone read it for me, please."

The noise of pages turning filled the sanctuary, and a man in his twenties read, "'And there were shepherds living out in the fields nearby, keeping watch over their flocks at night.'"

"Thank you Rick," said Benny. "If you read the rest of the story, you'll see these are the shepherds to whom the angels appeared to announce Christ's birth. Based on this, can we tell when Christ was born?" There was no answer from the group. "How about this? Can we tell, based on this one verse, when Christ wasn't born?"

"He wasn't born on December 25th," suggested this same man Rick.

"How can you say that with confidence?" asked Benny.

"Because the shepherds were living outside in the fields, as were the sheep. It seems unlikely they would be able to do that in winter."

"Correct!" said Benny. "But even still, unlikely as it is, the reason we know for sure that Christ's birthday isn't the twenty-fifth of December is because of the historical origin of the Christmas holiday. Even its name is reflective of who created it: it is Christ's Mass. The Catholic Church rededicated an existing pagan holiday as the time to celebrate the birth of the Son of God. Is that a surprise to anyone here?"

The group murmured "no" in soft agreement. Even Ruth was shaking her head to show she was aware of this already.

The pastor continued. "So I want you all to understand that what the Scriptures tell us, and what our world's churches tell us, are not always the same, and in fact are rarely the same. Can we all agree on that?"

A resounding "Amen" came from the group.

"Now, did you know that these wise men were not Jews? How can I know that? The Scriptures tell us that they were from the 'east,' not from Jerusalem or even a nearby region, but rather from a distant land, possibly what we know today as Iraq, maybe Iran, maybe as far away as India. We don't know for sure. But they traveled quite a distance to see the newborn king. And when they got there, did they ask 'Where is the Messiah?' Did they say, 'Where is our king?' No, rather, they asked, 'Where is the king of the Jews?' These people were not Jewish by blood, yet they knew about and sought after the Christ. How?"

"Maybe they heard a message at a synagogue in their own country?" offered a man sitting next to Christine.

Benny was surprised. "You know, in all the years of my ministry, I've never heard anyone give that answer before. Good for you. That's not right, of course," he said with a smile, and everyone laughed a little, "but I like your thinking. No, it wasn't from a synagogue. Non-Jews were not permitted in the synagogues at that time. The Jewish culture was very insular. Remember, even after Christ's resurrection and ascension, only one apostle preached the good news to the Gentiles, and it wasn't even one who had walked with Christ during His ministry! There was something about that culture at that time, and really for as long as it had existed, that was very reluctant to share with outsiders. This is why the torch had to be passed to another group, because God's chosen people were not living up to the task with which they had been entrusted. Paul, in his letter to the Roman believers, quotes Deuteronomy 32:21 about this topic, when God says, 'I will make you envious by those who are not a nation; I will make you angry by a nation that has no understanding.' Paul even criticizes his Jewish brethren, and remember he was Jewish himself, because they had studied this text for over a thousand years, and somehow didn't understand its message! No, Mark," said Benny, addressing the man who had last spoken, "the wise men knew of the God of Israel, but not from the Israelites. So, then, how?"

"From the Scriptures?" offered Christine.

"From the Scriptures," confirmed the pastor. "There is an Old Testament prophecy that points directly to the specific time frame of the coming of the Messiah's ministry.[12] How old was Jesus when he began His ministry?"

"Thirty," said Seth confidently.

"You know why he was thirty, young man?" questioned the pastor.

"No," admitted Seth.

---

12 This prophecy can be found in Daniel chapter 9.

"In Israel at that time, a person had to be thirty years of age before he could work as a rabbi. God, superior as He is over all societies, condescends to our level and meets us where we are. He preached freedom, but never against slavery. He preached monogamy, but gave rules to protect women in their polygamous society. God knows exactly who we are and how we like things and Jesus worked within the expectations of His own society, showing them their errors while walking among them. So, my point is, a baby cannot immediately enter ministry. So if these wise men knew when the Messiah's ministry would begin, then they knew approximately when he would be born. And they were looking for Him."

"Wow," said Ruth, astonished. This reminded her of how her new family was waiting and watching for Christ's return because of their knowledge of the Scriptures, just like the wise men had watched for His first coming.

"So it's always the Scriptures, and nothing but the Scriptures, that can teach us about God. And their power is not limited to which nationality of blood runs through our veins. To God, we are all His children, and we are all siblings. I don't imagine I'm saying anything groundbreaking today, right?"

The silence from the group answered his question for him.

"Yet I want to show you something that we as Christians, as Israelites by faith, even within our own denomination before it was so broken apart by the government, have repeatedly failed to realize from the Scriptures. Turn to Romans 5:1 and 2. I'll read it for you." He waited while everyone flipped their pages. "'Therefore, since we have been justified through faith, we have peace with God through our Lord Jesus Christ, through whom we have gained access by faith into this grace in which we now stand.' We throw that word around, 'grace,' a lot, or at least we used to. But can anyone tell me what it means?"

"Leniency by God," offered someone.

"Mercy," offered another.

"Undeserved mercy," said Josh.

"All those things are correct!" said the pastor. "God's law condemns all sinners to die, and yet by accepting God's own sacrifice of His very son, we allow Jesus to die in our place. God's wrath falls on Christ instead of on us, and we are shown grace. But I want us to think on this a little deeper today. When we are shown the amazing grace of God, whose life does God see when he looks at us?"

No answer.

"Does he still see us? Does he see the broken, imperfect lives we continue to lead each day? Are we still sinners in His eyes?"

"No," said Seth, "or we would have to die again."

"So if our sin is replaced by Christ's righteousness, then who does God see when he looks at us?"

"He sees Jesus Christ," said Ruth, more confidently than she expected.

"Amen, young sister!" cried the pastor. "Philippians 2:13 tells us that it is God who is at work in you, enabling you both to will and to work for His good pleasure. The Holy Spirit is strong in you," addressing Ruth, "and you who are so young in the faith. Praise God. So yes, he sees Christ in our place, because he loved us too much to allow us to die in our helplessness. So the verses from Romans tell us that it is Christ who has given us access to this grace of God. He is the key. He provided it, and we can partake of it by faith. But now what does that mean? How can we bring this grace into our lives?"

A quiet cacophony erupted as nearly all the people in the congregation offered their advice as to how to receive the grace of God. "Keep the Sabbath" was mixed with "Eat right and pray" and "Get baptized." Other suggestions were "Don't listen to bad music," "Get married before having sex," and "Go to church." There were other suggestions as well but Benny stopped listening. All these answers were wrong.

"Brethren, listen to yourselves. Think about this. Our Christ cried out to His Father for the forgiveness of the very men driving the nails into His hands and feet. He said He was glad to be having dinner with the man who would later betray Him. He came into a world filled with violence, decay and sin, and redeemed the human race though they had nothing to offer God at all. Each of us is a decrepit sinner, worth as much on our own as filthy rags. Redemption, salvation, even the very grace of God are all free gifts provided to an undeserving people by the Almighty God, and so accordingly Paul writes in Romans 5 that we HAVE BEEN justified through faith. Notice the tense there? Is it a future process? What does it mean when something 'has been' done?"

"It means it's done already. It's in the past," said Angelica.

"So when does justification happen?"

"It happens when we accept Christ's sacrifice," said Rick.

"Brother, hear your own words! How can justification happen as a result of something you've done, when it had already been provided to the world in the past tense, back in Paul's day?"

No response was forthcoming.

"Listen to me carefully," said the pastor. "There is nothing, nothing at all brethren, that we can possibly offer God to make Him think favorably toward us. We cannot keep enough Sabbaths to win His favor. We cannot spend enough time reading His Word. We cannot give enough time, enough energy, enough tithe even, to somehow win salvation. Christ came while we were yet sinners and died so that the entire world might be made right with God. To view Christ's mission as anything else is to accept the position of the government, of this Babylon, which says they are the only ones who provide access to God, and only by following their rules will God love you. God made all the stars and knows them each by name. You can offer such a being nothing in return, except your adoration. But He doesn't even need that. He died for you because he loves you, and it's as simple as that."

This confused Ruth, and she raised her hand. "If we don't have to do anything to earn God's love, then why do these Christians exist?"

"She means Babylon," offered Angelica.

"Right, them," said Ruth. "And all the churches I've ever heard have some list or task or something that we have to do to get to heaven. Like, I've heard about baptism for a few days now from Josh and Phoebe and them, so why would we ever be baptized if God loves us already?"

"Excellent question, young lady!" cried Benny, overjoyed. "Why don't you read for us the rest of Romans 5 verse 2? I only read the first part."

Ruth read, "'And we rejoice in the hope of the glory of God.'" She paused. "What does that mean?"

"How is God glorified?" asked Benny. "How would you be glorified?"

"You mean, like, how would I feel good about myself?"

"Sort of. What would be the kinds of things you feel would bring you glory?"

Ruth thought before answering. "Maybe if I was getting credit for something I've done."

"Okay, that's good. What about if others were so impressed by that thing you did that they followed in your example? Would you feel like they were giving you glory then?"

"I would feel very good about myself," she said. "I'd like that a lot."

"Apply that idea to God, then. What did God accomplish for us?"

When Ruth didn't answer right away, Josh offered some help. "He sent His son to die for us. Christ's mission was to glorify God by His obedience."

"So Christ, then, is the embodiment of God's glory. We, then, also glorify God when we follow in Christ's example. Sister Ruth, would you kindly read for us from John's gospel, chapter 14, verse 15?"

Ruth flipped there and read, "'"If you love me, you will obey what I command."' I guess that's Jesus speaking?"

Benny answered, "Hmm, I like the King James better. It says, '"If ye love me, keep my commandments."' Yes, Ruth, this is Christ speaking. He tells us that we can demonstrate our love for Him by being obedient, in the exact same way that He showed His love for the Father by being obedient to Him. This is why we do things like get baptized: not in order to be saved, but because we already are saved; not in order to earn God's grace, but because we have already received it. When we come to understand the amazing nature of God, His Spirit will work in us to create a desire to follow Him."

Ruth said, "That makes sense. But why are they out there killing people, then? I don't think Jesus said, 'If you love me, kill everyone else.'"

Benny answered, "I began this by stating that every religious group throughout all history, even including this one in its heyday, has stumbled over this principle of the free gift of grace, and of righteousness by pure faith. It is human nature to want to work toward something, and in fact to take credit for achieving something. We generally want our salvation to be as a result of something we've done, rather than giving all the credit to God for what He's done. When a religious system is so large and so powerful that the entire world bows down in homage to it, priorities can get skewed. The leadership in that church enjoys the homage they receive from everyone. You mark my words, and ask God in heaven when you see Him if I'm right: they know that what they're doing is against God and they just don't care. They enjoy the worship." He had been flipping pages in his Bible as he was speaking, and found his place right on time. "The book of Revelation says of these people, the leadership of this church: 'This title was written on her forehead: MYSTERY; BABYLON THE GREAT; THE MOTHER OF PROSTITUTES AND OF THE ABOMINATIONS OF THE EARTH. I saw that the woman was drunk with the blood of the saints, the blood of those who bore testimony to Jesus. When I saw her, I was greatly astonished.' So you see, the church itself is drunk with power. The Bible says so itself! Through persecution, it demands the worship of the inhabitants of the earth, and becomes drunk with it. What they are doing has nothing to do with the grace of God. They see their decision not to kill you as them showing you God's grace."

"Jesus loves you even when you disobey," said Phoebe, as a summary. "But they kill you when you disobey."

"And therefore," added the pastor, "which party inspires you to follow in its footsteps? God? Or an apostate church that bears God's name?"

"So God loves me even though I can't be baptized," stated Ruth, almost as a question, "because I have been justified through faith already."

"Can I get an Amen?!" shouted the pastor, ecstatic that his message had been so well received. The congregation cried 'Amen' in unison. "What an amazing faith statement! Young sister, if we had the means at our disposal, it would be my true honor and privilege to baptize you into Christ. But as you know, water is scarce these days. I hope you have peace knowing that God sees nothing but Jesus in you, whether you are baptized or not, because you have been justified by faith."

"Thank you, pastor. I wish I had met all of you before, when it would have been possible," said Ruth. Her heart longed to be obedient to her newly found Savior, but nonetheless she felt the promise of the Scripture verse they had read in Romans, and knew that she now had peace with God through Jesus Christ.

Barely had she said this when Seth, who had slipped away unbeknownst to the others, said from the hallway that lead to the library, "Um, pastor? Dad? Mom? You should come see this."

He then disappeared back down the dark hallway, and after a moment of confused silence, everyone got up to follow.

Chapter XXXI

Seth realized he needed to urinate in the middle of pastor Benny's sermon. That all-too-familiar discomfort in his bladder grew and grew until he just couldn't take it anymore.

Even still, he had a lot of respect for Benny and everyone else at the church, and did not want to make a scene or cause disruption about getting up to relieve himself, so he quietly slipped away during the sermon. He went to the main restroom that was accessible from the sanctuary itself, but when he opened the door he knew right away he couldn't use it. It had been destroyed; the sink and counter and urinal all looked as if a sledgehammer had been taken to them, and the floor was littered with shattered porcelain and other building materials. The room smelled musty, as if the water had pooled until it had been shut off, and never cleaned. He felt unhealthy just standing at the doorway.

He remembered that there was a second restroom in a more distant part of the church. Down the hallway, past the library, next to the pastor's office there was a smaller, more private rest area that he always assumed was just for Benny, since he never used it himself or saw anyone else use it. But desperate times call for desperate measures, and despite his discomfort at wandering off from the group and trespassing in someone else's private space, he nonetheless went there, in the darkness, because he just could not hold it in until he got home again.

He had successfully relieved himself there, with a fair amount of difficulty since it was pitch dark, and was on his way back to rejoin his family when he thought he heard something. There was a storage closet across the hallway from the restroom he had just used, and though he couldn't identify the sound he heard, and even began to question whether he had heard anything in the first place, he opened the closet door anyway. And that's when he saw it.

His young mind couldn't wrap itself around what he saw. It didn't make any sense. Had Benny planned it? If not, then how had it come to be? Should he tell others about it? Would they be mad at him for wandering off?

Yet he knew he must share.

He went back to the sanctuary and heard Ruth remarking, "I wish I had met all of you before, when it would have been possible." He felt like this was an important moment, and felt bad all over again for having missed it, and worse still for being about to interrupt it.

But he did anyway. "Um, pastor? Dad? Mom? You should come see this."

The short moment of non-response felt like a lifetime to the young man. In that short time he heard all sorts of reprimands in his head, and felt tremendous shame, though he didn't know why. He offered a quick and silent prayer that he hadn't made a mistake in drawing everyone's attention to himself. But there was nothing he could do about it now.

He turned and went back down the hallway, determined to make sure he hadn't hallucinated what he thought he saw. He heard the sounds of people following.

He stopped at the closet door, which was closed again. The group gathered around him, and Benny said to him, "What have you seen, son? Is everything okay?"

"Do you know what's in here already?" asked Seth. He still wasn't sure if he had stumbled on a surprise or not.

"There is lots of stuff in there, Seth," said the pastor. "I put a lot in there after the big raid. There are some Bibles, some shelving, some chairs, the baptistery, a few microphones. Don't know why I kept those," he added, almost as an afterthought.

Seth heard that word, *baptistery*, and still wasn't sure if he had made a mistake or not. But, resolved to push forward no matter what happened, he opened the closet door.

Inside the closet was more darkness, of course, but every person saw what he hoped they would see. In the darkness was a shimmer, as if non-existent light was somehow glancing off a reflective surface anyway.

Benny stood there in amazement. "Danny, go grab a candle, would you?" he said to another man standing with him, and this man ran back to the sanctuary to grab one. When he came back, Benny walked into the closet holding the candle, and its soft glow danced around the room along with the shadows it created, like a dark ballet. Benny walked right up to the baptistery and looked inside. It was filled about eighty percent with water.

The church had purchased this baptistery when they had first moved to this location more than ten years ago. They had been forced to move into this smaller building due to some financial restrictions placed upon them following an unfortunate decrease in membership size, and this current location did not have a permanent baptistery built into it. Not wanting to relinquish the right and ability to baptize others into Christ as the Spirit moved them to, they invested in a portable baptistery that could be filled and drained as needed, and stored away when not needed.

Benny had moved it into this closet during the several week cleanup effort after Babylon had trashed the church. He never saw himself using it again, because even if someone had the desire, the means simply no longer existed to fill it with water for a proper baptism by immersion. He figured it would simply live in this dark little room until Jesus returned. When he last saw it, a few weeks ago, it was dry as a bone.

Yet here it was, nearly full. How did this happen?

The pastor kept replaying his former words inside his head: *if we had the means at our disposal, it would be my true honor and privilege to baptize you into Christ.* Now here were the means, like a prophecy.

The small group uttered various words and phrases of praise and amazement at this discovery. Seth finally relaxed, a smile replacing his former look of concern.

Ruth turned to the pastor and asked emphatically, "Can you baptize me right now?"

Benny still was standing motionless at the edge of the water, stunned. He felt overwhelmed. He looked around for some clue as to how this had happened. He heard Ruth's question but he was in such shock he could not bring himself to answer. He raised and lowered his arm, moving the candle to illuminate various corners and shadows, attempting, as if it mattered, to find the water's source.

Glancing at the ceiling, he noticed that an exposed water pipe had a small crack in it, and a drop of water was dangling there, having seeped through. It wiggled with pressure, and fell down into the baptistery, causing a series of small ripples that emanated around the water's surface. Was this it? Had this pipe somehow cracked, and the water dripped a little at a time until it reached this level? As implausible as that seemed, it seemed more impossible still knowing that the water supply had been shut off to this building for months. Where had the water come from, even if it then leaked out through this pipe? Benny was shocked and amazed still, and all he could say was a simple and humble, "Praise God."

He turned to Josh, who had a position of leadership in the church back before the days of Babylon. "Do you know if we have baptismal robes still somewhere?" he asked.

Josh frowned slightly in concentration. "Unless they were taken or destroyed, I think they should be hanging in your office closet. Did you move them from there?"

Benny shook his head, he had not moved them or even touched them since the last time there had been a baptism, many months before the raid. "Go check," he said, and Josh left to retrieve them.

"Is that a 'yes'?" asked Ruth.

"Yes, sister, absolutely," said Benny. "When God provides so obviously, it would be foolish to say no."

From the pastor's office came Josh's voice, "They're here!"

Benny escorted Ruth into the office and handed her a robe, and took one himself. They took turns in the smaller bathroom that Seth had just used, changing from their clothes into the baptismal robes. Shortly, Benny climbed up the steps and waded down into the water. To his continued amazement, it was not even cold. Ruth followed him in. Everyone else was huddled around as best they could be, and kept quiet. Everyone knew they had stumbled onto a special moment. Not a single person there ever thought they would see another baptism again.

When both Ruth and the pastor were comfortable in the water, Benny turned to his congregation and began to speak. "My friends and brethren," he began, "you know as well as I do that God is here today. Our eyes have seen the amazing grace of the Lord shine through the darkness of this world and provide for the longing heart of His precious daughter, our sister Ruth. But as we stand here in awe, even myself, humbled anew by the Lord's mighty hand, we should remember not to be surprised that God would reach down and do for us what he has done for believers in the past."

Benny's mind raced in a million directions. Remembering the story of the baptism in the desert from Acts chapter 8, he said to Ruth, "You're the Ethiopian."

"What?" asked a confused Ruth.

"To my Philip," he said. "God gave us water just for you."[13]

Ruth smiled and said, "Okay," not caring at all that she didn't know what the pastor was talking about.

"Brothers and sisters, this calls to my mind Romans 6, which fits nicely with my message from before. Christ provided salvation for all mankind at Calvary's cross. It is an established fact, available for all who want it, and there is nothing we can do to earn it. But after we confess with our mouths that Jesus is the son of God, His grace propels us forward to grow in that same grace, to grow ever closer to the Lord through the indwelling of the Holy Spirit. Paul says, in Romans 6: 'Don't you know that all of us who were baptized into Christ Jesus were baptized into His death? We were therefore buried with Him through baptism into death in order that, just as Christ was raised from the dead through the glory of the Father, we too may live a new life. If we have been united with Him like this in His death, we will certainly also be united with Him in His resurrection.'

"So, Ruth, our newest sister, as you go under these waters, generously provided just for you by the Almighty Creator God, know that you are joining with the Lord Jesus in His death, being united in fact with the salvation He offered when He died on the cross. And, like Him, you can look forward to a new body, a heavenly body that can stand in the presence of divine holiness without being destroyed. Your life, whether Jesus comes today or next year, will never be the same. Therefore, it is my honor and my privilege today, to baptize you in the name of the Father, and of the Son, and of the Holy Spirit."

Benny leaned forward as Ruth leaned back. His left hand held her right arm, which she used to cover her face, and he supported the weight of her body with his right arm as she dipped beneath the water. After a short moment of immersion, he lifted her up again, and she came up out of the water, baptized into Christ.

The group erupted in applause, seeming to forget the danger that came with loud noises. Nothing mattered to anyone at that

---

13 The story which Benny is referencing can be found in Acts 8:26-40.

moment except the faith of their new sister, expressed by this outward and public showing of her acceptance of Jesus Christ as the Lord of her life.

Benny summed everything up then, as they prepared to exit the water and dry off. He said, "Just as Christ tells us in Luke's gospel, there is rejoicing in the presence of the angels of God over one sinner who repents. So, as you enter into your new life, Ruth, know that there is a party in heaven right now, and you are the center and focus of that party. Jesus is celebrating in victory over the enemy that you may be counted among the saints, clothed with His righteousness."

"Thank you, pastor," she said, and hugged him.

Again, the bystanders applauded. Everything was perfect in that moment.

Not one of them knew that several armed soldiers were plotting the deaths of everyone inside from just a thousand feet away, and only waiting for the signal to advance in their murderous intentions.

Everyone was still inside the church when that signal came.

Chapter XXXII

All the soldiers had checked their weapons and had been ready for action for going on half an hour. Tom, feeling more dead inside as each minute passed, steeling himself for the inhuman sorrow that he knew would accompany his action of robbing another person of his or her life, began to hope that the order would never come. Every minute that passed without the crackling of the radio brought new hope to him. Maybe a bigger threat had been found. Maybe these people would live to see another day.

But then, to Tom's unspeakable disappointment, the radio did, indeed, crackle with life, and the order came through from the powers that be. Tom resented that some faceless men could sit in a room somewhere and determine who lives and who dies. Yet he heard the order loud and clear, ringing in his ears. "Okay, men. Move out!"

His commanding officer stood up and shouted to his soldiers, "Alright! The order's come through! Front team, we're advancing straight down the hill. Rear team, flank the building. Backup team, you're following us at a perimeter of one hundred feet. I don't want one of these freaks leaving alive. You hear?"

"Sir, yes sir!" they shouted in unison, all except Tom. His hopes had been dashed again. He would get no sleep at all that night.

The commanding officer strapped a large bag to his back, checked his weapon a final time, and advanced. The adrenaline was rushing through each of their veins now, even Tom's. Each man felt it difficult to move forward at a slow pace and they found themselves virtually running down the hill toward the church filled with unsuspecting people.

A shrill noise could be heard from the air, approaching from somewhere. The soldiers heard this whine even above the noise of their advance. A vanguard drone had been sent to scout for any unforeseen obstacles. Tom watched as the drone came into view and slowed down, nearly hovering above the church. It was in reconnaissance mode. Then, just as quickly as it had appeared, it flew off.

***

From inside the church, the whine of the drone could be clearly heard. Benny and Ruth had left the baptistery and were drying off but were still in the robes when the noise came. Most everyone recognized the noise, but Ruth asked in alarm, "What's that?"

Benny, as solemn as Josh had ever seen him, answered simply, "I think we've been found."

***

Tom's thoughts were blank as he ran down the hill. The church building got closer and closer but all he could think of was the clanking of his weaponry. He heard the blood pounding in his head, and tried not to be reminded of the sound of blood escaping from a victim.

Each of the teams fell into their respective positions around the church. The front team, with Tom standing side-by-side with the officer in charge, ran right up to within ten feet of the front entrance of the church, and each dropped to one knee, leveling their weapons into the sanctuary. The backup team stopped a hundred feet behind them, and trained their weapons in the same direction from a standing position.

Tom's radio crackled as the rear team radioed in. "We're in position," they reported.

"Torches ready," he ordered. Each soldier had a very powerful flashlight that threw an amazing amount of light for hundreds of feet. These items had come to be known as 'torches' in Tom's company, since 'flashlight' just didn't seem to do justice to their incredible power. "On my mark."

The commanding officer turned to the rear team and motioned. A soldier from that team saw the signal and lifted the amplification device he had been carrying to his lips. Babylon had designed a bullhorn that fit in the pocket of their soldiers' uniforms. This man spoke into the bullhorn device, "You in the building, you are surrounded. By the authority of God spoken through His church, we order you to come out and surrender. You are accused of terrorism and heresy. If you surrender, you will not be harmed."

Tom found this lie so despicable he nearly laughed. No one ever left unharmed.

Tom lifted his radio to his mouth and said simply, "Shine."

Ten powerful torch lights shone simultaneously into every door and window the church had. The night and its darkness fled, as the entire scene was illuminated. The terrorists were caught, surrounded, and doomed. There was nowhere left for them to hide.

Chapter XXXIII

Inside the church, the entire congregation went into the sanctuary when they heard the whine of the drone. There was a door at the back of the church but it was small and buried in darkness, and besides they each knew that seeing a drone was usually the last thing a person ever did. In the sanctuary, at least they had the soft moonlight falling through the shattered front door and the soft candlelight from the tree, and room to be around each other without crowding.

When the whine of the drone moved off into the distance, there was a general sense of relief among the church, but it didn't last for long. They heard commotion outside, and they soon saw the shadows of men running toward them.

Everyone in the church shared thoughts of dread. They were trapped, and they knew it. Out front was a platoon of armed soldiers. Out back was probably the same. Inside the building, there was nowhere to hide. They would not all fit in the secret room behind the library, and the soldiers were likely to turn the entire building upside down anyway.

When the front line of soldiers approached the door and knelt down, Josh resigned himself to death. He had been permitted to live this long to bring Ruth to Christ, but now it was time to rest in the Lord and await his resurrection. He had thought of this moment many times over many years, and he felt peace within him. He truly was not scared to die. His family was with him now, and would be with him again when he heard the Lord's divine shout to raise him from the dead.

A booming voice seemed to fill the church from every direction as it bounced off the walls and ricocheted into everyone's minds. "You in the church, you are surrounded. By the authority of God spoken through His church, we order you to come out and surrender. You are accused of terrorism and heresy. If you surrender, you will not be harmed."

Rick, from the congregation, spoke up in support of their surrender. "We can't escape. We have to give up. They'll kill us if we don't!"

"They'll kill us even if we do," said Christine.

"They're going to have to earn our deaths," said Josh, resolved not to go down without a fight.

Phoebe was crying, "Daddy, I'm scared." She grabbed him around his leg and he hugged her head to comfort her.

"I know, darling, I know. God will take care of you, my love. God will escort you home."

"We're not giving up," said Benny, still in his damp baptismal robe. "Revelation tells us that Babylon will cause all who refused to worship the image to be killed. We're fulfilling God's Word here, brothers and sisters. Stand firm in the Lord."

The torch lights came on at that moment as if the sun suddenly rose in their midst. Every person shielded their eyes from the intense light. Blinded, Benny offered a prayer, loud enough to be heard by all. "'I have set the Lord always before me: because He is at my right hand, I shall not be moved.'"

"Amen," said Rick.

"Amen," said Christine.

To himself, Josh said, "Amen," and heard his precious daughter say the same, with her face buried into his hip.

They stood there, each one waiting for the crackle of gunfire or the shouts of the advancing soldiers. They prepared themselves to be beaten, tortured, raped, or killed. Tears came down the faces of many as they stood there, trapped and frozen in the illumination of death.

But the seconds kept passing, and nothing changed. Josh's eyes became accustomed to the brightness, and he saw the silhouettes of each of the men, still kneeling down at the door. They were not coming forward.

'Lord,' Josh said in prayer to his Father in heaven, 'what's going on?'

***

Tom could not believe what he saw. Each soldier's torch was shining directly into the open space in the church. He saw about twenty people standing there, defiant yet frozen, and none of his fellow soldiers seemed to notice.

"Maybe they're hiding," said the commanding officer to Tom. Before Tom could respond, the officer lifted the radio to his mouth and barked an order. "Capman," he said, "do a search."

A man from the backup team advanced slowly and surpassed the front team, then entered into the church through the broken front door. All the while, he kept his rifle up, pointed and ready to fire, as he swept through the sanctuary searching for signs of life. He moved to the back of the sanctuary and disappeared down the hall for about a minute. When he reemerged, his weapon was at his side and he looked relaxed. Confused, definitely, but relaxed.

He spoke into his radio for his companions to hear, "There's no one here. I searched every room."

The commanding officer swore. "Where did they go?" he demanded angrily.

Tom lowered his weapon. He felt like he was dreaming. He saw them all, young and old alike. He saw the water still glistening off Ruth's and Benny's heads, and the small puddles forming at their feet. But no one else did. He was afraid suddenly, and couldn't open his mouth to say anything.

"Vallor," shouted the commanding officer into the radio again, "go inside and make sure Capman's not retarded."

A soldier from the rear team broke through the door at the rear of the church and illuminated the hallway. He looked into each room, including the closet with the filled baptistery and evidence of recent use. He tore the curtains off the walls in the library, and even found the secret room. He knocked the Christmas tree to the ground, and the candles fell off their precarious perches but immediately extinguished when they hit the floor. He grabbed the tree, pulling it with him as he exited through the back door. But through all this, he did not see the people.

He radioed out, "There's no one here."

The commanding officer swore again, frustrated and scared.

Tom stood up slowly and walked toward the entrance. He stood next to the broken front door, in front of an intact window pane. He did not know what to make of what he saw. How could two of his highly trained companions be missing the couple dozen people standing right there in the middle of the biggest open space in the building? Yet he didn't want to say anything. For the first time in as long as he could remember, he felt true hope. Maybe he would sleep tonight after all.

***

"They're coming inside!" cried Rick. "Lord, help us!"

"Quiet!" ordered Benny. He called out in his own mind, 'Lord, may your will be done.'

The first soldier entered through the broken front door and swept through the sanctuary. As he approached one congregant, that person deftly stepped aside and let the soldier pass by. When he drew close to another member, that person too moved out of the way, and the soldier passed by without noticing. He moved directly at Josh, and Josh felt Phoebe's grip on his leg tighten. Josh moved himself and his daughter a step out of the way, as if in slow motion. He felt as if his movements were not even his own.

The first soldier gave up, and the second came crashing through the back door. Even still, Rick and a few others were visibly scared, despite the apparent miracle being wrought in their midst. After a few minutes of crashing around, they all heard the second soldier report, "There's no one here."

Benny watched as the soldier dragged the tree out the back with him and thought to himself, 'I guess that settles that problem.'

But he then fixed his gaze on the front line of soldiers, the only ones he could see against the intense light still shining in from the outside. He saw one of them stand up and approach the church slowly, not advancing in malice like the others, but moving forward as if bewildered.

Benny moved forward as well. Josh admonished him, "Pastor, what are you doing?"

"We have a brother in need," was the pastor's only response.

Benny walked right up to the inside of the window pane through which Tom was looking from the outside. The men looked into each others' eyes as if deep in communication, as if they'd known each other forever. Benny slowly raised his right hand and placed it against the glass. Tom raised his left hand and did the same. He wore on his arm the band of loyalty to Babylon, scarlet with a bright cross emblazoned on it, yellow like the sun. He had pledged his entire life to them. Yet Babylon had no place in this moment for him.

Tom's eyes revealed everything to Benny. The pastor had seen those eyes countless times before, in the faces of everyone who was searching for God even if he didn't know it. He felt tremendous compassion for this man, this lost soul who had gotten mixed up with the wrong crowd for a reason he probably didn't even understand himself. Benny wanted to cry out to this man, to welcome him into their congregation, to share the good news of the redemptive salvation of the Lord Jesus Christ. But instead he stood there, with his hand pressed against Tom's hand, separated only by a thin pane of glass.

Benny said, still looking directly into Tom's eyes, "God loves you, brother. Seek Him before it's too late."

Tom, on the outside, didn't audibly hear what the pastor said through the commotion around him. But somehow he knew exactly what had been said to him, and he slowly nodded his head in agreement. He didn't say a word.

"Morgan!" shouted the commanding officer to Tom. "Stop standing there like an idiot! Fall back!"

Tom knew what was coming. They would have to report back to their superiors that the targets had somehow disappeared. There would be an inquiry. There would certainly be blame placed upon them for something or other. Tom doubted that any one of the soldiers there that night would still be alive in two months after facing the reprimands of the horrible religious government, so thirsty for blood to augment its own power. Yet Tom felt within him that something had changed. He had seen a world unknown to him, only for a moment, but a moment of divinity can bear its mark for eternity. Ten minutes before, he had felt a longing for death, because he had felt dead on the inside for so long already. He lamented his every breath, and dreaded every action to come. His mind was so scarred by sin that the spark of hope had nearly gone out, and he felt alone even when in a crowded room. Now, he felt liberated. He did not know very much about God, but he knew unmistakably that it was God who had touched him. Like Nebuchadnezzar in the days of Daniel the prophet, who celebrated the liberation of his mind from the insanity of sin by praising the Almighty God, Tom cried out silently the best way he knew how, and his prayer ascended to the very throne of God: 'I praise and exalt and glorify the King of heaven, because everything He does is right and all His ways are just.'

Tom knew that whatever was coming, he was a changed man forever. He left the fateful church building to return to the wrath of the world, never feeling more at peace than at that very moment.

Inside, Josh felt completely broken to pieces. He had watched as if somehow separate from himself as the soldiers moved throughout the sanctuary, oblivious to the presence of the members around them. He saw himself move out of the pathways of the enemy effortlessly, as if his body was being moved for him. He saw several of his brethren in Christ sobbing in their invisibility as they experienced firsthand the amazing, unparalleled, unmatchable grace of the Almighty God. Josh himself had been crying nearly a minute before he even realized it. 'Heavenly Father,' he prayed in his mind, unsure if he could even speak any longer, 'I am so sorry for ever doubting your care for me. I see now that it's always been you, always you and never me, who has led me to safety and saved me from ruin. I thank you for your tender mercies toward us, your children, and I thank you especially for the sacrifice you made for us, to take our punishment for us, that we might live forever with you. I repent of my arrogance and I invite you in now Father. I give you permission to take over my life and use me to your glory. I cry out in my wretchedness: Woe is me! for I am undone; because I am a man of unclean lips, and I dwell in the midst of a people of unclean lips: for mine eyes have seen the King, the Lord of hosts.'

Josh remembered those terrible moments of pride: how he had rescued his family from persecution by recognizing the threat at the library and acting upon it; how he had provided food for his family through the terrible tribulation; how he had schemed to retrieve the water bag and then fill it; his idea to leave valuable items like the DVD player for looters to steal, so they would not search the house; his saving Peter from certain sacrificial death at his former home. Each of these moments had caused Josh to see himself as somehow a powerful man, or a smart man, or a man worthy of the grace of God. Yet in this moment at the church, watching divinity intermingle with humanity in a flawless, beautiful ballet of bloodless drama, Josh saw the grace that God has shown to all mankind, and realized more than ever that he, Josh, was no more worthy of God's amazing love than anyone else. Josh felt compassion for all these soldiers, even as they searched through the church looking to kill him. He saw them, lost in their ignorance, and wanted to reach out to share with them what he knew: that God has no pleasure in the death of the wicked; but that the wicked turn from his way and live.

In that moment Josh realized a glaring failure he had made. God brought back to his mind the crying woman in the field on the way to the river, the one whom Josh had chosen not to comfort. He felt his stomach tighten at this failure. Realizing that every step had been directed and watched over by God, he cursed his limited viewpoint and lack of faith. He should have held that woman, and shown her the loving arms of his Lord. Yet God's presence was so strong right now, standing in his church invisible to his enemies, that Josh felt comfort here as well. God knew enough to see that his children would fail from time to time. Josh felt the peace of God that surpasses all understanding and knew somehow that God had come to this woman's rescue in a way that he, Josh, had not. Josh fell to his knees in complete surrender. He realized anew that all he could ever hope to do was act to the best of his ability, and trust God to do the rest. He asked God to introduce him to this woman in heaven, and felt assured that his request was granted.

When Benny removed his hand from against the glass at the front of the church, and the soldiers withdrew, no one in the church moved for some time. Benny, typically an upbeat man no matter what, seemed about to burst open with joy. He took a few steps back into the church, toward his stunned and motionless congregants, and stopped. He was moving as if in slow motion. His smile seemed so big against his otherwise small head that Benny himself wondered if he would be able to wear any other expression ever again. Benny closed his eyes and knelt down. He threw his head back, raised his arms to the sky and, through tears that were falling unrestrained from his eyes, cried, "Halleluiah!"

One at a time, each of the other members dropped to his or her knees as well, each with a shout or a murmur, or whatever the

Spirit moved them to say in appreciation to their Lord and Savior in that moment. They fell into prayerful, joyful worship in that very room where they had been attacked, and against all odds survived. Josh saw through his own tears that every one of them had wet faces of their own.

The words of the Lord flowed freely in and out of each person's mind that night: "Fear them not: for I have delivered them into thine hand; there shall not a man of them stand before thee."

Epilogue

Josh and his family returned home later that night by the same cautious route primarily through the woods that they had used to reach the church, and that they would continue to use to reach the church for as long as they continued to go. Yet as they traveled home the journey was much different. They felt confident about everything, despite the continued hardship. Each of them, even Ruth, knew by faith that God would resolve the Great Controversy the best possible way, and that they would all get to meet Him, and live with Him forever, soon. The Ragizzo family and their new sister Ruth lived out the rest of earth's days in a firm trust that any hardship that befell them would be met by a mighty and able God who lived only to serve His people.

That was the very last time the world ever celebrated Christmas. Early on in the new year, growing skepticism about Babylon's ability to follow through on their promises to return the world to order and peace led to an amazing wave of violence against not only the keepers of the Sabbath, but also against growing numbers of the Loyalists as well. The heart of every fallen man was only violence all the time. Satan reigned with mighty force in a final attempt to rid the world of God's people once and for all. But the heavenly sanctuary was cleansed, probation was closed, and the Lord prepared to return to collect the harvest of His people.

Through the trials of the worst persecution ever to befall mankind around the globe, God's people in all nations had learned to trust completely in the Lord, and how to live free from sin. Pleased that His church on earth should finally reflect His own character, God finished His redemptive work in the heavenly sanctuary and called out to the universe that the plan of salvation had ended: *He that is unjust, let him be unjust still: and he which is filthy, let him be filthy still: and he that is righteous, let him be righteous still: and he that is holy, let him be holy still.* Everyone on earth had chosen which side he would be on, forever, and there would be no more crossing between camps.

On the earth, the plagues erupted across the globe. At this time, the Ragizzos and Ruth grew in confidence and ventured back out into the world, to join the others who were emerging in victory. The world died around them, but they lived. All men and women who had chosen against God became filled with sores all over their bodies; the waters of the earth turned to blood, and all aquatic creatures perished; the sun, after having received for so long the worship that belongs only to the Most High God, filled the earth with its scorching heat; light evacuated from the planet and a palpable darkness remained despite the searing heat; and all support for Babylon disappeared. The greatest earthquake ever known to man shook the planet to its very core: cities crumbled and islands disappeared. The silence of the universal global shock at the devastation was broken only by the hail and wind storms that followed, seeming to lay waste to all that remained after the shaking. But as the fallen populace of the world cried out to be hidden from the One whose wrath was causing this destruction, calling indeed for the mountains and rocks to fall on them as a better alternative than looking God in the eye, the skies parted like a scroll, the heavens disappeared, and the King of Kings and Lord of Lords returned to the earth that He had made to deliver His people from the enemy and bring them to heaven, to the mansions that He had prepared for them. Each person from the beginning of time who had called out to the God of heaven for His mercy, and by faith accepted that His mercy was theirs to take, was wed to the Lamb of God and was restored to his or her rightful place in the universe as heirs to God's eternal, perfect kingdom. After the destruction of sin and the re-creation of the earth, the universe was again in harmony, and was forever free from rebellion.

Each of these people: Phoebe, Seth, Angelica, Josh, Ruth, Benny, Tom; each of these had sinned in the eyes of God. Each deserved the death of the wicked. Each deserved to share in the same fate as the former earth. Yet they lived, not by works and not by adherence to any religious doctrine. They lived by faith, and faith alone. They confessed that they were strangers and foreigners on the earth, and that they desired a better country for their own, a heavenly one. Our just and mighty God heard these confessions and heartfelt desires for a heavenly kingdom, as He does even for you and me, and therefore God was not ashamed to be called their God: indeed, He had prepared a city for them, the heavenly New Jerusalem.

Let every man and woman know that God is calling us for this final struggle and warning us of its dangers. He begs for us to seek Him and longs for everyone to experience His salvation and amazing grace. He took on flesh, He became as one of us, to remove our punishment from upon us and take it upon Himself, all so that we, the lowly and wretched sinners that we are, should spend eternity in the divine city He has prepared with His own mighty hands. There is no one on earth too sinful for the Lord to redeem. There is no one left out of His promise to save mankind. Only by our rebellion and refusal of His free gift can we be absent from His divine kingdom.

> Whoever is thirsty, let him come; and whoever wishes, let him take the free gift of the water of life.

The invitation is extended to everyone. Even you.

Do you hear the Lord calling you now, as you read this? Will you accept His free gift of eternal life? I believe, by faith, that you will. Praise God!

Let us borrow the hopeful ending of the very Word itself: 'He who testifies to these things says, "Yes, I am coming soon." Amen. Come, Lord Jesus. The grace of the Lord Jesus be with God's people. Amen.'

Notes: Scripture references

Chapter 1

Babylon   See **Revelation 14:8 ; 16:19 ; 17:5 ; 18:2, 10, 21.**
This term is used interchangeably in all references. We find the
fullest description of Babylon in **Revelation chapter 17.**

Chapter 3

*And there shall be a time of trouble, such as never was since there was
a nation even to that same time.* **Daniel 12:1 KJV** (King James
Version)
*For then shall be great tribulation, such as was not since the beginning
of the world to this time, no, nor ever shall be.* **Matthew 24:21
KJV**

Chapter 4

*The earth shall reel to and fro like a drunkard, and shall totter like a
hut; its transgression shall be heavy upon it, and it will fall, and not
rise again.* **Isaiah 24:20 NKJV** (New King James Version)*
...enter also into the glorious land. **Daniel 11:41 KJV**
...set out in a great rage to destroy and annihilate many. **Daniel
11:44 NIV** (New International Version)
...he shall come to his end, and none shall help him. **Daniel 11:45
KJV**

Chapter 5

*'I tell you, I will never again drink of this fruit of the vine until that
day when I drink it new with you in my Father's kingdom.'* **Matthew
26:29 NRSV** (New Revised Standard Version)

And the four and twenty elders and the four beasts fell down and worshipped God that sat on the throne, saying Amen; Alleluia. And a voice came out of the throne, saying Praise our God, all ye His servants, and ye that fear Him, both small and great. And I heard as it were the voice of a great multitude, and as the voice of many waters, and as the voice of mighty thunderings, saying, Alleluia: for the Lord God omnipotent reigneth. **Revelation 19:4-6 KJV**
In the beginning was the Word, and the Word was with God, and the Word was God. The same was in the beginning with God. **John 1:1-2 KJV**

Chapter 6

...reserved for fire, being kept until the day of judgment and destruction of the godless. **2 Peter 3:7 NRSV**

Chapter 8

'Your sons and your daughters will prophesy.' **Joel 2:28 NIV**

Chapter 13

God is faithful, and He will not let you be tested beyond your strength, but with the testing He will also provide the way out so that you may be able to endure it. **1 Corinthians 10:13 NRSV**
'For then shall be great tribulation, such as was not since the beginning of the world to this time, no, nor ever shall be.' **Matthew 24:21 KJV**

Chapter 14

'But I say to you, love your enemies, bless those who curse you, do good to those who hate you, and pray for those who spitefully use you and persecute you. Therefore you shall be perfect, just as your Father in heaven is perfect.' **Matthew 5:44, 48 NKJV***
To every thing there is a season, and a time to every purpose under the heaven. **Ecclesiastes 3:1 KJV**

Chapter 17

In the beginning God created the heaven and the earth. And the earth was without form, and void; and darkness was upon the face of the deep. And the Spirit of God moved upon the face of the waters. **Genesis 1:1-2 KJV**
Now the serpent was more crafty than any other wild animal that the Lord God had made. **Genesis 3:1 NRSV**
'You were the model of perfection, full of wisdom and perfect in beauty. You were in Eden, the garden of God; every precious stone adorned you: ruby, topaz and emerald, chrysolite, onyx and jasper, sapphire, turquoise and beryl. Your settings and mountings were made of gold; on the day you were created they were prepared. You were anointed as a guardian cherub, for so I ordained you. You were on the holy mount of God; you walked among the fiery stones. You were blameless in your ways from the day you were created till wickedness was found in you.' **Ezekiel 28:12-15 NIV**
How you are fallen from heaven, O Lucifer, son of the morning! How you are cut down to the ground, you who weakened the nations! For you have said in your heart: 'I will ascend into heaven, I will exalt my throne above the stars of God; I will also sit on the mount of the congregation on the farthest sides of the north; I will ascend above the heights of the clouds, I will be like the Most High.' **Isaiah 14:12-14 NKJV***
And another sign appeared in heaven: behold, a great, fiery red dragon having seven heads and ten horns, and seven diadems on his heads. His tail drew a third of the stars of heaven and threw them to the earth. And the dragon stood before the woman who was ready to give birth, to devour her Child as soon as it was born. **Revelation 12:3-4 NKJV***
But you are cast out, away from your grave, like loathsome carrion, clothed with the dead, those pierced by the sword, who go down to the stones of the pit, like a corpse trampled underfoot. **Isaiah 14:19 NRSV**

...death and hell were cast into the lake of fire. This is the second death. **Revelation 20:14 KJV**
And God shall wipe away all tears from their eyes; and there shall be no more death, neither sorrow, nor crying, neither shall there be any more pain: for the former things are passed away. **Revelation 21:4 KJV**
And no marvel; for Satan himself is transformed into an angel of light. **2 Corinthians 11:14 KJV**
For we wrestle not against flesh and blood, but against principalities, against powers, against the rulers of the darkness of this world, against spiritual wickedness in high places. **Ephesians 6:12 KJV**
For our struggle is not against enemies of blood and flesh, but against the rulers, against the authorities, against the cosmic powers of this present darkness, against the spiritual forces of evil in the heavenly places. **Ephesians 6:12 NRSV**

Chapter 18

The words of the Lord are pure words, like silver tried in a furnace of earth, purified seven times. You shall keep them, O Lord, you shall preserve them from this generation forever. **Psalm 12:6-7 NKJV***

Chapter 19

'Babylon the great is fallen, is fallen.' **Revelation 18:2 KJV**
From the sky huge hailstones of about a hundred pounds each fell upon men. And they cursed God on account of the plague of hail, because the plague was so terrible. **Revelation 16:21 NIV**
I saw heaven standing open and there before me was a white horse, whose rider is called Faithful and True. With justice He judges and makes war. His eyes are like blazing fire, and on His head are many crowns. He has a name written on Him that no one knows but He Himself. He is dressed in a robe dipped in blood, and His name is the Word of God. The armies of heaven were following Him, riding on white horses and dressed in fine linen, white and clean. Out of His mouth comes a sharp sword with which to strike down the nations.

"He will rule them with an iron scepter." He treads the winepress of the fury of the wrath of God Almighty. On His robe and on His thigh He has this name written: KING OF KINGS, AND LORD OF LORDS. **Revelation 19:11-18 NIV**

The clamor shall resound to the ends of the earth, for the Lord has an indictment against the nations; He is entering into judgment with all flesh, and the guilty He will put to the sword, says the Lord. **Jeremiah 25:31 NRSV**

The slain of the Lord shall be at that day from one end of the earth even unto the other end of the earth: they shall not be lamented, neither gathered, nor buried; they shall be dung upon the ground. **Jeremiah 25:33 KJV**

Chapter 20

First of all, you must understand that in the last days scoffers will come, scoffing and following their own evil desires. They will say, "Where is this 'coming' He promised? Ever since our fathers died, everything goes on as it has since the beginning of creation." But they deliberately forget that long ago by God's word the heavens existed and the earth was formed out of water and by water. By these waters also the world of that time was deluged and destroyed. By the same word the present heavens and earth are reserved for fire, being kept for the day of judgment and destruction of ungodly men. **2 Peter 3:3-7 NIV**

But do not forget this one thing, dear friends: With the Lord a day is like a thousand years, and a thousand years are like a day. The Lord is not slow in keeping His promise, as some understand slowness. He is patient with you, not wanting anyone to perish, but everyone to come to repentance. **2 Peter 3:8-9 NIV**

But the day of the Lord will come like a thief. The heavens will disappear with a roar; the elements will be destroyed by fire, and the earth and everything in it will be laid bare. **2 Peter 3:10 NIV**

Chapter 21

...seven heads and ten horns, and upon his horns ten crowns, and upon his heads the name of blasphemy. **Revelation 13:1 KJV**
And I saw one of his heads as it were wounded to death; and his deadly wound was healed. **Revelation 13:3 KJV**
The whole world was astonished and followed the beast. Men worshipped the dragon because he had given authority to the beast, and they also worshipped the beast and asked, "Who is like the beast? Who can make war against him?" **Revelation 13:3-4 NIV**
And all that dwell upon the earth shall worship him whose names are not written in the book of life of the Lamb slain from the foundation of the world. If any man have an ear, let him hear. **Revelation 13:8-9 KJV**
...exercised all the authority of the first beast on his behalf, and made the earth and its inhabitants worship the first beast, whose fatal wound had been healed. **Revelation 13:12 NIV**
...cause all who refused to worship the image to be killed. He also forced everyone, small and great, rich and poor, free and slave, to receive a mark on his right hand or on his forehead, so that no one could buy or sell unless he had the mark, which is the name of the beast or the number of his name. **Revelation 13:15-17 NIV**
In all the squares there shall be wailing; and in all the streets they shall say, "Alas! alas!" They shall call the farmers to mourning, and those skilled in lamentation, to wailing. **Amos 5:16 NRSV**
The day of the Lord is darkness, and not light. As if a man did flee from a lion, and a bear met him; or went into the house, and leaned his hand on the wall, and a serpent bit him. **Amos 5:18-19 KJV**
Will not the day of the Lord be darkness, not light – pitch-dark, without a ray of brightness? **Amos 5:20 NIV**
In that day I will restore David's fallen tent. I will repair its broken places, restore its ruins, and build it as it used to be. **Amos 9:11 NIV**
...which came out of great tribulation, and have washed their robes, and made them white in the blood of the Lamb. Therefore are they

before the throne of God, and serve Him day and night in His temple: and He that sitteth on the throne shall dwell among them. **Revelation 7:14-15 KJV**
They shall hunger no more, neither thirst any more; neither shall the sun light on them, nor any heat. For the Lamb which is in the midst of the throne shall feed them, and shall lead them unto living fountains of waters: and God shall wipe away all tears from their eyes. **Revelation 7:16-17 KJV**

Chapter 22

"For there shall arise false Christs, and false prophets, and shall [show] great signs and wonders; insomuch that, if it were possible, they shall deceive the very elect. Behold, I have told you before." **Matthew 24:24-25 KJV**
"...the Alpha and the Omega, the Beginning and the End ... who is and who was and who is to come, the Almighty." **Revelation 1:8 NKJV***
For the living know that they will die, but the dead know nothing, and they have no more reward, for the memory of them is forgotten. Also their love, their hatred, and their envy have now perished. Nevermore will they have a share in anything done under the sun. **Ecclesiastes 9:5-6 NKJV***
Whatever your hand finds to do, do it with your might; for there is no work or device or knowledge or wisdom in the grave where you are going. **Ecclesiastes 9:10 NKJV***
"Ye shall not surely die." **Genesis 3:4 KJV**

Chapter 23

The kings of the earth, and their armies, gathered together to make war against Him who sat on the horse and against His army. **Revelation 19:19 NKJV***
But after these things he must be released for a little while. **Revelation 20:3 NKJV***

The rest of the dead did not come to life until the thousand years were ended. **Revelation 20:5 NIV**

…surrounded the camp of the saints and the beloved city. **Revelation 20:9 NKJV***

Then I saw a great white throne and Him who was seated on it. Earth and sky fled from His presence, and there was no place for them. And I saw the dead, great and small, standing before the throne, and books were opened. Another book was opened, which is the book of life. The dead were judged according to what they had done as recorded in the books. **Revelation 20:11-12 NIV**

All those who go down to the dust shall bow before Him, even he who cannot keep himself alive. **Psalm 22:29 NKJV***

Then I saw a new heaven and a new earth, for the first heaven and the first earth had passed away, and there was no longer any sea. I saw the Holy City, the new Jerusalem, coming down out of heaven from God, prepared as a bride beautifully dressed for her husband. And I heard a loud voice from the throne saying, "Now the dwelling of God is with men, and He will live with them. They will be His people, and God Himself will be with them and be their God. He will wipe every tear from their eyes. There will be no more death or mourning or crying or pain, for the old order of things has passed away." He who was seated on the throne said, "I am making everything new!" Then He said, "Write this down, for these words are trustworthy and true." He said to me: "It is done. I am the Alpha and the Omega, the Beginning and the End. To him who is thirsty I will give to drink without cost from the spring of the water of life. He who overcomes will inherit all this, and I will be his God and he will be my son." **Revelation 21:1-7 NIV**

You defiled your sanctuaries by the multitude of your iniquities, by the iniquity of your trading; therefore I brought fire from your midst; it devoured you, and I turned you to ashes upon the earth in the sight of all who saw you. All who knew you among the peoples are astonished at you; you have become a horror, and shall be no more forever. **Ezekiel 28:18-19 NKJV***

Chapter 24

"The wind blows wherever it pleases. You hear its sound, but you cannot tell where it comes from or where it is going. So it is with everyone born of the Spirit." **John 3:8 NIV**

"Don't urge me to leave you or to turn back from you. Where you go I will go, and where you stay I will stay. Your people will be my people and your God my God." **Ruth 1:16 NIV**

Chapter 25

And God said, "Let there be lights in the dome of the sky to separate the day from the night; and let them be for signs and for seasons and for days and years, and let them be lights in the dome of the sky to give light upon the earth." And it was so. God made the two great lights – the greater light to rule the day and the lesser light to rule the night – and the stars. God set them in the dome of the sky to give light upon the earth, to rule over the day and over the night, and to separate the light from the darkness. And God saw that it was good. **Genesis 1:14-18 NRSV**

"Let there be lights in the firmament of the heaven to divide the day from the night." **Genesis 1:14 KJV**

For the Lord God had not caused it to rain upon the earth, and there was no one to till the ground; but a stream would rise from the earth, and water the whole face of the ground. **Genesis 2:5-6 NRSV**

There went up a mist from the earth, and watered the whole face of the ground. **Genesis 2:6 KJV**

In the six hundredth year of Noah's life, in the second month, on the seventeenth day of the month, on that day all the fountains of the great deep burst forth, and the windows of the heavens were opened. The rain fell on the earth forty days and forty nights. **Genesis 7:11-12 NRSV**

God said, "This is the sign of the covenant that I make between me and you and every living creature that is with you, for all future generations: I have set my bow in the clouds, and it shall be a sign of the covenant between me and the earth. When I bring clouds over the earth and the bow is seen in the clouds, I will remember my covenant that is between me and you and every living creature of all flesh; and the waters shall never again become a flood to destroy all flesh." **Genesis 9:12-15 NRSV**

Thus the heavens and the earth were finished, and all their multitude. And on the seventh day God finished the work that He had done, and He rested on the seventh day from all the work that He had done. So God blessed the seventh day and hallowed it, because on it God rested from all the work that He had done in creation. **Genesis 2:1-3 NRSV**

Remember the Sabbath day, and keep it holy. Six days you shall labor and do all your work. But the seventh day is a Sabbath to the Lord your God; you shall not do any work – you, your son or your daughter, your male or female slave, your livestock, or the alien resident in your towns. For in six days the Lord made heaven and earth, the sea, and all that is in them, but rested the seventh day; therefore the Lord blessed the Sabbath day and consecrated it. **Exodus 20:8-11 NRSV**

When the Sabbath was over, Mary Magdalene, and Mary the mother of James, and Salome bought spices, so that they might go and anoint Him. And very early on the first day of the week, when the sun had risen, they went to the tomb. **Mark 16:1-2 NRSV**

"Think not that I am come to destroy the law, or the prophets: I am not come to destroy, but to fulfill. For verily I say unto you, till heaven and earth pass, one jot or one tittle shall in no wise pass from the law, till all be fulfilled. Whosoever therefore shall break one of these least commandments, and shall teach men so, he shall be called the least in the kingdom of heaven: but whosoever shall do and teach them, the same shall be called great in the kingdom of heaven." **Matthew 5:17-19 KJV**

The Lord said to Moses: You yourself are to speak to the Israelites: "You shall keep my Sabbaths, for this is a sign between me and you throughout your generations, given in order that you may know that I, the Lord, sanctify you." **Exodus 31:12-13 NRSV**

"Therefore the Israelites shall keep the Sabbath, observing the Sabbath throughout their generations, as a perpetual covenant. It is a sign forever between me and the people of Israel that in six days the Lord made heaven and earth, and on the seventh day He rested, and was refreshed." **Exodus 31:16-17 NRSV**

Chapter 29

And there were shepherds living out in the fields nearby, keeping watch over their flocks at night. **Luke 2:8 NIV**
I will make you envious by those who are not a nation; I will make you angry by a nation that has no understanding. **Romans 10:19 NIV**
Therefore, since we have been justified through faith, we have peace with God through our Lord Jesus Christ, through whom we have gained access by faith into this grace in which we now stand. **Romans 5:1-2 NIV**
...it is God who is at work in you, enabling you both to will and to work for His good pleasure. **Philippians 2:13 NRSV**
And we rejoice in the hope of the glory of God. **Romans 5:2 NIV**
"If you love me, you will obey what I command." **John 14:15 NIV**
"If ye love me, keep my commandments." **John 14:15 KJV**
This title was written on her forehead: MYSTERY; BABYLON THE GREAT; THE MOTHER OF PROSTITUTES AND OF THE ABOMINATIONS OF THE EARTH. I saw that the woman was drunk with the blood of the saints, the blood of those who bore testimony to Jesus. When I saw her, I was greatly astonished. **Revelation 17:5-6 NIV**

Chapter 31

Don't you know that all of us who were baptized into Christ Jesus were baptized into His death? We were therefore buried with Him through baptism into death in order that, just as Christ was raised from the dead through the glory of the Father, we too may live a new life. If we have been united with Him like this in His death, we will

certainly also be united with Him in His resurrection. **Romans 6:3-5 NIV**
"...there is rejoicing in the presence of the angels of God over one sinner who repents." **Luke 15:10 NIV**

Chapter 33

I have set the Lord always before me: because He is at my right hand, I shall not be moved. **Psalm 16:8 KJV**
I ... praise and exalt and glorify the King of heaven, because everything He does is right and all His ways are just. **Daniel 4:37 NIV**
"Woe is me! for I am undone; because I am a man of unclean lips, and I dwell in the midst of a people of unclean lips: for mine eyes have seen the King, the Lord of hosts." **Isaiah 6:5 KJV**
...no pleasure in the death of the wicked; but that the wicked turn from his way and live. **Ezekiel 33:11 KJV**
"Fear them not: for I have delivered them into thine hand; there shall not a man of them stand before thee." **Joshua 10:8 KJV**

Epilogue

He that is unjust, let him be unjust still: and he which is filthy, let him be filthy still: and he that is righteous, let him be righteous still: and he that is holy, let him be holy still. **Revelation 22:11 KJV**
Whoever is thirsty, let him come; and whoever wishes, let him take the free gift of the water of life. **Revelation 22:17 NIV**
He who testifies to these things says, "Yes, I am coming soon." Amen. Come, Lord Jesus. The grace of the Lord Jesus be with God's people. Amen. **Revelation 22:20-21 NIV**